CHOMP!

Charlie Carter and
the Monster Pike

For my dad.

I've finally written, it, dad! Sorry it took so long.

David x

With many grateful thanks to:

Siobhán O'Brien Holmes at *Writer and the Wolf* for the rather wonderful development edit. Find her at: www.writerandthewolf.com

Katherine for designing the interior. You can find her at fiverr.com/iamgigpower

Websites: www.facebook.com/ChompCharlieCarterAndTheMonsterPike
www.Instagram.com/CharlieCarterAdventures
www.CharlieCarterAdventures.com

CHOMP!

Charlie Carter and
the Monster Pike

David Rogers

INTRODUCTION

Immerse yourself in a tale like no other....
A chilling *Creature Feature* for
kids of all ages!

There's something in the water.

Something big. Something deadly.

When people start going missing on the Thames, the Police think it's the work of a maniac serial killer. Then a national newspaper THE DAILY ECHO gets wind of a rumour that there's a **monster pike** on the loose and puts up a bounty of £1M for anyone who can catch it. The papers call it *The English Jaws* and a crazy free-for-all monster hunt ensues.

But can the **net** be closed on the Monster Pike or is something **fishy** going on? Will the Newspapers ever stop **carping** on about it? Will the bumbling Police be in the right **plaice** for once or will they get **school**ed? Why are the Special Agents from the mysterious Fizz trying to **mussel** their way in? And will Charlie Carter help them all out just for the **halibut** or is that just a **fishcious** rumour?

It's not until Charlie Carter and his two schoolfriends Jazz and Sam discover the mangled remains of a whale with massive bite-marks washed up at low tide on the Thames that they realise that the killer won't be found on the land - but in the water. The killer is also off the **scales** – it's over twenty-feet long with four-inch long razor-sharp teeth, and it can sink a speedboat by ramming it at thirty miles per hour.

But will three schoolkids ever be listened to or will they just **flounder**? And **cod** alone knows where this nightmare creature came from. More to the point, how the **hake** do you catch a monster fish like this in the busy River Thames which is 250 miles long and 80 feet deep?

Can the bungling River Police, a Marine Biologist and a heavily armed gung-ho Trophy Hunter catch the Monster Pike, or will it be **turtle** disaster? Are they all **livebait** to be picked off one by one?

Will Charlie Carter have the oppor**tuna**ty to save the day? Who will be the **sole** survivor?

Any **fin** is possible in this book!

Contents

Prologue

The Escape

It couldn't tell how huge it was.

The beast had never seen itself and probably never would. It didn't know it was one of a kind, totally unique. Some people might call it a miracle of science. Some might call it a monster. In itself, it felt strong. Powerful. Much more so than the strange little things on two legs that hurried and scurried around its tank made of thick armoured glass day and night, injecting it with a glowing green liquid: monitoring it, measuring it, examining it. Making it grow.

The beast hated these smaller things – things with white laboratory coats on, things with bright lights and boxes that made strange sounds. These things that didn't need water to breathe. Things that hurt it. It wanted to kill these things.

Every day a huge metal cover behind a rusty metal grill would open and fresh water would rush in, water that would surge around its gills and clean out the old stale water. Day in, day out, ever since the beast had first been caught. It had been much smaller then of course, but now its fins pressed against each side of the huge tank that was its home. With no room to even turn around, the beast recalled a different world outside its tank. A world without end, a world without pain, where it could swim and eat without thought or fear. It waited, knowing the right moment to strike would come.

The metal cover opened again, and this time it didn't close quite so quickly. With a swish of its mighty tail the beast propelled itself through the rusty grill and into a long subterranean tube. A hundred metres later it was out in open water. Free. It could feel that it was back in its own world. Free to roam wherever it wanted. Free to hunt. Free to kill.

And the beast was hungry.

1

Tsunami

It was the height of a long hot summer and Charlie was noticing things that he'd never even seen before. It made his pain less real.

A million gossamer seeds floated lazily by on the warm evening breeze. Birds were singing their final songs of the day and all too soon, that distant orange ball of fire we know as the sun would start to dip below the tall whispering masts of the yachts that dotted the busy marina pontoons. In the local park, proud mums and dads watched their kids with ice cream lips playing 'jumpers for goalposts' and all too soon they'd be off to play 'happy families' and have dinner in front of the tv.

That had been Charlie, once.

But not anymore.

Not since *'you know what'* had happened. Now he didn't care about anyone or anything. Not really. Charlie certainly didn't care about his stupid Uncle Keith or his Uncle's stupid old 4X4 that he was helping to unload in the marina carpark.

'This stuff stinks!' said Charlie, trying to turn his face away from about three tons of smelly old fishing gear he was trying to squeeze onto two old dilapidated fishing trollies.

'Yeah, it's great isn't it! I love the smell of maggots in the evening, don't you, Charlie?'

'No. Seriously – the back of your car stinks. Has something died in there?'

'I'll meet you over there,' said his Uncle, ignoring Charlie's moans and gripes completely. 'Can you remember our usual fishing spot? Get off the pontoons at the end and you'll see me on the riverbank. I'll get the kettle on.'

And that was that. Charlie's Uncle darted on ahead with the lightest fishing trolley and left Charlie to struggle with the heaviest one. It had been about a year that they'd gone fishing together, but since *'you know what'* had happened Charlie's Uncle Keith was trying to help take Charlie's mind off things.

Fat chance.

His Uncle's whole car smelled like death and the last thing Charlie wanted to do was to spend the night on a stiflingly hot riverbank waiting for a float to bob up and down in the water signalling that a fish had been caught. He certainly didn't want to be responsible for hurting a poor little fish, or worse, killing it. Especially not now.

He'd had enough of death to last him a lifetime.

Charlie went to close the 4X4's back door but a pile of newspapers in the boot caught his eye. The top paper was yesterday's edition and the front page read:

THE DAILY ECHO

Britain's biggest and brightest Newspaper | Still only 20p!

MORE MYSTERIOUS DISAPPEARANCES!

Two more swimmers have gone missing in the Thames over the Bank Holiday weekend.

A midnight swim looks to have turned to yet another tragedy as two more swimmers have been reported missing, presumed drowned. DI Williams of the Metropolitan Police Marine Policing Unit (commonly known as the River Police) has repeated official advice and issued the following statement: 'The Police would like to remind everyone that it is dangerous to swim in the Thames as the water is very cold even at this time of year. There are many dangerous undercurrents and boat movements of all shapes and sizes throughout the day.'

DI Williams has yet to bow to public pressure and hold an official Press Conference, despite heavy criticism about all the missing persons recently. The latest disappearances now bring the total to five in the last month, but the real total...

Contd. Inside on page 2

A deckchair, yesterday, as the scorching nationwide Heatwave continues

Bank Holiday Scorcher!

Hotter than Spain! The summer heatwave continues as families flock to parks, rivers and beaches across the UK. Temperatures continue to rise and is due to hit a sweltering 21degrees this Bank Holiday weekend.

Slip – Slap - Slop

If you go out in the sun today, don't forget to follow Government Guidelines and:

SLIP on a t-shirt,
SLAP on a hat,
SLOP on some Factor 50+ sunscreen.

Swim Safely

The nationwide 'Swim Safely' campaign launches inside. During the hot weather, the Public are reminded of the dangers of swimming in deep, cold water. The Metropolitan Police Marine Policing Unit (the River Police) have launched a campaign to keep everyone safe. *Campaign details on p12*

Convicted Axe-Murderer has escaped: On the run in London

John Burns, 57, otherwise known as 'Mad Dog' has escaped and is believed to be on the run somewhere in London or the Thames Valley.

Mad Dog is considered highly dangerous and possibly armed. The Public are urged not to approach him but call 999 instead. Possible reward for information leading to his recapture.

Mad Dog was serving life after being proved guilty of second-degree murder, after a brief argument with his neighbour about a tree. He was being transferred to a Maximum-Security prison when he overpowered his guards and made good his escape. This is his second escape attempt this year.

Have you seen this man?

Police issued a Photofit of Cyril 'Hatchet' McNee, a well-known accomplice to Mad Dog, who hasn't been seen for 3 months. An official spokesperson said

yesterday, 'Obviously under official guidelines we're not allowed to publish his face to protect his human rights.'

Contd. on Page 3 inside

Derby Winners announced! Full story on inside back pages
Tomorrow's Lottery Results Today! Why wait? We predict the winning lines inside!
All the latest football results – 'We were robbed!' says Bournemouth United FC coach

'Hurry up, Charlie!' shouted his Uncle from somewhere up ahead. 'Stop dawdling!'

'Yeah, okay, okay. I'm going as fast as I can!' lied Charlie. The less time he had to spend with his Uncle Keith the better he thought, as his jokes were often dire and Charlie was definitely not in the mood for laughing right now. Then he slammed the back door of the car shut as hard as he could.

Squeak Squeak Squeak

'This trolley is RUBBISH!' puffed Charlie. 'How come I've got the heavy one? Do you know that one of these wheels is about to fall off? It's REALLY annoying!'

Squeak Squeak Squeak

Up ahead on the pontoons, Uncle Keith rolled his eyes and ignored Charlie some more. It was true, though. Charlie was dawdling a bit. Ever since *'you know what'* had happened he'd lost all inclination to do anything. But he'd started appreciating things in a different way. But he certainly wasn't going to tell anyone this. The whole world was against him, of that he was quite sure.

'Ah, there you are at last,' said Uncle Keith as Charlie came into view at the end of the pontoons. 'Fancy a cheese and pickle sandwich?'

'Yuk!' Charlie blurted out, looking at the squishy bread in his Uncle's hand. 'No I don't.' He was really *Starvin' Marvin* but he wasn't going to let on.

'I made them myself, just for us.' His Uncle Keith looked crushed. 'No? Okay then. Use those pontoon steps over there to get down – I've already set the camping stove up so perhaps you can show off your cooking skills instead. Your mum said you were a great cook... oh, sorry.'

Charlie forced a half-smile, hoping his Uncle wouldn't notice his eyes filling up as he bounced the trolley down the moss-covered green slippery steps.

'Looks a great place. Not. I'm really looking forward to spending all night watching nothing happen. Eurgh. This place smells awful as well.' moaned Charlie as he trudged over to where his Uncle had set up. 'Ground swallow me up now!' he silently wished.

Charlie noticed that there was a heavy smell of diesel

at this far end of the marina, and even in the dusk he could see rainbows glistening and spiralling on the surface of the water. The tide was out, and one side of the pontoon was resting on the ground. The water on the other side of the pontoon was deeper and it was here that a couple of big motorboats were moored.

'You know, Charlie, it's been six months since...'

'Hey look - I think one of those speedboats has got a leak. Have you seen that one? Look – it's got three engines.' said Charlie, changing the subject fast.

'Floating gin palaces!' scoffed his Uncle. 'They're always like that. Blooming things leaking oil and diesel into the river. Who can afford one of them, anyway? Pah. Waste of money. Sit down and I'll pour you some tea. Or would you prefer some cola? I've got...'

'I know you're doing my Dad a favour in taking me out fishing, but honestly, I'm fine. You don't have to keep looking after me. I can look after myself you know.'

'Hah! Yes, I know you can,' his Uncle sighed. 'But we're all feeling it, Charlie. Your mum was my sister, after all. It hurts me as well. Things like this leave a huge gap in people's lives, including your dad's. You shouldn't be so off with him all the time...'

'You don't understand! Nobody does! Things like this don't happen in real life. Not to me! I'm Charlie Carter. I'm the Head Boy at school. I'm the Captain of the football team. People rely on me to be... to be...'

The tears came then, and Charlie let his Uncle pull him close and rub his hair in that 'don't worry, it'll be alright' fashion that he always did. But Charlie knew it wouldn't be alright. It wouldn't get better and it wouldn't go away.

'All my dad cares about is sorting out the farm, now. I never wanted to move there anyway. I just wanted to help him with his stupid inventions and stuff. Now he doesn't even notice if I'm there or not. Stupid inventions. Stupid farm.'

'Your dad's going through a lot, Charlie. I know he cares for you but he's dealing with, you know, *things* in his own way, too. He was really looking forward to retiring and getting rid of all that stress to spend more time with you and your mum. Just give him a chance, that's all. Then I know you two will be building all sorts of crazy things together again. He loves you and would do anything for you. I *know* that, Charlie, believe me.'

'I was hoping to see more of him now, too. He was always working away doing whatever it was he did before he retired. I don't even know what job he retired from. Mum would never tell me, before...you know. She used to say *'One day, I'll tell you when you're old enough, Charlie...'* but that day never came did it? Now it's too late. Then once in a Blue Moon when my Dad did come home from abroad, he'd always say *'I could tell you what I do for a living - but I'd have to shoot you.'* which never made any sense to me whatsoever.'

'So, you really don't know what your Dad used to do?'

'Well, I think he was something like an Astronaut, wasn't he?'

'Nah. He said that job didn't have enough

atmosphere,' smiled Charlie's Uncle.

Charlie groaned. 'Here come the bad jokes,' he thought. 'Was he a famous Secret Spy?'

'Well, I don't think anyone could be famous *and* a secret spy, Charlie...'

'Was he a Daredevil Motorbike Stuntman?'

'Only for a while – but he got the high jump.'

'A Rocket Scientist?'

'Nope. That job never got off the ground.'

'Was he a world-famous Magician that could make millions of pounds worth of diamonds disappear, never to be found again...?' said Charlie, half-hoping that his Dad had a stash of diamonds and jewels hidden somewhere.

'That job disappeared in a puff of smoke. But now you're just messing me about, although that does remind me - your Dad asked me to give you this. I put it on for safekeeping...'

Charlie's Uncle adjusted the collar on his fishing jacket and took out a silver necklace. There was a small silver locket on it, but before he could show it to

Charlie there was a loud **GLOMP!** and one of the floats disappeared beneath the surface of the water.

'Yes! We've got one! Come on, Charlie - I'm going to catch a big one tonight, I can feel it in my water!' shouted his Uncle as he dived towards his fishing rods.

Charlie shook his head and gave a little laugh as he looked at the back of his Uncle's smelly fishing jacket. In great big embroidered letters, it said:

KEITH THE CARP

His Uncle loved that nickname which the members of his Angling Club had bestowed upon him. His Uncle thought it was because of all the record-breaking carp he'd caught over the years, but one of the members had let on to Charlie one day, that they only called his Uncle Keith 'Keith the Carp' because he always smelt like an old fish.

The moon rose and Charlie looked more bored than a bored thing on National Being Bored Day. He'd managed to get the camping stove going and was watching the little fish his Uncle had caught slowly sizzling in the frying pan.

'Poor fish,' said Charlie. 'You know, my Dad taught me some basic survival skills. I can extract water out of a cactus, I can catch Witchetty Grubs if I'm lost and miles from anywhere and really hungry. I can even make a tent out of old leaves and some string - but now I'm stuck here on the wild and remote banks of the River Thames in the centre of London, where all I need to know is which gas setting I need to put the burner on.'

'And your point is...?' asked his Uncle.

'Well it's hardly Bear Grylls, is it?'

'I've got survival skills, too, you know, Charlie. I can make popcorn!'

'Really?' said Charlie, really not interested.

'Yeah, watch this!' said his uncle, and gleefully threw a handful of live maggots into the frying pan. He laughed as the maggots heated up and flew like popcorn over their heads with a loud **POP POP POP**. 'Bet Bear Grylls wouldn't teach you how to do that, now, eh?'

'Bet you wouldn't like it if Bear Grylls threw YOU in there,' scowled Charlie.

'Oh, come on and lighten up, Charlie. You're a right misery pants, aren't you? Fishing trips are supposed to be fun, you know. Two guys fending for themselves out in the wilderness, eating only what they can catch with their bare hands, fighting off bears, marauding wolves and lions...'

'We're only a couple of miles from London Bridge. There's not many bears in this neck of the woods. Look. There's even a Chippy over there. Hardly the Wilds of Outer Mongolia, is it?'

'Blimey, Charlie. Moan, moan, moan. All you've done today is moan.' His Uncle was silent for a moment, then he remembered.

'Ah, I was going to give you this. This will brighten you up a bit I hope...'

Uncle Keith reached for the necklace and the silver locket sparkled in the moonlight. He pressed a clasp on one side and the locket sprang open. Charlie looked at what was inside, and what he saw made his heart miss a beat. It was the most beautiful thing he'd ever seen.

On one side of the open locket was an old photo of his mum and dad holding a baby. On the other side, difficult to read in the moonlight, Charlie could just make out the engraving which said: 'Charlie's First Year'.

'That's you and your mum. Oh, and your dad of course.'

'I've...I've never seen that photo before,' stuttered Charlie.

'Your mum used to wear this locket all the time. Your dad was going through some paperwork stuff with the solicitors the other day. She'd left you this in her will. It's yours...'

'She did? Wow. That's amazing. I... don't know what to say. Thank you...'

Charlie went to reach for the silver locket, but his Uncle snatched it away and tucked the chain back down his neck out of Charlie's reach.

'Ah, you can't have it yet. You can have it later – as long as you lighten up, that is.'

'Hey! That's not fair – that's mine, not yours. Give me it!'

'Uh uh uh...' teased his uncle. 'Not yet. You can have it when we leave - if you promise to stop being a pain.'

Charlie was about to say something he shouldn't, but then a loud **SPLASH** out in the middle of the river caused them both to start. The line on one of the fishing rods started whizzing out faster than Charlie had ever seen it go before.

'Wow, what's that? That sounded like a monster!' whispered Charlie.

'Get up on the pontoons, take some action shots of me landing it!' shouted his Uncle.

Charlie ran up onto the pontoons as his uncle took a step into the water and heaved back on the fishing rod. This one was really putting up a fight. Charlie whipped out his mobile phone and switched the camera on. He steadied himself against the back of the speedboat with the three engines but had to stifle a laugh when his Uncle made a schoolboy error and took one step out too far. Water filled over the top of his uncle's wellies and Charlie could hear him muttering silent curses under his breath.

Charlie took a few shots – his phone was okay at taking photos in low darkness but just to be on the safe side he turned on the flash. He couldn't wait to show his mates at school what a berk his uncle was. The flash lit up the night as Charlie ran off loads of shots in burst mode – which made his uncle appear as though he was moving in a silent film.

Then it happened.

A loud **WHOOSHING** sound like a boat had just been launched made Charlie squint hard into the darkness. But what he saw made his blood run cold.

From the middle of the river, a four-foot high wave of foaming water made straight for his uncle, who tried to take a step back but couldn't move. Both of his wellies were now held tight in the Thames mud. Panic set in. A little bit of poo plopped out of the bottom of one his trouser legs and floated to the surface with a little *plop.*

Both Charlie and his uncle screamed at the same time. Charlie watched in horror as a huge glistening shape lined with dark green stripes zig-zagged towards the shore and a huge set of jaws full of razor-sharp teeth appeared out of the foaming river. A wall of freezing cold water cascaded over the pontoons and knocked Charlie off his feet and onto the speedboat.

'Holy Macaroni!' he shouted.

Cold foamy spray spat at Charlie's face forcing him to hide under the speedboat's dry covers. He was soaked to the skin. He curled up into a tight little ball, closing his eyes, not believing what he'd just seen.

But he couldn't close his ears as his uncle's screams were cut short by a mighty...

!!CHOMP!!

After what seemed an eternity, Charlie peered out from under the speedboat's covers. Small waves lapped at the shore. His uncle had disappeared. Well, most of him. All that was left were the two lower parts of his legs sticking out of two green wellies which were still stuck in the mud.

A small plume of dark red blood spurted out of each wellie where Keith the Carp had once stood.

But as for the rest of him...

...it was **fish food**.

2

Agent Blue

'What?' said Agent Blue.

3

Agent Ochre

'Huh?' said Agent Ochre.

4

Pitch Black

'I said 'What?' Jeremiah. What do you want?' hissed Agent Blue.

'Oh. Sorry, I didn't hear you properly.' whispered the muscular Agent Ochre, flicking his dreadlocks to the side. 'But hey - don't call me by my real name.'

'Oh yes. Sorry. I keep forgetting about that, Jere....er, I mean, Agent Ochre.' apologised Agent Blue. 'Shall we start again?'

'Yeah,' nodded Agent Ochre. 'I think that's a good idea. We seem to have messed it all up so far. It's so dark now I can't see what I'm doing anyway. Hang on, I'll get my head-torch. Shall I start the engines?'

'Okay,' but don't turn the lights on yet.'

From out of the darkness three big outboard engines thudded into life. An array of bright underwater lights lit up the river underneath the sleek motorboat and a huge spotlight illuminated the marina and half the Thames.

'Turn them off, you idiot! If the River Police see us, we're done for!' hissed Agent Blue.

It all went dark again.

5

Agent Ogre

Old Father Thames snaked its way across the darkening summer landscape like a huge silver adder looking for its last kill of the day.

With the onset of darkness, the capital's glossy buildings started to hide their features from the cold heart of the city. Creatures far more poisonous and toxic than any serpent slithered out of their daytime hideaways. The city's neon streets were dangerous after dark and out on the fast-flowing, cold waters of the Thames if you didn't know what you were doing, if you got disorientated by the bright city lights reflecting off the water or forgot which way the strong unforgiving currents were flowing, then you could get yourself into a whole lot of trouble. Big trouble. Very quickly.

Charlie groggily rubbed his eyes open but couldn't see a thing. In a panic he went to stand up, but vinyl covers overhead stopped him. He had to make do with half-crouching instead, which was fairly uncomfortable. Heavy vibrations were going right through his body, and not far away he could hear two angry voices shouting at each other over what sounded like a thunderstorm. Then Charlie remembered.

He'd cried himself to sleep on the speedboat with three engines.

But now the speedboat was moving.

Supressing the desire to shout out for help, Charlie tried to collect his jumbled thoughts. He'd just seen his Uncle eaten by a... a what? Some big monster fish? It seemed impossible but he'd seen it with his own eyes. He really wanted his mum – but he knew that was *really* impossible. Even a precious memory of her – the locket she always used to wear – had been cruelly taken away when it was almost within his reach. The locket? Wow, that photo! Unique. He had to get it back. But how? Here he was in the middle of the Thames onboard a moving speedboat with strangers who were trying to hide something from the police. Charlie put the thoughts about the locket to one side: He knew he was in *big* trouble.

'Get a grip, Charlie Carter. Don't panic! Think about this,' he whispered to himself. 'What would Tom Bruise do?'

Tom Bruise was a real-life Hollywood Hero. Tom was always leaping out of planes, blowing things up, shooting the bad guys. He'd probably just burst out of hiding and kick the baddies over the side of the boat.

Charlie checked his phone – the feint glow said 2:34am. It was the middle of the night! The glow from his phone also lit up what he was sitting on. It said:

LIFE-RAFT: DANGER – PULL TOGGLE TO

AUTO-INFLATE

in great big red letters on the side. And then in smaller letters underneath:

DO NOT USE INDOORS.

'Good job I'm not indoors then,' thought Charlie. 'There's nothing else for it but I'll just have to burst out. Surprise the baddies. Throw them over the side of the boat. Hand them in to the police. Collect huge reward. Become a national hero. Be famous on Twitter, Facebook, Instagram, Snapchat, all that. Be in the papers. Maybe even become so famous I'll star in Tom Bruise's next film *Mission Implausible 6*. Sounds like a good plan.' Charlie said to himself. 'Let's do it!'

Cautiously he peered out from under the covers. The stars shone down from a cloudless summer night sky. Two silhouettes moved against the city lights: one tiny figure, one massive. Neither of them looked very pleasant and both were trying to stay hidden in the shadows. They were definitely up to something.

'I might have to resort to some king-fu!' thought

Charlie as he tensed in readiness to leap out, his legs like jelly. At the last second, he saw the flash of a gun under the big man's jacket.

PRRRRRP!

A loud noise like a squelchy bottom burp split the darkness. Charlie froze. Luckily, the two men were making so much noise themselves they hadn't noticed the rather rude noise Charlie's jeans had made as they rubbed against the yellow rubber life-raft.

'A gun? On a speedboat? What on earth are these two up to? Okay. I might need a re-think here.' thought Charlie to himself. 'What are my options?'

He listed them all in his head:

Option 1: Call Tom Bruise? Nope, too far away. Also, he might be at some big Hollywood Party and wouldn't appreciate me calling him after work.

Option 2: Call home, get my Dad to help? You must be joking! He'll probably be too busy anyway or ground me for a week when he finds out about Uncle Keith.

Option 3: Call the Police? Definitely no! They're always turning up and ruining my fun. It wasn't my fault I blew the shed up. Mind you, one of these guys *has* got a gun. Hmm? Blowing things up – ah, that might be the answer.

Option 4: Call the SAS to blow the boat up. Yes! That's it. No, wait, hang on. That wouldn't be a good idea. I'm still on the boat. And I don't think I've got the number for the SAS anyway. This is hard! But I have to think.

Whichever way he looked at it, Charlie realised he was going to be in deep deep *deep* trouble, that's for sure. Who would be able to help? Who wouldn't mind him texting them in the middle of the night? Who would be pleased to hear from him? There was only one thing for it. He only had one option really. He sent a text to one of his best friends, Jasmin.

For a girl, she was alright.

CHARLIE MOB:	**'Jazz! U wake? I'm on a speedbot sumwher on Thames. Need ur held!**

A slight pause. Then Charlie's phone gently vibrated and lit up.

JAZZ MOB:	**'It's half past two in the morning u doughnut!! Of course I'm not awake. I know I said I'd be there 4u anytime but it's the middle of the night. Anyway, what do u need holding? Your spelling is atrocious. PS: How's fishing trip with ur Uncle Keith the Crap? Say hi from me.'**
CHARLIE MOB:	**'U mean Keith the Carp. Well lets just say its been an interesting night so far. But I didn't mean held, I meant help. HELP!'**

JAZZ MOB:	'What? Go away! I'm asleep!!!'
CHARLIE MOB:	'I'm in trouble. Serious! Really need ur help. Think I'm being kidnapped on boat on thams. Not much signal here'
JAZZ MOB:	'Tell me tomoz. Get ur Uncle Fishface to help u. Night'
CHARLIE MOB:	'No, I can't get him 2help because…'

Charlie's thumb hovered over his phone's keypad. What was he supposed to tell her? That his uncle had just been eaten by Jaws? That he's just had the second most traumatic and terrible experience of his entire life?

| CHARLIE MOB: | 'Because he's not here. Im trapped on a speedboat. Two dodgy looking guys on it, up to something. One of them has a gun!!!' |
| JAZZ MOB: | OMG! Charlie! Wat u going 2do? |

CHARLIE MOB:	**Not sure. Think I'm going2capture them but might need you and Sam 2help. This is not a bloke. Very series. Come 2towerbridge asap!'**

Time was running out. He checked what he'd text over to Jazz and tutted to himself.

CHARLIE MOB:	**'I meant joke, not bloke. And VERY serious.'**

There was a longer pause this time. Charlie felt the speedboat slow down at the same time he felt his phone vibrate.

JAZZ MOB:	**'Don't worry about saying please, will you, Charlie? Anyway, Ive got hold of Sam. We're coming 2help. What do u want us 2do? Shall I call police?**

CHARLIE MOB:	'No don't call Police. Mind you, 1of these guys has gun. Maybe u should. Let me have a think.'
SAM MOB:	'Hi Charlie. Jazz just txt. Hows it going?'
CHARLIE MOB:	'No time 2explain much Sam. Fone signal bad. Ive been kidnapped by 2blokes. On Thames by Tower Bridge'
SAM MOB:	'Cool! Sounds like another brill adventure! Do u want me to come and bash them up? You'll be safe as houses with me there!'
CHARLIE MOB:	'No u doughnut!!! One guy is 7 feet tall. U r only3 feet tall. He looks like he eats kids like us for breakfast!'
SAM MOB:	'Wat shall i do then?'
CHARLIE MOB:	'Tell Jazz I'm on a speed badger with 3 engines.'
SAM MOBI:	'A speed badger?'

CHARLIE MOB:	**'No not a badger. I meant BOAT!'**

For the first time in his life, Charlie missed his friends Jazz and Sam. He felt alone. His best friends weren't there for him, and he didn't like it. Whatever he was going to do, he was going to have to do it all by himself.

CHARLIE MOB:	**'Don't worry. Can't wait anymore. I've got this!'**
JAZZ MOB:	**U serious????!! Don't' do anything u numpty. I'm going to call the Police.'**
CHARLIE MOB:	**'If you must. Get them to meet me at Tower Bridge. I'll handle this until they get here.'**
JAZZ MOB:	**'Don't do anything silly like u usually do. If this is a windup Charlie u r going 2b sorry! Shall I call ur Dad2?'**

CHARLIE MOB:	**'No! Don't call him. I'll be ok'**
	JAZZ MOB: 'Look I'm going to call the Police now. Don't go away'
CHARLIE MOB:	**'I'm not going anywhere. I'm going to...'**

The little aerial logo flashed on Charlies phone. The signal had gone completely. Shaking it didn't help.

'Great. Middle of London. No signal. Love modern tech.' he thought. 'Okay. I'm on my own. Nothing else for it: Wait for right moment to catch them off guard. Leap out. Then POW! Two right hooks. Make Citizen's Arrest. Hero in all the papers. Hand them over to Police. Yup. Easy. Obviously the only sensible thing to do.'

Charlie shivered. It was the middle of summer but out here on the water it was *sooooo* cold. But maybe it was more that the cold which was causing him to shake uncontrollably.

PRRRRPPPP!

'Oops! Sit still, Charlie and listen. Listen!' he told himself over and over, trying not to move anymore.

He peeked out through a small hole in the covers and could just about see movement in the boat's cockpit. The smaller man was at the helm and guiding the sleek-looking powerboat over to a small orange buoy in the centre of the river. In the moonlight he could see a tattooed hand pull a lever which cut the purring engines and heard the splash of a heavy anchor being dropped overboard. Both men were dressed in smart black suits and ties. The bigger man was wearing an expensive looking head-torch.

'Bet they're cold' Charlie thought to himself, shivering.

The big man switched his head-torch on. The brightest LEDs you've ever seen lit up half of London and Charlie winced instinctively.

'Owww! Agent Ochre, you imbecile! Get those lights out of my face!' cried the smaller man. 'I can't see where *anything* is now!' He paused for effect then said 'Imbecile!' again.

'Hey, I ain't no inner seal, inbred seal, well, whatever it was you called me, Agent Blue. You're an inner seal yourself, just for not coming prepared.'

'Yahhh, just 'cos you got some fancy utility belt under your suit, doesn't make you a better Agent than me.'

'You're just jealous! You ain't got no head-torch, and I have. These are milly-terry Grade one-oh-one dijjy-tail L-E-D's. Got them from the Fizz. Brightest on the planet. The best head-torch you can steal, er, buy!' bellowed Agent Ochre, proudly, and let out a deep belly-laugh that sounded like a charging bull.

Agent Blue flicked the remains of a cigarette overboard. 'Stop making such a racket, Jeremiah. I got us here okay, didn't I?'

'Hey, I said don't call me by my real name, Agent Blue,' hissed the big man. 'I keep telling you – when we're out on a mission for The Fizzle-illity then you've got to refer to me by my official codename, as in: Agent Ochre. You're obviously Agent *Dimlo*, I think.'

The smaller man laughed. 'The *Fizzle-illity*? Hoo

boy! At least learn to pronounce your employer's name right. You mean The Facility. *Fah-silly-tea*. And hah hah to Agent Dimlo. Yeah, you're very funny, Agent *Ogre*. Not.'

Agent Blue pulled a face to make himself look like an ogre but froze when the man-mountain known as Agent Ochre leant over him menacingly. Agent Ochre wasn't laughing.

'Let's just agree to call them *The Fizz*.' he growled, low and mean like a grizzly bear with a sore head.

Agent Blue swallowed hard and changed the subject. 'Word has it that you used to be a champion Cage Fighter, but you gave it all up because you lost a fight.'

'I lost. Just once.' growled Agent Ochre. 'Out of forty fights. Thirty-nine wins and people only remember the one I lost. So I swore then that I'd never lose another fight – no matter how big my opponent is.' His muscles were flexing under his suit.

'Okay, okay. Calm down, calm down, Agent Ogre, erm, Ochre. Sheesh. I'm sorry.'

The big Agent backed off and smiled to himself as he grabbed a rope going over the side of the boat.

'Now, as we're both friends again,' sighed a very relieved Agent Blue, 'Can you help me pull these things up, please, huh? Slowly! Slowly! Jeez – do you know how much these cylinders are worth?'

'Yeah, course I do,' bristled Agent Ochre, his muscles visibly sweating with the exertion of pulling on the rope. 'I know each one is worth a lot more than what The Fizz pay me each year, and I know they're not worth me asking too many questions about what's in them, that's what I know. And something else I know – if we don't get these cylinders back to the Fizz tonight then the Boss is going to have our guts for garters!'

'Yeah, I bet she will. If we mess up, we'll both end up on the wrong end of a firing squad for sure. Or worse!'

'What's worse than a firing squad?' Agent Ochre looked puzzled.

'Oh, she'll think of something, believe you me.'

'Well hurry up and get those cylinders onboard. Then

we can get out of here and back to base where it's warm. Hurry up!'

The two argumentative Agents grabbed the blue fishing rope together and hauled the luminous orange buoy onboard. But then the rope snagged on something deep underwater.

'Are you pulling, you big lump? Ooof! This rope's well and truly stuck on something.'

'Of course I'm pulling. I'm 6'6' of pure muscle! See – it's free now. Here it comes...'

'I think that muscle takes up too much space in your head which don't leave much room for your brain,' scowled Agent Blue quietly, to himself.

Agent Ochre heaved on the rope again. With each pull Agent Blue was lifted off his feet. From Charlie's hiding place he watched as the two men hauled in the first of their illicit horde: Two military-grade shiny aluminium cylinders, each about two feet long. They looked brand new as though they hadn't been underwater long and had the word REJOOV with a 'toxic' stamp stencilled on each side.

REJOOV ☠

Both Agents swiftly unhooked the two cylinders from the rope.

'Hey! One of these things is leaking on my boat!' bellowed Jeremiah, looking down with disgust at the fluorescent green liquid now spreading slowly over the polished wooden deck.

'Don't sweat it. We've only got one more cylinder to go. The Fizz won't care, as long as we bring all of three cylinders back, they probably won't even notice that one of them is leaking. It's only a small leak anyway. Stop moaning.'

The rest of the fishing rope was still submerged in the water, but as the two men went to pull the rope, it went taut and the boat took off backwards down the Thames. Charlie nearly screamed out loud as huge amounts of icy cold water splashed over the back of the boat where he was hiding.

Both men fell on their backs and struggled to their feet.

'What on earth....? Think we've caught a submarine!' shouted Agent Blue.

'Cut the rope! Cut the rope!' Agent Ochre quickly reached into his suit and pulled out a large and ferocious-looking commando knife from his utility belt.

But, just as suddenly as it had begun, the boat stopped. Agent Ochre grabbed onto a handrail, but Agent Blue wasn't so lucky and lurched forward, almost doing a half-run as he tried to stop himself from being propelled towards the back of the boat.

But it was too late.

Charlie had to put his hand over his own mouth to stifle a laugh as he watched Agent Blue perform a perfect somersault into the river.

Agent Ochre let out a huge belly laugh as Agent Blue came to the surface, spitting out half the Thames.

'Plahhhggg!

Splurrrff!

Uggggh!

Spppluffft!'

Charlie bit his hand hard to avoid laughing. But then the urge to laugh went away completely when Agent Ochre pulled out the gun and pointed it directly towards where Charlie was hiding.

'Got you right where I want you, you little squirt!' Agent Ochre said with an evil laugh.

Oh no! thought Charlie. *That's it then. They've found me. Game Over.* Charlie went to move the covers back from over his head and put his hands up.

'Now that you're in there, you might as well find out what the ropes snagged on. We gotta get that last cylinder!' grunted Agent Ochre.

Luckily, Agent Ochre hadn't seen Charlie at all, but was pointing the gun at Agent Blue, who was now living up to his name by turning slowly blue in the cold waters of the Thames.

PLARRRPPFF!

Charlie bit his lip. That wasn't the rubber life-raft

this time. For a fraction of a second, Agent Ochre glanced in Charlie's direction, but luckily, he was shrouded in shadows. But that's when Charlie knew he had to get off this boat. Fast.

Even if he had to swim for it.

Even though

    Charlie

        knew

            what

                was

                    down

                        there.

6

Terror from the Deep

Agent Blue wasn't happy to say the least.

'This water tastes foul, you idiot!!!' he spluttered, treading water. 'And its freezing you complete and utter div-head! Plufffshhh!'

Charlie peeked out and watched as one of Agent Blue's shoes bobbed off downriver in the fast-moving tide.

Agent Ochre couldn't help himself and the big man roared with laughter. 'Go see what the rope's snagged on! And get a move on ya little squirt – time's a wasting.'

'But I can't see anything down there!' shouted Agent

Blue 'And what if there's sharks?'

Agent Ochre guffawed. 'This is the Thames! There ain't no sharks in the Thames! The worst you'll get is an eel up your trouser-leg.'

Agent Blue looked down in horror. 'What????!!!! E-eels??!!' he squealed loudly.

'Electric eels!' shouted Agent Ochre gleefully. 'Or a Lamprey Eel and they're even nastier! There might even be imber-*ceels* down there!'

'Nooooo!' wailed Agent Blue. 'I knew I should have just stayed in tonight. I could be playing Half-Life or FIFA instead. They don't pay me enough for this.'

'You're going to have a half-life if you don't untangle that rope!' Jeremiah snapped, then glanced around furtively. 'For an undercover Operation for the Fizz, this ain't going well,' he growled to himself. 'Stop shouting. Here. Take this.' Agent Ochre took off his head-torch, attached it to a long boathook and passed it down to Agent Blue who was treading water and turning bluer by the minute.

'This is my own head-torch so don't lose it. Like I said, it's Military Grade and cost me an arm and a leg. You lose it and that'll be the last thing you ever do!'

Agent Blue put the head-torch on then angrily punched the water, splashing the unimpressed Agent Ochre looking down from the nice dry boat. 'I'm telling you: this rope is caught on something solid. It ain't shifting.'

Agent Ochre waved the large commando-style knife threateningly at Agent Blue. 'Then go down and cut the last cylinder free, Agent BlueInTheFace, unless you want me to cut you an extra-wide smirk.' but then he switched the blade round and gently handed Agent Blue the knife, handle first. 'And seriously, get a move on. I'm freezing my bottom off up here.'

Agent Blue rolled his eyes and gripped the knife in between his teeth. Charlie couldn't quite make out what he was saying, but if you put your fingers in between your own teeth, it sounded a bit like this: *'OOO c-colb? Um b-b-bloomin f-f-feezin in ere, jub u wait u st-st-stoopid iddy-iddy ot!'*

Agent Blue drew in a big breath and disappeared, pulling himself down the rope, circling ever downwards into the cold, gloomy depths of the River Thames. Charlie shivered to himself. Agent Ochre found a discarded cigarette packet, lit one, then coughed his guts up.

'Bloomin' awful cancer stick! They'll be the death of me,' coughed Agent Ochre.

He felt the blue rope going over the side of the speedboat. It was still tight where it was snagged on something, but then the rope went loose. 'Ah well done, squirt. You got it.'

Just as Agent Ochre said that, the rope took off again at thirty-miles-an-hour, pulling the speedboat backwards and sending the big man crashing to the floor for the second time.

'Owww! Not again!'

The whole back of the boat was submerged with water. The big man struggled to get back on his feet and felt for his knife, silently cursing when he realised it wasn't there. On his hands and knees, he desperately rummaged around in one of the boat's lockers, found an axe and half-stood up. He raised the axe high above his head and swung it down in a powerful arc towards the fishing rope. With a mighty blow Agent Ochre missed the fishing rope completely and instead severed one of the three fuel lines to the engines. Gallons and gallons of red diesel spilled across the floor of the boat. With the second swing of the axe he only succeeded in embedding the sharp metal axe into his foot.

'YOWWWW!'

Screaming in pain, the big man hopped into the Skipper's seat and gunned all three engines into life. Two engines answered with a mighty roar, but the third engine spluttered loudly due to lack of fuel - which was spilling out onto the deck of the speedboat.. Agent Ochre wrenched the throttles open to their fullest extent, but despite this the boat was being pulled backwards by a huge underwater force.

'Whoah! Whoahhh!!! Whoahhhhhh!!!!' implored

Agent Ochre, still with a lit cigarette in his mouth. He desperately stood up to lean his full weight onto the throttles. More fuel spilled out.

Then a lot of things happened at once.

Charlie could smell the fuel and knew it was his time to act. It was now or never.

He burst out from underneath the covers and shouted, 'HANDS UP!!!!' in the deepest, boomiest, scariest voice he could muster, hoping he sounded just like Tom Bruise, Secret Agent.

Charlie held his mobile phone inside his coat pocket like it was a hidden gun. Agent Ochre looked at Charlie in total surprise. He'd never seen a twelve-year old kid pull a gun on him before. He wasn't sure if he should laugh or really put his hands up.

And that's all the time that either of them had together.

As Charlie leapt out of hiding, the toggle on the end of the life-raft pull-cord caught on his jeans and the small explosive charge in the life-raft (only to be used in emergencics, of course) caused the life-raft to inflate. Violently.

All that took just a couple of seconds - so in reality, it went a bit like this:

'HANDS UP!'

'EH?'

! ! B O O O O O O O O M – SSSSPPPPPHHHFTTTT!!

But after that, everything seemed to happen in slow-motion.

One of the last things Charlie saw was Agent Ochre looking up at him in total amazement as Charlie was catapulted upside down over the Agent's head towards the front of the boat, quickly followed by the self-inflating life-raft which Charlie was still attached to.

'Holyyyyyyy Macaroniiiiiiiiiiii!' screamed Charlie.

At that very same moment, the rope went slack, and the speedboat stopped surging backwards. Agent Ochre screamed and stumbled helplessly towards the back of the boat. Charlie watched in wide-eyed horror as the cigarette tumbled out of Agent Ochre's mouth towards the floor of the boat which was full of gushing fuel.

As Agent Ochre made his ungainly and uncontrolled way out of the back of the boat, he grabbed hold of the boathook to try and stop himself - but it was useless. Just like Agent Blue had done only a few minutes previously, so the big man violently somersaulted off the back of the boat and into the Thames. The two silver cylinders of Rejoov quickly followed and disappeared off into the depths.

Both Charlie and Agent Ochre hit the water at the same time. Charlie at the front of the boat, the Agent at the back. The self-inflating life-raft was now fully inflated and fell over Charlie as a huge fireball erupted overhead, lighting the depths momentarily and forcing a huge grey cloud upwards into the purple night sky. A kazillion plastic shards showered the water as the speedboat blew up.

KAAAA-

BLAMM!

In a Security Operations Room not too far away, a Security Guard was gawping open-mouthed at his bank of infra-red TV monitors. Each monitor displayed a slightly different view of the impressive explosion and recorded it for posterity. The Guard hit a big red button.

‼WAAAP WAAAP WAAAP WAAAP‼

All Charlie could hear across the water were sirens going mad. He nervously peered out from underneath the upside-down life-raft and watched all the red and blue flashing lights in the distance getting closer.

'Well, that went well.' Charlie said to himself. 'At least the cavalry is coming.'

The bottom half of the speedboat was still afloat, but on fire. The heat was intense, so Charlie ducked back under his life-raft. One of its clear plastic windows was resting on the water and Charlie put his face up to it. He immediately wished he hadn't.

One of the bright underwater LED spotlights from what remained of the speedboat's hull shone downwards, illuminating a dreadful scene. The water had a fluorescent green tint to it from the leaking cylinder. Agent Ochre was still very much alive and pulling determinedly on the blue rope which extended out of vision and into the depths. He was going to get that last cylinder no matter what and was wearing a small yellow dive-mask with a mini-scuba tank attached over his mouth which read 'Emergency Air'. The tank was only about a foot long and designed to give about six minutes of oxygen in an emergency. Charlie had seen Tom Bruise wear similar emergency air tanks in Mission Implausible 2. Or was it Mission Implausible 3? Anyway, it was definitely Tom Bruise in the film.

Agent Ochre must have sensed he was being watched and looked up to see Charlie's face looking down at him. Even with the dive-mask on you could tell Agent Ochre was grinning as a silver cylinder attached to the blue rope appeared from out of the depths. He held it up to show

Charlie as though he'd just won the World Cup. But then Agent Ochre's grin changed to a frown as he looked at Charlie, who now had a look of sheer terror on his face.

But Charlie wasn't looking at Agent Ochre.

He was looking at what was behind him.

The blue rope was still coming up out of the depths but what Charlie saw attached to it made his eyes pop. Agent Ochre turned round to see what Charlie was looking at, and a few bubbles escaped from the back of his trousers. It was a dreadful, grisly sight that slowly floated up out of the debris and darkness of the Thames.

Agent Ochre was staring face to face with the severed head and torso of Agent Blue. Everything below Agent Blue's waist was gone and all that was left was a jagged, bloody gash with guts spilling out of the open stomach area. Air bubbles still escaped from Agent Blue's mouth which was frozen open in a silent scream, whilst on his head the precious head-torch still shone brightly.

The bleeding half-corpse bumped into Agent Ochre as he inadvertently pulled the rope harder towards himself. The bright beam highlighted things that Charlie would remember for the rest of his life. Which, as Charlie saw what was rushing upwards below Agent Ochre, he thought probably wouldn't be for that much longer.

A vast shape covered with dark green stripes like some sort of underwater tiger surged vertically up out of the depths. In his haste to get away, Agent Ochre dropped the silver cylinder which disappeared into a cavernous mouth lined with razor-sharp teeth. Then the jaws clamped around what was left of poor Agent Blue and swallowed his remains whole.

It was a huge fish.

A pike to be exact. A freshwater fish full of sharp, needle-like teeth. But this one was of monstrous size. Something that, by rights, shouldn't exist. Except of course – it did. Charlie knew what it was straight away despite its vast, freakish size. It was the same thing that had taken his uncle.

The same thing that had taken his mum's locket.

But now Charlie had a clear view of the pike as it just

hung there in front of him, it's great weight supported by the water as it chomped on the remains of Agent Blue. It guzzled the dead agent deeper and deeper into its stomach.

Uncle Keith used to catch pike all the time. Those ones were only about three or four feet long – but even they had still put up a massive fight. His landing net had been full of snapping teeth and anger. Pike had lots of vicious energy and tempers to match. Charlie had learnt the hard way that you had to use special metal pliers to get the hooks out of their mouths. There was blood, sweat and tears on that fishing trip.

But this pike had to be over twenty feet long, maybe even twenty-five feet. Nearly as long as Charlie's school mini-bus. Charlie reckoned that each one of its razor-sharp teeth were as long as one of his fingers, and its huge eyes were alight with a green hellish glow from within.

Agent Ochre was struggling to swim away but the blue rope was tangled round his legs.

Charlie shook his head but couldn't tear his eyes away from this gruesome scene.

'Maybe I'm just dreaming. Maybe it's just oxygen deprivation.' he thought, as his brain politely informed him that his brain cells were starting to deplete and die from, yup, oxygen deprivation.

Charlie drew his gaze away from the underwater horror story and took a deep breath of plastic-smelling air underneath his life-raft. He shook his head to clear his thoughts and a couple of the braincells bouncing around inside his skull must have collided - Charlie had a brainwave. He fumbled for his phone but in his panic took twenty photos of the inside of his jean's pocket. Then, when he finally managed to get his phone out, he took about twenty close-up shots of his own terrified face.

KCHA KCHA KCHA KCHA KCHA KCHA KCHA KCHA KCHA KCHA KCHA KCHA KCHA KCHA KCHA KCHA KCHA KCHA KCHA KCHA KCHA

Temporarily dazzled, Charlie dropped his phone and it slowly sank away from him in the fluorescent green water. He made a mad grab for it and got it. Then it plopped out of his grasp again. He snatched it back and somehow switched the camera over to video. At least it was waterproof. Charlie pointed his phone back towards where he'd last seen Agent Ochre but then silently screamed as the monster pike shot past him just an arm's-length away. For a split second, its huge eye seemed to look deep into Charlie's soul.

Charlie could see the head and shoulders of Agent Blue stuck inside its cavernous mouth. The pike swam off in a large circle then whooshed back and lunged towards Agent Ochre who was holding the boathook out in front of him. Agent Ochre closed his eyes in readiness for the inevitable deadly bite from the twin rows of four-inch long teeth rushing towards him.

But the bite didn't come.

Agent Ochre opened his eyes.

He was being propelled through the water at a high rate of knots. The huge pike's jaws were just inches from his head. Luckily, its jaws had been jammed wide open by the boathook that Agent Ochre was holding - but the thin wooden pole was flexing. Any second now it would surely break. Agent Ochre held onto the boathook for all he was worth as the huge fish shook its head from side to side, trying to dislodge him. He could see the top of Agent Blue's head – it was still wearing his expensive LED head-torch. The blinding light was shining brightly out of the colossal pike's mouth.

Agent Blue's cold dead hand was beckoning to Agent Ochre, silently willing him to come closer... closer. Agent Ochre stared at his beloved head-torch inside the rows of razor-sharp teeth and Charlie realised what he was thinking. It really wasn't that far away, surely? Why should some blooming great fish have my beautiful new LED head-torch? No way!

Agent Ochre reached into the huge pike's mouth. His whole arm was inside the mighty jaws now.

'Wow. He REALLY wants his torch back,' thought Charlie.

Agent Ochre's fingers... could... just... about....reach... his head-torch...

With onc last huge effort Agent Ochre managed to wrench his torch off Agent Blue's ice-cold head inside the pike's jaws...

...and that's when the boathook snapped.

7

Befuddled Brian

Summer in the City was always a delight to behold.

Charlie found it spellbinding and loved to watch and listen to the hustle and bustle of it all as London woke up. Birds sang their little hearts out, trees offered their shady canopies to people out walking their dogs, and the little cafes and bars that dotted the shimmering city streets laid out their finest tableware. Early-bird shoppers looked down from bright red buses at the Mudlarks scattered along the shoreline and joggers pounded the pavements before the heat of the sun drove them all away. It was a beautiful start to the weekend.

Innumerable club dinghies, racing canoes and motley craft of all shapes and sizes were already bobbing about on the bright water, whizzing to and fro. Enthusiastic members of the *London Rowing Club* set about preparing their long wooden Gigs for a sweaty training day out on the water. Anglers cast their rods out onto the shimmering water and twenty members of the *Earls Court Junior Swimming Club* donned their rubber-caps and dipped their toes into the deceptively chilly water, egged on by proud parents.

Twice a day the Thames in London rose as much as twenty-three feet (or 'seven yards in old money' as Charlie's dad would say in typical bad *Dad-Joke* fashion, which Charlie never understood) with a tidal swell right up to the swirling waters of Teddington Lock. In that swell was washed up centuries of history – personal possessions that people over the years had lost or simply tossed away without a second thought into the river.

Charlie watched it all.

He could see it, hear it... even *smell* it. But he didn't

care about it. He knew he should have been shouting at everyone. Warning them about what was in the water. But he couldn't even move. His mouth felt as dry as the bottom of a parrot's cage and his skin was clammy despite the sun's warming rays. All he could do was keep a tight death-grip on the life-raft he was holding whilst his scrambled brain tried to make sense of what had happened last night.

He was safe now.

Safe, sitting next to a concrete boat ramp on the muddy banks of the Thames. He was watching the Fire Brigade trying to hook up the remains of a burnt-out powerboat to a large mobile crane. There wasn't much left of the boat – just the bottom of the thick GRP fibreglass hull and one engine hanging down from it. But at least Charlie wasn't in the water anymore. They'd fished him out and somebody had wrapped him up in a silver foil blanket. The tide was out and that... that *thing* in the water, that *monster* - well, it couldn't get hold of him now. But still his mind raced. Round and round and round it went, tormenting him with random questions and visions of horror. He shook his head trying to piece it all together, but nothing made much sense. The outside world felt far away.

Jazz had to shout three times before Charlie's befuddled brain even realised there was somebody standing right next to him.

'Charlie! Charlie! *Charlie...!!??* You okay?' she said.

Charlie recognised the voice, but it sounded extremely far away, like a bad memory. Too many bad memories at the moment, he thought. That voice again. Nope. He just couldn't put a face to it. He just sat on the riverbank shivering and staring straight ahead, holding on to the life-raft as though his life still depended on it.

'I don't think he even knows we're here,' sighed Jazz.

'So - what actually happened last night then?' asked a puzzled-looking Sam standing next to her, wrinkling up his nose.

'I don't really know,' she replied. 'He hasn't said a word since the River Police brought him ashore. All I know is that he was going fishing with his Uncle, next I'm getting some random texts from him in the middle of the night saying he was in trouble and he could see someone with a gun. I didn't know whether to believe him or not – you know what he's like – but he didn't seem to be telling a whopper this time.'

'Charlie doesn't tell whoppers!' said Sam indignantly, still wrinkling his nose up.

Charlie could hear his friend and gave a thin smile. 'Good ol' Sam. Always defending me,' he thought.

'Hmm. Well I don't know about that,' huffed Jazz. 'But he really sounded like he was in trouble, so I called...'

'Me!' beamed Sam.

'No, not you. Well okay yes, I did call you but then I called... the Police.'

'What? *You* called the Police? You know Charlie doesn't like the Police to be involved in our adventures. They always put a stop to our fun.'

'Er, Sam. Hello? Look at the state of him. I'm glad

I did. And will you stop wrinkling your nose up all the time!'

'I can't help it – my nose is itchy. I think its hay fever.'

'Well, scratch it then.'

'I can't get my finger that far up.'

'You're disgusting,' said Jazz.

'Yeah well, he should have called me first. I would have come down here and helped Charlie duff 'em all up.'

Jazz rolled her eyes. 'Your mum wouldn't even let you out until you'd had your breakfast this morning. Some help you were. But neither of us were there for him. He needed us last night and we let him down. Look at him - he looks half-drowned. Could have gotten himself killed. I wish this ambulance would hurry up.'

'Heh! I know. He never does anything by halves does he?' smiled Sam proudly, looking round at the remains of the speedboat being lifted out of the water. 'Cool crane, huh? Not much left of that boat – looks like Charlie had a brilliant time!'

'Yeah, it's cool. As soon as got off the bus I saw all the blue lights. Knew it had to be Charlie. Fire Brigade, River Police boats, that big crane thing – the whole lot were here, pretty much. There's an ambulance on its way, too. One of the Policemen radioed for it.'

'I'm not a Policeman, young lady. I'm a Detective Inspector.' said a craggy-faced man. He looked tired and the shabby blue suit he was wearing looked as though hc'd slept in it. He brushed Jazz and Sam to one side and stared down at the bedraggled Charlie, who still hadn't moved. 'In fact, I should inform you that I am Detective Inspector Williams of the *Metropolitan Police Marine Policing Unit* to be precise, not the River Police.'

Sam looked at Jazz and silently mouthed *'River Police!'* to her. She stifled a giggle.

'The Thames is our jurisdiction – what happens on it, in it, under it or by the side of it - is our business. Your friend, what did you say his name was again? Let's have a look at my notebook. Ah yes, Charlie Carter. Well, Charlie's in shock. Not too bad, but we've got to keep him warm until the ambulance gets here. Has he said anything yet?'

'Not a word' said Jazz.

'What about his next of kin? Has he got any parents or *anyone* at all willing to admit that he belongs to them?'

'Yes, of course he has. He's not some waif and stray you know. I've called Charlie's dad and I've got to let him know which hospital he'll be in.'

'Huh,' Sam grumbled under his breath. 'River Police. Not even the real Police. Pushing us around like that. Who does he think he is? Needs to buy himself an iron. And one for his suit.' Sam giggled at his own joke. 'I might have to show him some of my kung-fu moves...'

Jazz put a calming hand on Sam's arm. 'Hush up. The ambulance is taking its time, DI Williams, Sir' she said politely. 'Do you know which hospital they'll take him too, please...?

'I think it'll be....OH NO!' muttered DI Williams as a 'Daily Echo News Team' van with a massive satellite dish on its roof appeared at the top of the boat ramp. 'That's the last thing I need.'

Charlie watched without emotion as a DENT Cameraman and a grey-haired DENT Reporter jumped out of the van and DI Williams rushed up the boat ramp to usher them away. Charlie could hear a few snatched bits of their conversation. DI Williams wasn't in the mood to answer any questions and had a face on him like he'd just swallowed a wasp. The acronym DENT was written in big letters on the side of the microphone which was thrust into DI Williams face.

'Has last night's events got anything to do with the swimmers that have mysteriously gone missing over the last few weeks?' enquired the DENT Reporter loudly.

'No comment. This is an official Police matter and we're still continuing our investigations. Now, if you'll kindly...'

'There have been four swimmers reported missing in the last month alone, Sergeant. The public have a right to know what's going on. What are the River

Police doing about the missing angler, that is, if you're actually doing anything at all?'

DI Williams didn't take the bait. 'All in good time, all in good time. These sorts of things happen sometimes – the Thames is a dangerous place. The General Public are reminded to follow official guidelines and...'

'Would you like to tell viewers what caused the explosion last night?' demanded the DENT Reporter.

'Look, I'm due to give a Press Conference later this week, I'll answer all your questions then. For now, though, please let us get on with our job. You can see we have an injured person here and our priority is to get him away to hospital as soon as possible.'

'Oh yes, look! There's an injured boy!' shouted the DENT Reporter, dashing past DI Williams with the cameraman in tow.

DI Williams shouted after them 'And I'm NOT a Sergeant and we're NOT the River Police. I'm DI Williams of the *Metropolitan Police Marine Policing Unit* and I'm....'

The big mobile crane revved up and the rest of his words were drowned out. One of the straps that the Fire Brigade had put around the still smoking shell of the speedboat had come off, and the Chief Fire Officer was shouting at the crane driver.

The DENT news team thrust their camera and microphone in Charlie's face.

'Are you a witness? Did you see the explosion earlier this morning? Are you injured? What happened?'

'This,' said Sam in a grand voice. 'Is the one and only Charlie Carter.'

The camera zoomed in on Sam. The DENT Reporter wrote down *'Charlie Carter'* in his notebook.

'He lives on a great big farm the other side of Heathrow Airport. He's a brilliant inventor and nearly thirteen years old. Quite possibly a child-genius. Not unlike my good self. Oh, I'm Sam by the way. Samuel Curtis. I'm his best friend. Make sure you write that bit down, please.'

'Okay, carry on,' said the DENT Reporter, furiously scribbling down notes.

'He was abducted by aliens last night, but this morning they returned him for a refund.'

The DENT Reporter wrote down *'Abducted by al....'* then stopped writing.

DI Williams appeared. 'That's quite enough of that. Please, thank you, thank you....' and a couple of uniformed Police Officers herded the DENT News Team away.

'Huh. Well, I hope they got my name right...' huffed Sam.

'Ssh!' Jazz hissed. 'I can hear...'

Charlie could hear the ambulance siren as well. The shrill wail reverberated around the banks of the Thames and rattled painfully around his skull. He noticed that all the other Police cars, Police boats and Fire Engines assembled around the top and bottom of the slipway all had their sirens turned off, although their lights were still flashing. DI Williams ran off and directed the ambulance in.

'I suppose they don't need their sirens on unless

they're moving through traffic,' thought Charlie. 'Hey! I just had a proper, sensible thought!'

Charlie looked up and tried to smile at the girl standing next to him. The smile was more of a grimace. 'Well, I think I'm returning to normal. Is that you, Jazz? What are you doing here? Hey, you've brought Sam along as well. What's going on?'

'Ah, at last. Hello, Charlie. Welcome back to the real world. Are you warm enough? Do you want another silver blanket? You can let go of that life-raft now if you want to. The ambulance is here at last and I've phoned your Dad to let him know you're alright, he's going to meet you in hospital. I've also let the school know that you won't be making the Riverboat Shuffle tonight. Think you'll still be in hospital, I dare say. But we'll come and pick you up when they say you can go home. I was going to get you a cup of tea, but they wouldn't let me. How are you feeling?'

'Whoah, whoah. TMI, Jazz!' said Charlie. 'Say all that again, but slower. You know it took my mum's locket.'

'What did?'

'And it took my Uncle.'

'Have you banged your head?' asked Jazz. 'I was saying...'

'Jazz. Stop fussing round him,' interrupted Sam. 'Give him a chance to speak!'

'Well, he hasn't got anyone to make a fuss of him now, has he? Only his Dad and he's all 'stiff upper lip' and all that nonsense.'

'Give him some air, Jazz. He doesn't want to answer any silly questions right now. Hey Charlie! Did you watch the football, last night? It was brilliant!'

Jazz rolled her eyes.

Charlie gave a little snort. He knew he shouldn't be rotten to his best mate. Normally he could never be down and unhappy around Sam as he never took life that seriously. But just of late, all Charlie wanted to do was punch him, although he didn't know why.

'No Sam, no I didn't watch the bloomin' football last night, you doofus!' said Charlie. 'I had better things to do. Although for the life of me I can't remember *what* I was doing, exactly. What's going on, mum? Who's all this lot? What are they doing with that boat? Actually, where IS here? My head hurts. I think my brian might be a little befuddled but it's get get getting betterrrrrr undiscombumbumhotrodspitfireWOWbigfish!' Charlie frowned. 'Oh no. Wait. Hang on a minute. Perhaps my brian, I mean, my *brain* isn't quite back to normal yet,' he groaned.

Jazz flashed Sam a worried look as the Paramedics strapped Charlie onto a large wheeled stretcher.

'Kablaaaamm!' shouted Charlie as they wheeled him up the slipway.

'You'll be okay!' Jazz called after him, uncertainty in her voice.

'Giant inflatable fish!' Charlie shouted. 'Top Secret cylinders with glowing eyes! Rejoov! Holy Macaroni, Jazz. There's a monster down there. THERE'S A MONSTER IN THE THAMES! YOU'VE GOT TO WARN EVERYBODY!'

'What WAS he going on about, Jazz?' asked Sam. 'And I thought *my* story about the aliens was far-fetched.'

'Think he's banged his head.' she sighed.

'Sounds quite exciting!' said Sam.

And judging by the frantic scribbling in his notebook, the grey-haired DENT Reporter listening nearby also thought it sounded quite exciting.

8

A Fishy Tale

Jazz frowned, not sure what to say next about Charlie's crazy outbursts. Just before the Paramedics wheeled him into the ambulance, Charlie continued shouting.

'WAIT, WAIT! I'VE GOT TO TELL JAZZ SOMETHING...'

'Okay, said the Paramedic. 'But don't be long. We've got to run some tests on you yet before we can take you to hospital.'

'Jazz,' said Charlie. 'Come here! I'm starting to remember things...'

'I think the word you're looking for is *please*,' said Jazz, pretending to be quite cross. She bent down at the side of Charlie's stretcher and he started whispering to her quite animatedly, telling her everything. Sam skulked off to find somebody else to talk to.

There was action going on all around. DI Williams was trying to direct a crowd of sightseers away from the mobile crane which was revving its engine and belching great clouds of grey smoke out of its tall exhaust pipes. The Fire Brigade had managed to get the remnants of the burnt-out speedboat halfway up the steep ramp. Rainbow coloured water ran down the ramp and into the Thames.

Charlie carried on babbling away to Jazz about what had happened. Neither of them noticed the grey-haired Reporter lurking nearby and writing down their every word.

Sam stuck his head in the back of the ambulance.

'Hello, Doctor!' said Sam loudly, making the Paramedic jump. 'I'm Sam, Charlie's best friend. You know - Charlie Carter. He's famous. That's him over there. You've probably heard of him...?'

'Nope,' shrugged the paramedic. 'Never heard of him, not until just now. What's he famous for?'

'Erm... he's a famous inventor, just like his Dad. His Dad's brilliant. He was the first man in space, you know!' said Sam, proudly.

'What? You mean his Dad's Yuri Gagarin?'

'Er, no, no. Perhaps his Dad must have discovered Gravity, then. He's very important.'

'That was Isaac Newton. He died in 1727.'

'Ah. Probably not Charlie's dad then. Don't think he's quite that old. Nearly, but not quite. He used to have a very important job in the City, but I can't remember what it was. Anyway, he says he's retired now, but he's not really, and he's just bought a great big farm that Charlie lives on and when I go round, me an' Charlie try out all his inventions, then one day one blew up and...'

'Can I actually help you with anything, young man?' interrupted the Paramedic.

'I was just wondering how long you were going to keep Charlie for, that's all really. Only we've got some serious stuff to do today,' said Sam as he read through some medical leaflets in the ambulance.

The Paramedic gave an impromptu laugh.

'Well, young man, as soon as we can get him in here, we can run a few tests before we take him off to Hospital,' she said.

'What sort of tests? Palpitation tests?' asked Sam, reading a leaflet.

'Yes, probably but...'

'Conjunctivitis tests?'

'Erm, no. I don't think we'll be testing him for con...'

'What about Glutinosity?'

'No.'

'Collywobbles?'

'Definitely not.' she said, patience wearing wafer-thin.

'Hypotension-itis?' continued Sam. 'Tennis Elbow? Morgellons....?'

'No, no and no. Oh my word, stop!' shouted the

Paramedic, clearly rattled by Sam's incessant questions. She tried to regain her professionalism. 'We won't be doing those sorts of tests on your friend. We'll have in here for about twenty minutes, then we'll take him off to hospital – I daresay he'll be in overnight. Got to make sure he's back to normal, first.'

'Normal? Who, Charlie? Good luck with that, then!' laughed Sam.

'Maybe he can come out to play with you tomorrow,' she said.

'Come out to *play*?' said Sam. 'We're not kids you know.'

'How old are you, then?'

'I'm 12 and Charlie's nearly 13.'

'Oh, right. Sorry,' apologised the Paramedic, raising her eyebrows and giving Sam an incredulous look. 'What's this 'serious stuff' you're going off to do, then?'

'Treasure Hunting!' beamed Sam.

'Treasure hu....?' began the Paramedic, then stopped herself. She bit her lip and tried not to laugh.

'Yeah, Charlie's dad made us some proper metal detectors last week, and we're going to be famous millionaires when we dig up all the treasure down here.'

'Ah. I see. What you really mean is that you're going mud-larking,' said the Paramedic.

'TREASURE HUNTING' corrected Sam.

Then he spelt it out for the poor lady Paramedic, who obviously couldn't understand the exciting concept of hunting for buried treasure and becoming a zillionaire in the process.

'T-R-E-S-H-A-H-U-N-G-T-I-N. I saw a brilliant programme on tv about it. This archy, er, archangel, no, archaeopteryx...'

'Archaeologist?' enquired the Paramedic.

'Yes. That's him. He said there's loads of treasure from Kings and Queens from centuries ago down here, all buried along the Thames when the tide goes out – so we're going to find it and be RICH!' Sam could tell that the lady Paramedic wasn't that impressed, so he sniffed and added: 'We don't do mud-larking. That's for amateurs.'

'Hmm. Okay,' she sighed. 'I'm sure you'll have lots of fun, young man. Now excuse me, but I've got to get back to work. I have to look after your friend.'

The wheels of Charlie's stretcher clunked into place as they brought him in to the ambulance, and the lady Paramedic started strapping all kinds of tubes and pipes and plasters on, connecting him up to lots of beeping instruments. Sam watched the procedure in awe.

'Hey Charlie!' shouted Sam. 'I'm going to be an Ambulance Driver when I grow up. Bet it's great fun! I was just telling the Doctor here all about...'

'Paramedic,' corrected the Paramedic.

'Sorry,' said Sam. I was just telling Doctor Paramedic here about the time when we...'

'Yes, yes, yes,' said the Paramedic, ushering the non-stop talking machine known as Sam out of the back of the ambulance. 'We've got to look after your friend, now, young man.' and reached over and shut the ambulance doors in Sam's face.

'I see you've met Sam,' apologised Charlie. 'He's a

good kid, really. Heart of gold. Just doesn't know when to shut up.'

'Yes, he was a bit non-stop.'

'You know Doc, it's funny,' Charlie continued as the Paramedic started taking readings from all the dials and gauges. 'Look at them all trying to get what's left of that speedboat up the ramp. There were two people in that – three if you count me. But both of them died. Don't know how I didn't. Just lucky, I guess. It chose them, not me. That boat ramp is meant to be used for having fun. It's meant for launching brilliant dinghy's from or racing canoes or even hovercraft! It's for families to get out onto the water and have fun – you know. It's meant for good times, not bad. But I guess you can't have good without bad, can you? Otherwise how do you know what good is? So I really need to warn people about the monster mmmk blllub ummmk...'

The lady Paramedic quickly strapped an oxygen mask on Charlie and tightened it so that he couldn't talk anymore.

'Sheesh. You kids!' she sighed. 'Do you all talk non-stop?'

Charlie got the message and sat there in a huff. But all he could think about was the giant fish with teeth as long as his hand, exploding speedboats, mysterious silver cylinders full of Rejoov whatever that was, and Secret Agents up to no good. But most of all the locket his Uncle had shown him. The locket with the photo of Charlie and his mum in it. His mum's locket. *Charlie's* locket. It wasn't his Uncles. And it certainly didn't belong to some overgrown stickleback. Round and round and round his thoughts went. What on earth did it all mean? And who, or what was The Fizz? His brain was tired and started to whirl again. It needed a rest and Charlie let it. He slowly drifted off to sleep.

'I guess with me going to spend yet another night in hospital, I'm not going to solve this mystery anytime soon,' yawned Charlie, closing his eyes. 'At least I've told Jazz pretty much everything. I can rely on her. Luckily, she believed every word I said, especially when I told her that we have no choice to get my mum's locket back...

We HAVE to catch the monster pike.'

9

A Gruesome Discovery

'Charlie Carter's such a liar!' said Jazz.

'What are you on about? Charlie's brilliant!' said Sam.

'A brilliant liar, maybe.'

'He never lies! Anyway, what did he come out with this time, then?' asked Sam.

'Oh, he gave me some fishy story like he usually does, that's all.'

'Cool. Let's hear it then.'

'He said he'd seen a monster.'

'The Loch Ness Monster?'

'No, moron. What would the Loch Ness Monster be doing in the Thames?'

'Might be on holiday.'

'I despair, I really do,' said Jazz shaking her head. 'You're just as bad as Charlie, sometimes.'

'I'm really going to miss him.'

'They're only taking him in for one night. Shame he's going to miss the Riverboat Shuffle tonight, though – he always makes me laugh when he tries to dance. Still, we can all visit him in hospital tomorrow and bring him back home. His Dad said he'll give us a lift.'

'I'm going to be an ambulance driver when I grow up!' said Sam excitedly.

'You? An ambulance driver? Pfft!' laughed Jazz. 'Seriously? You'd only be taking Charlie backwards and forwards to hospital and nobody else. You'd end up seeing each other even more than you do now.'

'That'd be cool! How many times did we visit Charlie in hospital last year?'

Jazz shrugged. 'Ten? Twelve? He had about one major accident every month, I think.'

'I know! Charlie's awesome, isn't he?' exclaimed Sam. 'Remember that time when Charlie's dad invented that rocket-powered jetpack and Charlie borrowed it but melted a hole in the roof of his Dad's cowshed and then Charlie fell through it and got covered in...'

'Yes, I remember that,' giggled Jazz at the thought. Charlie was an idiot sometimes, but he did get up to some funny stuff. 'I thought his Dad was going to go mad at us for that – but I think he laughed more than we did!'

'Until he realised that one of Charlie's feet was facing the wrong way!' laughed Sam.

Jazz tutted at the memory but let out a little laugh.

'Charlie's brilliant!' laughed Sam. 'And what about that time when it snowed, and Charlie helped his Dad invent that car with tank tracks? Then Charlie borrowed it and rolled it over. That was a right laugh!'

'Yes. Although he did break his arm in two places.'

'I know. Cool, eh?' beamed Sam. 'Charlie's just like

his Dad, isn't he?' Jazz was just about to agree with him when Sam added, 'A complete loon! Wish I lived on a farm.'

'My mum said that everyone in the hospital knows Charlie by name, as he's there more often than the doctors and nurses.' laughed Jazz.

'What *did* happen to his mum?' asked Sam in a quiet voice.

Jazz stopped mid-laugh and took a deep breath. 'My mum said not to worry about it. She said Charlie would tell us in his own time. It's such a shame. He was very close to his mum.'

'Oh,' said Sam.

'I don't know what it must feel like to lose a parent,' sighed Jazz. 'Neither of us do, do we? Charlie does now, though, and I feel so sorry for him. I just don't know what to do for the best. Ignore it for now, I guess. I hope we never have to find out what it feels like.'

Sam looked dejected and Jazz though he was about to cry.

'Anyway!' shouted Sam suddenly, making Jazz jump. 'Come on, we've got some serious work to do! I brought the metal detectors with me!'

Sam ran off to where two rucksacks were lying next to the slipway and Jazz ran after him.

'Charlie takes too many risks sometimes and that's why he ends up hurting himself. But I'm glad you two boneheads let me come along on your crazy adventures,' she laughed.

The shadow of a crumpled blue suit and the smell of clothes left too long in the washing machine loomed over them both as they took the metal detectors out.

'Where are you two little Herberts off to now, then?' said DI Williams doing his detective bit.

Sam bristled. 'Nowhere,' he shrugged.

'What was Charlie saying to you, young lady?' asked the detective.

'We don't know,' said Sam.

DI Williams gave a little laugh. 'I wasn't talking to you, young man. I was talking to the young lady here, erm...' DI Williams got out his crumpled notebook. 'Let me see now, what's your name again, young lady?'

'Don't tell him, Jazz!' shouted Sam.

'Ah yes, that's it, thank you. Jazz.'

Jazz gave Sam a withering look.

'Hmm. I couldn't get anything out of young Charlie when I tried speaking to him just now. He's going through a lot, isn't he? We found his Uncle by the Marina. Well, what's left of him, anyway. Not a pretty sight, I can tell you.'

'I think Charlie must have banged his head,' lied Jazz. 'He was talking complete nonsense.'

'He does that a lot anyway!' laughed Sam.

DI Williams turned towards Sam and peered down at him closely, trying to look threatening, but he didn't pull it off very well. He looked more like a friendly Uncle rather than an actual detective.

'This is a serious Police matter,' said DI Williams in a gentle but serious voice. 'What's *your* name, just for my notes, please, young man?' he tucked his chin in and raised one eyebrow towards Sam.

Sam tucked his chin in and raised one eyebrow as well. 'I'll tell you my name if you tell me yours,' he said.

'I asked first.'

'I asked second.'

The DI gave Jazz a sideways look and a wink. 'Is he always this difficult?' he smiled.

Jazz shrugged her shoulders. Inside she was cringing. Sam might have been little, but he had no fear. Or respect for Authority, for that matter.

'Sam!' she whispered. 'Don't be a doob!'

'I've told you once, anyway. I'm DI Williams.'

'Are you Welsh?' asked Sam.

'No, I'm not Welsh!' said DI Williams incredulously. 'D dot I dot Williams. Not *Dai* Williams! DI stands for Detective Inspector. I wasn't born DI Williams, was I? Hrumph. Now then. Who are you?'

'Samuel Curtis, Sir,' said Sam, saluting. 'Known as Sam to my friends. S dot A dot M. You can call me Samuel.'

DI Williams was about to take the bait when a loud ***graunching*** noise and lots of shouting from the slipway disturbed the peace. He looked round and saw that the still-smouldering remains of the speedboat had detached itself from the crane's ropes. It shot back down the slipway at speed, hitting the water with a loud **HISSSSSSsssss**

DI Williams dashed off, shouting and waving his fists at the crane driver and his crew. All the Emergency crews began scurrying around as well, and DI Williams was pointing at things then holding his head with both hands in rapid succession.

'Idiots. Some numpty's in big trouble,' said Jazz as she turned to Sam. 'That wasn't funny, you know. DI Williams seems to be a nice man, really. He's only doing his job.'

'Well, I don't like him. He's the numpty. He shouldn't have pushed you earlier. I bet Charlie would have given him what for if he'd seen that.'

'Oh, it's always *'Charlie this'* and *'Charlie that'* with you, isn't it? And anyway, he didn't really push me, did he? It was only a nudge.'

Sam didn't look convinced. A loud noise and more shouting from the boat ramp stopped him from saying what he was thinking.

CRRRACKKK!

'Whoah! Look at that, Jazz! Awesome!' Sam pointed at the smouldering remains of the speedboat which had just embedded itself into the side of one of the Police boats.

Both boats slowly started sinking below the surface of the Thames and more rainbows formed in the water as their lifeblood spilled out. The River Police were shouting at the Fire Brigade, the Fire Brigade officers were shouting at the mobile crane driver and DI Williams was shouting at everyone.

'Shall we just leave them all too it?' suggested Jazz.

Sam nodded and pulled a 'Let's get outta here!' face.

Down on the muddy riverbank the tide was out but it would soon be creeping back in.

'Hey, look at this!' shouted Sam. 'Look where the

high tide mark is – it's about three times higher than me!' He pointed to a thick green slimy line way above his outstretched hands. 'Amazing to think that all this will be under water again in a couple of hours!'

'Yeah. Amazing,' shrugged Jazz. 'You get excited about anything don't you?'

Jazz was carefully sweeping her metal detector to and fro across the muddy shoreline. Its slow and steady **beep** meant it hadn't detected anything metal yet. Sam was waving his metal detector in front of him like a demented Ghostbuster.

'Hey look, Jazz, I ain't afraid of no ghost!' shouted Sam as he sloshed around in the mud.

On the side of each amazing beeping contraption, painted in Charlie's scrawl, were the words 'The Carter USM6'.

'What's USM6 stand for, Sam?'

'Charlie said it's the 'Ultra-Sonic Machine Version Number 6'.

'Version Number 6? You mean his Dad's made five previous versions?'

'Yup. But they all blew up.'

'Blew up?' Jazz looked at the metal detector she was using and carefully held it away from her as far as she could.

BWEEP * BWEEP * BWEEP * BWEEP * BWEEP * BWEEP * BWEEP

'My detector won't stop beeping!' exclaimed Sam. 'There must be buried treasure EVERYWHERE down here! Bet it's the Crown Jewels, or a chest full of pirate treasure!' he squealed excitedly and pulled a little shovel out of his backpack.

'Don't think so!' Jazz laughed. 'Knowing you, it's probably an old unexploded bomb from World War Two.'

Sam pulled a comical 'Oh my god!' face at Jazz. 'Yeah! That would be brilliant!'

'Until it blew your legs off.'

Sam started to dig little holes all around himself, which quickly filled up with water.

'I think I've dug up half the Thames, you know.' He said disappointedly. 'Haven't found a single thing yet -

but I reckon I'm going to find a Lancaster bomber. That'd be worth a fortune on eBay! Charlie said people keep seeing the ghost of a World War 2 bomber flying about, so I reckon it must have crashed right here...'

'I don't think you'll find an old Warplane round here,' Jazz sighed. 'Not 75 years after the war, anyway.'

BWEEP * BWEEP * BWEEP * BWEEP * BWEEP * BWEEP

'Well, it's either that or my detector must be on the blink then.' said Sam.

'We've only been down here five minutes, give it a chance. Try over there. Hey look - they haven't even taken Charlie away yet. They're taking ages with him.'

Sam looked over to the slipway and could see all sorts of people and vehicles moving around where the ambulance was still parked. 'Yes, they're giving him a test for Morgellons,' he said with great authority. 'They'll give him a thorough test for Encephalitis Lethargica before they take him away, as well.'

'Really,' said Jazz not believing a word. 'He just

banged his head and started seeing things, that's all.'

'Well he did get kidnapped by aliens and blow up a speedboat.'

'Pfftt! No, he didn't. Kidnapped by...! Hah!' Scoffed Jazz. 'All he did was bang his head, fall in the water and the River Police had to fish him out. He's obviously got concussion, that's all, the rubbish he was coming out with.'

'Really? What did he tell you then?'

'Well, for a start he told me that there were Secret Agents on that speedboat. And they were smuggling some green liquid stuff called Rejoov into the country by night. One of them even had a gun. Then he said that they were attacked by a... a...'

'What?'

'He told me that he saw a pike. A giant one. And it ate both of the Secret Agents.'

'Sounds plausible' nodded Sam.

'No, it doesn't, you bonehead!' exclaimed Jazz. 'How does ANY of that sound true in the slightest? There's no

Secret Agents, no Rejoov or whatever it's called, and no such thing as a giant pike.'

'Well, I believe him.'

'Well, you would,' she pouted.

'Jazz?'

'Yes?' she snapped impatiently.

'What's a pike?'

'You see! How can you believe ANY of that pack of lies when you don't even know what a pike is? Pike! You know, P-I-K-E.' she spelt it out for him. 'It's a fish. Everyone catches them round here.'

'Thank you. I was only asking.... A-S-K-I-N-G. How big's a pike then?'

Jazz calmed down. 'Well, they're only about this big,' she said holding her arms up. 'About three or four feet long.'

'That's not very big.'

'That's big enough. They're vicious things with a bad temper. Charlie caught one once and it was huge – nearly four feet long and full of teeth. It bit him when he tried to take the hook out and it gashed his hand wide open.'

'Cool!' exclaimed Sam.

'Except that...'

'What?'

'Charlie said the one he saw last night was twenty feet long.'

Sam looked at Jazz, open mouthed. He didn't say a word and slowly lost his grip on the metal detector which slipped down to his feet.

BWEEP!!

Jazz and Sam both jumped at the same time.

BWEEP * BWEEP * BWEEP * BWEEP * BWEEP * BWEEP * BWEEP * BWEEP *

'Buried treasure!' shouted Sam.

Jazz wasn't so sure. 'Er, Sam....?' she asked, looking down at the boots Sam was wearing. 'Have you got steel-toecap boots on?'

'Yeah, of course. I always wear them. They keep my feet safe.'

He swung his metal detector over his boots.

BWEEP * BWEEP * BWEEP * BWEEP * BWEEP * BWEEP * BWEEP * BWEEP *

Sam lifted his detector up. It stopped beeping. He waved it over his boots again.

BWEEP * BWEEP * BWEEP * BWEEP * BWEEP * BWEEP * BWEEP * BWEEP *

Sam gave Jazz a big sheepish grin.

'Doughnut!' she laughed and walked off.

She'd only taken a few steps when her own metal detector went into overdrive and started to beep and ping loudly.

BEEWEEEEP! PYOW! PYOW!

Jazz looked down. There was something shiny sticking up out of the mud and weeds. She moved her metal detector out of the way and lifted the small metal object up.

'This is heavier than it looks,' she said and gave it a tug to free it from the weeds and mud or whatever it was caught up on.

Sam bounded excitedly towards Jazz, then stopped, almost mid-bound.

'Look!' Jazz said proudly. 'It's a head-torch I think – but it's really heavy.'

Sam stared at her, wide-eyed and open mouthed. He looked at the head-torch, then at Jazz, then back at the torch.

'Drop it, Jazz! Drop it! Look!'

Jazz looked down, and everything went into that kind of slow-motion effect like in the films. She wanted to run but her feet wouldn't listen. It was like she was stuck in some kind of nightmare where the axe-murderer is getting closer and closer and you're running and running but getting nowhere.

'Yeeeeeeaaaiiiiii!' Jazz screamed out loud and stared in horror at the weeds still attached to the head-torch she was holding. But no. No! They weren't long weeds. They were fingers. Human fingers. And the fingers were still gripping the strap of the head-torch. And those fingers were attached to a hand which was attached to an arm which was attached to... nothing. It was a severed arm holding onto the shiny new head-torch.

The world came back to Jazz at full speed. She flinched instinctively and threw the head-torch and dismembered human arm away as far as she could. The grisly relic fell with a loud **splat** between her and Sam, who could only stare at it in silent horror.

A deep, gravelly voice interrupted the silence.

'Hey. That's MY torch.'

Jazz and Sam looked slowly round to where the voice was coming from.

A large man in a smart suit covered in mud was lying an arm's throw away.

Jazz looked at Sam.

Sam looked at Jazz.

They both looked at the one-armed man lying there in the mud.

'And I think that's my arm, too,' groaned Agent Ochre.

Then Jazz and Sam screamed together at the top of their lungs.

10

Agent Purple

The ambulance finally pulled away from the top of the slipway, sirens blaring and lights flashing. Its 'blues and twos' echoed around the tall offices and dilapidated warehouses. A man in a crumpled blue suit jumped in front of it and slapped the bonnet hard.

'Stop! Stop!' shouted DI Williams.

Inside, Charlie woke up with a start as the back doors to his ambulance burst open. Two Police Officers holding a man on a makeshift stretcher stood there. Each of them was covered in mud from head to toe and it was difficult to tell them apart. DI Williams looked like he was holding... what was that? An arm?

'Doctor! Thank god you haven't left yet! I'm DI Williams from the Marine Policing Unit....'

'You mean the River Police?' asked the creepy-looking male Paramedic sitting next to Charlie. He had black hair full of Brylcreem. There was no sign of the lady Paramedic.

'No, not the River... anyway, that doesn't matter. This is a REAL emergency - this man has lost an arm!'

'Oh okay. Which one?' shrugged the Paramedic, clearly not that bothered.

'It's this one here,' said DI Williams, pointing Agent Ochre's arm at the creepy Paramedic. 'Oh I see, you mean which *person*? The big man. It's his right arm. He needs to get to hospital straight away. Might still be able to re-attach it.'

'Erm, we're a bit busy in here really...'

'What? But you're an ambulance!'

'Not much room, really...' said the Paramedic.

'You've got two stretchers in there! Take him to hospital, NOW! That's an order!' barked DI Williams.

Charlie watched as the Police lifted the semi-conscious figure of the big man he'd seen on the speedboat the night before, into the ambulance and onto the spare stretcher. Then they laid something that looked like a cow's leg on top of his chest.

Charlie stared at Agent Ochre's dismembered arm and felt a bit sick. It was still holding onto the head-torch.

'Thought he'd lost that.' Charlie said to the creepy-looking male Paramedic. He looked a bit sick, too.

'Bet you've seen worse than that,' said Charlie.

'True,' replied the Paramedic, then to DI Williams, 'Where did you find him?'

'*We* didn't find him. *We* couldn't find a barn door if it were right there in front of us, could we?' said DI Williams as he glared at his Police Officers. They all looked the other way. 'Absolutely useless, this lot. No, *we* didn't find him - those two did.'

DI Williams nodded in the direction of Sam and Jazz.

Both looked a bit ill. Sam waved at Charlie, then made a 'being sick' sign. Charlie nodded.

'They found him near to where we found Charlie, just down there on the shoreline.' said DI Williams. Then in a softer tone, turned to Charlie and asked, 'How you feeling, lad?'

'Mmmm. Ib fime. Glmmm...' mumbled Charlie and loosened his oxygen mask.

'Good, good. Right then – you'd best get on your way to hospital.' DI Williams went to slam the back door of the ambulance shut, but stopped just in time as Sam stuck his head in.

'See you at the hospital later, Charlie,' said Sam. 'At least you'll be safe as houses there.'

'It worries me when you say that!' said Charlie. 'It's like an omen.'

'A what?'

'Whenever you tell me I'll be safe, I'm usually anything but.'

'Come on you two, this ambulance has got to go.'

Sam smiled and waved a cheery 'goodbye' to Charlie, and Charlie gave a feeble wave back. But then he noticed a curious look on Sam's face. Sam was staring at the male Paramedic.

'Sam? You okay?'

'Charlie, that para...'

'Goodbye!' said DI Williams and prodded Sam out of the way. He slammed the back doors of the ambulance shut and slapped them hard, twice. As the ambulance drove off, DI Williams stuck his tongue out at Sam and walked off.

'Child,' muttered Sam under his breath.

Agent Ochre looked round at his blurry new surroundings. He peered hard at Charlie then gave him a weak nod.

'Ohhh. Hey. You okay?'

'Hi,' said Charlie. 'I'm okay, I think.'

'You're the kid from last night, aren't you?'

'Guess so,' said Charlie. 'I'm Charlie. Charlie Carter. You're not going to try and kill me, are you?'

'Heh! No, kid I'm not going to try and kill you.'

'Why are you called Agent Ochre?'

'That's just the codename the Fizz gave me, kid. My real name's Jeremiah. Pleased to me you... OWWW!' He went to try and shake Charlie's hand but then looked down to see his missing arm. 'Oh wow, what happened last night? It's all a bit of a blur.'

'Tell me about it,' said Charlie.

'I remember being on my speedboat. Then Agent Blue fell in the water. Then you appeared and... and... wasn't there some big explosion?'

'Certainly was,' said Charlie.

'Hmmm. How *is* my speedboat?'

'I think you might need to get a new one.'

'It's starting to come back to me now...' groaned Jeremiah. 'Hey! It was you! YOU blew up my speedboat!'

'Me? No, I didn't! I knew you'd blame me for that. It was...'

'And there was... something in the water. It was huge. What was it...? OWWWW!'

Jeremiah winced again and scratched his torn-off arm with his good hand.

'You've got a phantom pain,' said Charlie.

'A what?'

'Some people can still feel a phantom pain in a limb that's not there anymore,' said Charlie. 'I saw it on a programme once.'

'Oh, right. But scratching it makes it feel better! Hey, Doc,' he called over to the Paramedic, 'Have you got any more painkillers on this bus?'

'Just a minute,' said the Paramedic with his back towards them. 'I've got something here that will help.' He rattled around in a drawer full of syringes and drugs.

Charlie saw Jeremiah look at the Paramedic and a strange look came over his face. It was like Jeremiah could only half-remember something that was tantalisingly just out of reach, almost on the tip of his tongue but not quite. Charlie knew how he felt. They'd both been through quite an ordeal last night. But then Jeremiah seemed to have a lightbulb moment and a look of recognition flashed across his bloodshot eyes. He stared hard at the black-haired Paramedic and Charlie thought he was about to say something profound....

'SHARRRRRKKKKK!!!!!'

screamed Jeremiah at the top of his voice.

The Paramedic plunged a hypodermic syringe into Jeremiah, who was flailing around all over the place. It sent him off to sleep almost immediately with a quiet gurgle.

'No, don't worry,' said Charlie, turning to the Paramedic. 'It wasn't a shark. He's got that totally wrong.'

'I know,' said the Paramedic.

'Nah, it wasn't a shark.' Charlie said, casually. 'It was a PIKE. A real monster. About twenty-five feet long.'

'Yup. I know,' said the Paramedic again.

Charlie relaxed. He felt safe now, here in the back of an ambulance. He was on his way to hospital where he'd be looked after. He'd probably be out in a day or two. Everything would be okay. Jeremiah was snoring on his own stretcher. Even the Paramedic was chilled out. Charlie noticed he was changing out of his work clothes and taking off the green NHS paramedic uniform. Underneath he was wearing a nice smart black suit. Charlie absent-mindedly watched the London streets pass by the ambulance windows. The blues and greens of the Thames slowly gave way to the browns and greys of the big city and...hey. Wait a minute. Why was the Paramedic changing into a black suit? Charlie didn't understand.

His mobile phone beeped.

JAZZ MOB:	Get off the ambulance now!
CHARLIE MOB:	We're not at the hospital yet.
JAZZ MOB:	Police just found the ambulance crew tied up!!!
CHARLIE MOB:	What r u talking about?

JAZZ MOB:	**Sam told Police that your paramedic wasn't the same one he spoke to earlier. DI Williams did a search and found the real ambulance crew! Your Paramedic isn't a Paramedic! Get out Charlie!**
CHARLIE MOB:	**Calm down, Jazz, it's all fine here and…**

A gloved hand took the phone from Charlie's grip. He looked up and the creepy-looking Paramedic was standing over him with an evil glint in his eye. He had Charlie's phone in one hand and a hypodermic syringe that Charlie didn't like the look of *at all* in his other hand.

'Sorry, kid – but we can't have any witnesses.'

He went to plunge the syringe into Charlie's arm but just then the ambulance lurched violently around a corner and the man in the black suit fell backwards over Jeremiah, who grunted loudly in his sleep. The syringe dropped to the floor and rolled away. Charlie leapt up, trying to get as far away from the strange Paramedic as he could and pressed himself against the rear doors. He could hear sirens in the distance. The glass partition opened at the front of the ambulance and another man in a black suit peered through.

'Agent Purple! They're onto us!'

'Just drive, you idiot!' shouted Agent Purple as he desperately tried to retrieve the syringe as it rolled around the floor.

The driver did what he was told and floored it. The ambulance surged forward, and Charlie's face thudded against the back windows. He looked out and could see a line of Police cars zigzagging through the traffic behind the ambulance. DI Williams was in the first Police car, quickly catching up. There were at least two or three other Police cars behind him. The ambulance lurched violently again throwing medical equipment everywhere. Jeremiah's spare arm fell on top of Agent Purple's head.

'Oof!'

'That was impressive,' thought Charlie. 'Jeremiah's

just managed to punch someone even though he was asleep. Cool!'

Charlie peeled his squashed face off the back window. Behind the line of Police Cars was the DENT news van desperately trying to keep up. Charlie thought he went weightless at one point as the ambulance swerved and skidded all over the road. They were going at breakneck speed through London traffic. Through red lights. Through speed cameras. Driving on the wrong side of the road. They even went through a stack of cardboard boxes at one point. The screaming sirens were loud and piercing as the ambulance cornered hard and Agent Purple fell across Charlie's empty stretcher. The sudden weight caused the stretcher's wheels to come loose from its floor clips. Just for a moment, the stretcher wedged itself sideways between Charlie and Agent Purple.

Something rolled against Charlie's foot.

'Give me that syringe, kid!' hissed Agent Purple.

Charlie watched in horror as Agent Purple grabbed hold of the stretcher and crushed the metal bars with his bare hands. He was a LOT stronger than he looked.

'Think Charlie, think!' He said to himself as he looked around at all the pressure gauges, oxygen tanks, monitors and who knows what else all now shaking itself loose. The only thing that wasn't shaking and clattering about was a fire extinguisher by the back door. Charlie listed his options.

Option 1: Call Tom Bruise for real, this time? Nah. There's no time for that.

Option 2: Leap out onto the bonnet of the nearest Police Car? Nah, I'd probably miss, and they'd run me over.

Option 3: Stab Agent Purple with his own hypodermic syringe? Well, that would be funny, and I've seen that done in lots of those old films my Dad loves. What are they called? Oh yes – the *Carry On* films. Brilliant. Bit impractical in an ambulance doing ninety miles an hour though.

Option 4: I could...

'Kid! I said give me that syringe, NOW!' shouted Agent Purple and lunged towards Charlie. He tripped and fell hard on the floor. Charlie seized his chance and grabbed the fire extinguisher off the wall, hitting Agent Purple's head with it as hard as he could, exactly in the same spot where Jeremiah had given him a 'phantom punch' only moments before.

'Ow! Ow! Ow!!!!' shouted Agent Purple. He stood up in front of Charlie and rubbed his head hard. Then he grinned and held up the syringe in front of Charlie's vanishing smile.

'Look what I found!' he gave a cold and hollow laugh.

'Yeah? Well look what *I* found!' shouted Charlie as he pressed the trigger on the fire extinguisher. A huge cloud of CO_2 gas filled the back of the ambulance. Charlie couldn't see a thing – but that was good as it meant that neither could Agent Purple. Charlie bent down and scrambled through Agent Purple's legs towards the front of the ambulance. Agent Purple turned around, coughing his guts up.

'Where are you? Come here!' he shouted, angrily rubbing his eyes and waving the syringe about, trying to find Charlie. As the CO_2 gas cleared, a large shadow loomed up in front of him. A massive fist hit Agent Purple square between the eyes.

WHUMMP!!

Agent Purple fell hard against the rear doors and one burst open, causing him to nearly fall out. The road sped past in a crazy blur below.

'Pick on someone your own size,' said a gruff voice out of the fog.

Jeremiah was holding his severed right arm with his one good hand, and punched Agent Purple with it again, twice, just for good measure.

'OOOOF!!! OOOOF!!!'

Charlie was amazed to see that the hand on his severed arm was still holding onto the head-torch. Agent Purple was lifted off his feet by the final blow and literally flew backwards out of the ambulance doors. But just as he fell, Agent Purple managed to grab onto the strap of Jeremiah's head-torch which stretched out until it was about a centimetre thin.

Agent Purple was now completely hanging out the back of the speeding ambulance. His feet were resting on the back bumper, the rest of him was at forty-five degrees holding onto the strap of the head-torch for dear life. He stared down at the road as it roared past underneath him.

Charlie was just about holding on to his sanity.

'Look out!' shouted Charlie and kicked the empty stretcher on wheels towards the back doors. The stretcher flew out of the ambulance and hit Agent Purple hard. He fell on top of it and sparks flew from its wheels as it was towed behind the ambulance bouncing and careering all over the place. Agent Purple screamed but still held onto the strap of the head-torch for all he was worth.

'Let... go... of... my... torch!' shouted Jeremiah at Agent Purple.

'Jeremiah! I've got an idea!' shouted Charlie.

'Do something, kid, quick!'

Charlie reached over and tickled Jeremiah's severed arm. The arm flinched and Jeremiah giggled. The 'phantom tickle' worked! The fingers on his arm released their hold on the strap. As the ambulance whizzed across a bridge, Agent Purple on the stretcher came off the road at about sixty miles an hour, bounced over the kerb, screeched across the pavement and disappeared over the railings.

Realising that all was lost, the ambulance driver skidded hard and came to a shuddering stop. Charlie, Jeremiah and about three hundred bits of ambulance kit all landed in a crumpled heap at the front of the ambulance. Charlie nearly fell out the side door along with half the medical equipment. It was a right mess.

Two Armed Police Officers made their way to the front of the ambulance. The driver's door was swinging open. The cab was empty.

Charlie disentangled himself from hordes of boxes, bandages, tape, tubes and bottles. He walked over to where DI Williams was looking over the side of the wall.

The River Thames was far below. Agent Purple had disappeared into the swirling water.

A Police Boat motored into view.

'KKcchkk. Are you there, Boss, over?' crackled a tinny voice from nowhere.

DI Williams pulled out his two-way radio and pressed a switch on its side.

'Yeah, I'm here. Can you see anything, or anyone, down there. Over?'

'KKcchkk. Can't see a thing, boss. Over.'

DI Williams shook his head at Charlie. 'Honestly, this lot are a shambles.'

Charlie bit his lip and thought it best to say nothing. DI Williams pressed the switch on his walkie-talkie again.

'Are you sure? Over.'

'KKcchkk. Nope. Nothing down here but water, Boss. Not even a giant shark. Over'

'Yes, yes, okay, Number Two. There are no such thing as giant sharks, or alligators or even monster goldfish in there. But thanks for checking, over.'

'KKcchkk. Can I go back to base now, please, Boss, over?'

'Yes you can, Number Two. Thanks for your help. Just don't let anyone hear your talking about giant sharks and that, okay? Over.' sighed a deeply disappointed DI Williams.

'KKcchkk. Sorry, boss. Over and Out.'

'No, Number Two. You can't say over *and* out on the radio. Saying *Over* means you're asking me to respond. Saying *Out* means that you're ending the conversation. Do you see what I mean? Over.'

'KKcchkk. Okay, boss. Over.'

'Oh. And one other thing, Number Two, over....' said DI Williams.

'KKcchkk. Yes, Boss?'

'Can you stop saying KKcchkk on the radio, please?'

'KKcch.... Oh. Sorry, Boss. I thought you had to say that on the radio?'

'No of course you don't!' sighed the exasperated DI, giving Charlie a silent 'I don't believe what I'm hearing' gesture.

Charlie gave him a shrug. He felt exhausted. He looked over to where the Police and some *real* paramedics were helping Jeremiah out of the stolen ambulance and into the back of a proper one.

'Hey, kid! Charlie!' shouted the big man.

'Yes?'

'You owe me a torch!' Jeremiah looked at Charlie with a stern face for a second – then gave out a great big laugh. 'Ha ha ha!' he bellowed. 'Just kidding, kid! See you in hospital! Ha ha ha!'

He was still laughing his great big booming laugh as they shut the doors of the real ambulance. Charlie shook his head at Jeremiah's rubbish attempt at winding him up. And for what felt like the first time in six long months, Charlie laughed, too.

DI Williams ruffled Charlie's hair. 'You're alright, kid. Well done – good work. We could hear Agent Purple threatening you over the radio. I thought it was curtains for you.'

'Agent Purple will have to try harder than that,' said

Charlie with false bravado. 'But I think I'll be glad to go to hospital for real, this time, sir.'

'I'll give you a lift,' said DI Williams. 'Just to make sure you get there this time.'

'Good idea,' said Charlie.

Shortly after the hubbub had died down and the Police had left the scene, a lone figure watched the wrecked ambulance being towed away. The grey-haired Reporter looked down at the few bits and pieces that hadn't been tidied up. A bandage here. A rubber glove there.

And that's when he found it. A little metal device lying forgotten on the pavement.

He picked up Charlie's mobile phone and quickly walked away.

11

Riverboat Shuffle

Night on the river was always colder than a normal night elsewhere, even in the height of summer. Landmarks from the water were always hard to see and it was difficult to tell how far something was away. Or how close it was.

Twice a year, once in Summer and then once again just before Christmas, Charlie's school always organised a 'Riverboat Shuffle'. It was basically an excuse for the teachers to let their hair down and have a party onboard a boat with loud disco music. Some years the DJ would play dance music so loud it almost made your ear's bleed, this year the DJ appeared to have favoured Heavy Rock music from the 80s. This meant that there was a sum total of two people on the dancefloor, both of them teachers - and one of them looked like he'd been taught to dance by a chicken who'd eaten too many vindaloos.

'Shame Charlie's missing the *Vomit Comet* tonight,' said Sam holding a glass full of fizzy pop.

'Ssshh!' whispered Jazz. 'Don't let the teachers hear you call it that!'

'Well, this boat makes me feel ill,' said Sam, pretending to throw up. 'All I can smell is diesel fumes and what with that and this boat juddering all down the river – I feel a bit seasick.'

'I think a few people do' said Jazz, looking at a couple of other pupils leaning over the side of the boat.

'And those people walking past...' pointed Sam at a couple walking their dog on the riverbank.

'What about them?'

'They've overtaken us once already. Not exactly a speedboat, is it?'

'The speed limit on this river is only five miles an hour,' said Jazz as she watched a speed limit sign trundle past at a snail's pace.

The deep **BOOM BOOM BOOM** of the bass reverberated deep into the dark waters of the Thames and the flashing red, green and blue disco lights attracted all sorts of creatures – insects, moths and bats circled the boat. Along with something much bigger.

Jazz and Sam strolled to the back of the boat where a small group of their schoolfriends were having a friendly argument. Sam leant on the hinges of the large wooden gangplank, folded up now that the boat was under way.

'I can swim a hundred metres breast-stroke in about a minute,' boasted Royston.

'A minute? No way! I've seen you swim and that'd take you about an hour!' scoffed his mate Andy.

'Yeah right, I'm easily the fastest swimmer in school,' said Royston.

'You're rubbish!' Andy laughed. 'Anyone in Year 9 could beat you. Even Sam here!'

Sam bristled a bit at the light-hearted jibe, but he kept his cool.

'Sam doesn't have to prove anything to you lot,' said Jazz. She whispered to Sam, 'Don't take any notice of that doob.'

'Yeah, well actually, I'm the fastest swimmer,' said Sam, ignoring Jazz completely. 'I even beat Charlie once swimming ten lengths.'

Jazz rolled her eyes silently.

'Huh! That's not difficult,' said Royston. 'Charlie swims like a brick!'

'Yeah, well don't pick on someone who's not here to defend themselves,' said Sam angrily. 'I could swim faster than you with one arm tied behind my back.'

'That would just make you swim round in circles, you derp!' laughed Royston along with everyone else.

'Who you calling a derp, you din?' said Sam.

'You, you derp!' laughed Royston and gave Sam a playful shove.

For a second Sam managed to steady himself against

the hinged gangplank. His head was over the back of the boat and he looked down into the dark frothing waves in amazement. It looked like there were two huge round torches following the boat underwater, getting closer and closer.

'Oh wow. Bio-luminescence,' Sam muttered, then went 'Whoahhhhh!!!!!' as the gangplank gave way and launched him into the river.

He surfaced quickly and looked towards the slowly disappearing boat as it chugged its merry way downriver. Already he could hear Jazz shouting for the boat to be stopped. Then she appeared at the back, next to the gangplank which was trailing behind the boat in the water. Jazz had seen it, too. Just before Sam fell – a huge glowing shape underwater which had rapidly swum off, momentarily frightened by the gangplank hitting the water, closely followed by 'derp' boy.

Now she could see the shape swimming in a big circle, back to where Sam was treading water.

'Sam! Swim for it! Swim to the gangplank!' Jazz shouted.

'What?' said Sam as he looked around·and realised the danger he was in. Two large orbs of green light were slowly making their way towards him underwater. He started swimming. Fast.

'That's it! Swim!' shouted Jazz and Royston together. 'Don't look back!'

Sam swam as though his very life depended on it. Which, of course, it did.

The monster pike closed in, slowly. It wasn't in a rush. Its belly was probably full and a little thing like Sam in the water didn't stand a chance. It was more of a primordial feeling that the pike had in the pit of its stomach: It wasn't hungry - but it would kill this little thing, just because that's what it did. That's what it was designed to do by Mother Nature. The fact that Man had made it a freak of nature was neither here nor there.

'Sam, so help me! Swim! Come on!' Jazz was halfway down the gangplank now, with Royston at the top holding on to stop her from falling in, too. Her arm was stretched out as far as she could get it, her hand desperately reaching for Sam as he swam towards the boat.

Twenty metres.

'Come on, Sam!'

Ten metres.

'Swim! Swimmmm!'

Three metres.... Sam was nearly there.

He reached for the gangplank.

The huge fish made a sudden lunge towards him. Then it crashed back into the river sending an enormous wave over the back of the riverboat, soaking everyone. As the water subsided and the boat stopped rocking, twenty schoolkids looked down at Royston, still leaning over the top of the gangplank. Royston looked down at Jazz who he was still holding onto halfway down the gangplank. Jazz looked down to see that she was holding onto...

Sam.

He was gripping onto her arm for all he was worth, both his feet tucked up on the gangplank. His face was ashen - but he was smiling.

'You see. I told you!' gasped Sam, struggling to get his

words out. 'I told you I'm the fastest swimmer in school.'

'You are mate, you are!' sighed a very relieved Royston.

A huge shout split the night air: 'He's ALIVE!!!' they all cheered, and a hundred text messages ping-pinged their way to friends and relatives about the giant fish.

The Riverboat partied on into the darkness.

12

The Brain Sploosher

The digital clock on the wall told Charlie he'd been awake for far too long.

2:04am in any hospital was a lonely place to be. Charlie groaned to himself. The clock was annoying. The stifling summer heat was annoying. The blip-blip-blipping of the monitors above his head were annoying. The big man snoring in the room next door to him was REALLY annoying. The nurses had been great though, and they'd looked after Charlie and Jeremiah, putting them in different rooms and given them a bowl of fruit each. Not that Charlie liked fruit that much - and the two uniformed Police Officers sitting guard outside in the corridor had stolen all their grapes. All that was left were a couple of oranges and a melon each.

Who eats a melon in hospital? wondered Charlie.

He stared at the digital clock on the wall. It blinked 2:05am back at him. Charlie sighed and thought about his mum's locket. That was REALLY annoying, he thought. No, not annoying, it was *much* worse than that – it was almost a physical pain, deep inside. The pain of losing it had kept him awake.

Charlie lifted the corner of his curtain and watched the big hulk of a man sleeping soundly next door. Even through a thick pane of glass, Jeremiah's snoring made the walls shake. Jeremiah was sweating and every now and again he'd jump in his sleep and his one good arm would twitch about, then he'd quieten down for a while as his bad dream subsided. Charlie noticed that Jeremiah's unattached arm lay next to Jeremiah on a special trolley. It was wrapped in clingfilm and surrounded by ice like a joint of meat in the Supermarket. According to the nurses who Charlie had spoken to earlier, the doctors were going to operate on Jeremiah and re-attach his arm first thing in the morning.

'The morning?' Charlie sighed. 'How long was that away? Well, at least I get to go home tomorrow.'

The annoying clock on the wall now said 2:06 and Charlie sighed to himself again. Bored. Bored. Bored. Charlie couldn't wait to see Jazz and Sam. He knew his Dad would bring both his friends with him tomorrow – take Charlie back home, back to watching TV in bed for a couple of days and beating everyone on the PlayStation whilst he thought of a plan to somehow get his locket back. But all that was for tomorrow. Right now, all he wanted to do was sleep. Charlie let go of the curtain and rolled over, willing himself to go to sleep. His eyes slowly closed...

'!!SHARRRRR

RRRRKKKKK!!'

The scream rang out from Jeremiah's tonsils as he woke up drenched in a cold sweat. Charlie nearly fell out of bed.

'Well there's no way I'm going back to sleep now, is there?' said a wide-eyed Charlie. He peered back through the curtains.

Two Police Officers rushed into Jeremiah's room and struggled to hold the big man down, then a nurse and a senior Matron rushed in to help. Luckily, as they'd considered him to be possibly quite a dangerous person even with one arm, they'd taken the precaution of strapping Jeremiah to the bed with thick leather straps. Thick leather straps which were now straining to keep hold of Jeremiah as he twisted from side to side.

'It was a SHARK! I swear it was! A giant green shark and its eyes were on fire! ITS EYES WERE BURNING

WITH GREEN FIRE FROM THE DEPTHS OF HELL!!!'

Charlie guessed that the Matron had seen it all before as she didn't seem fazed by Jeremiah's screams. She simply tutted, said 'There there, I'm sure it was' and rolled him over on his side before stabbing a large needle as hard as she could into the big man's exposed buttocks.

'Owww!!!

Oww!

Owwwwwwww'

'Ooh, I felt that myself,' winced Charlie. 'I wouldn't want to meet her down a dark alley at night. Mind you, I wouldn't want to meet her in broad daylight, to be fair.'

Jeremiah quietened down at last and closed his eyes with a big gurggly grin on his dribbly face. Everybody relaxed. The Matron and the nurse left Jeremiah's room and the two Police Officers went back to their seats in the corridor and continued reading their books.

Outside, the bright full moon and a gentle night breeze made tree branches cast eerie shadows on the hospital walls. Other shadows moved in the moonlight.

There was a dull thud in the corridor outside Charlie's room. Then another. Charlie squinted out from under his bedcovers.

Through the heavily frosted glass door to his room, Charlie could see a silhouette move against the yellow light of the hospital corridor. A disjointed, shadowy figure of a tall thin man appeared. A door creaked open. Charlie froze – for a second, he thought that somebody was coming into his room, but the noise came from Jeremiah's room next door. Charlie slowly lifted up the corner of the adjoining curtain again.

The tall, thin man edged slowly into Jeremiah's room, stepping over the legs of the two Police Officers lying unconscious in the corridor. The man was wearing a smart suit and sunglasses even though it was night-time. A fresh, ugly wound ran down the length of his cheek and from inside the wound a tinge of luminous green shone through.

Charlie watched, unable to move, as Agent Purple

snuck into Jeremiah's room like a slimy, furtive snake creeping ever closer to the big snoring figure. Agent Purple was sweating profusely - he'd already tangled with Jeremiah once and came off worse. Whatever he was up to, his nerves were showing.

Then another similarly dressed man entered the room. He was stocky but a lot shorter than Agent Purple. Charlie recognised him straight away as man who was driving the ambulance.

Agent Purple touched the leather straps securing Jeremiah and gave a visible sigh of relief. 'We'll only need the Truth Serum this time, Agent Red. But give him a big dose,' hissed Agent Purple. 'We can't afford to mess up again.'

'Okay, Sir.' Agent Red did as he was told and took a small hypodermic syringe out of a leather case and inserted it into Jeremiah's arm.

'Ow!' said Jeremiah as he spluttered back into the waking world. 'Not another injection, I'm... oh wow, look at the crazy colours!' and he started smiling at the two mysterious men standing over his bed. 'I love those colours you're wearing!'

The two Agents looked down at themselves. They were dressed entirely in black.

'Quieten down, Jeremiah. We've got some questions for you.'

Jeremiah shook his head and tried to focus on the two men.

'You two look like you should be in some old gangster movie,' sniggered Jeremiah. 'You're going in and out of focus. It looks like you're fizzing and crackling like in one of those old films they show late at night – you know, before they get digitally restored?'

'Probably just a trick of the light,' whispered Agent Purple, trying to be patient.

'I think I might have given him a bit *too* much,' apologised Agent Red, peering at the syringe.

'Hey! I know you guys! You're from the Fizz. You were in the ambulance. I *love* you guys!' shouted Jeremiah. 'Although – didn't you try to kill me?'

'No, no, Agent Ochre, or should I say, Jeremiah. We'd never try and do that, would we? We're your *friends* from The Facility – or the Fizz if that's what you want to call it,' slimed Agent Purple, his voice oozing with insincerity. 'And Agent Red here has got some *friendly* questions for you...'

'Great! I love a pub quiz!' beamed Jeremiah.

Agent Red sidled up to the bed and in a gentle voice, said 'Hello - my name is Agent Red.'

'Pfftt! That's a funny name! But I love you, anyway!'

'That's very nice to hear, Jeremiah. I love you, too.' Agent Red grimaced at Agent Purple, who glowered back at him.

'Get on with it!' hissed Agent Purple.

'I need you to answer some questions, please, Jeremiah, is that okay?' continued Agent Red, trying to remain patient.

'Yeah, that's fine. How much do I win? Can I phone a friend? 50/50? Ask the Audience?'

'Er, no, no, none of those options I'm afraid, Jeremiah. And you don't get *any* lifelines.'

'Huh. This is a rubbish gameshow.'

Okay then. What we need to know, Jeremiah, is the whereabouts of our three cylinders? Our *awfully expensive cylinders* of Rejoov,' whispered Agent Red gently. 'We have to get them back to the Fizz. You know SHE won't be happy if you've lost them.'

Jeremiah looked startled. The injection had woken him up and made him quite happy in a delirious sort of way, but his blood still ran cold at the thought of upsetting the boss of The Fizz. Many people had. Many people had mysteriously disappeared.

'Ahh, well, there's only cylinder left, not three. But I know exactly where it is, although you're not going to believe me....'

'Don't worry, Jeremiah, I've given you enough truth serum for a horse, so I'm sure that me and Agent Purple here will believe everything you say.'

'Jeremiah, my friend, tell us exactly why there's only ONE cylinder left,' smiled Agent Purple. 'We'll believe you...'

Jeremiah shook his head, then blurted out really fast:

'No no nope no way there is NO way I'm going to tell you anything - okay so the Top Secret REJOOV cylinders worth ten million pounds each that come in from Europe and dropped off at the Top Secret collection point in the Thames which you get us to collect in the middle of the night - well we were collecting the latest batch and we got two of them onboard but one was leaking this green stuff all over my boat then I thought we got hit by a submarine and we got towed for about a mile along the Thames and Agent Blue fell out trying to get the other cylinder which was caught on the bottom - not his bottom - the bottom of the Thames then this kid called Charlie Carter appeared out of nowhere and blew up my speedboat so it was his fault that those two cylinders were blown to smithereens and then this giant shark ate Agent Blue so I'm really sorry about that but it wasn't my fault but the good thing is I DO know exactly where the third cylinder is...'

Jeremiah paused for breath at last and took a big

gulp of air. He looked puzzled. He wasn't going to tell them anything - but now he'd told them pretty much everything. That truth serum was obviously powerful stuff.

'What a load of rubbish!' said Agent Red.

'I didn't believe a word of that,' hissed Agent Purple. 'I bet he's hidden them somewhere to sell on the black market. Give him a bit more truth serum and make him tell us where!'

'Well, that was quite a story, Jeremiah, but you've got to tell us the truth, please,' said Agent Red preparing another dose of truth serum.

Jeremiah looked hurt. 'That *was* the truth! But okay. I didn't want to tell you this, so come closer...' he whispered, looking around to check that nobody else was listening.

'Go on. Just tell us the truth, Jeremiah' said Agent Red, leaning in close.

'Well, for a start, your breath smells.' Jeremiah giggled.

The smile froze on Agent Red's face.

'And I think you both need a makeover – those black suits are so last year.'

From behind his curtain, Charlie had to stop himself from laughing out loud.

'One other thing…' Jeremiah whispered into Agent Red's ear.

'What's that, my friend?'

'You've got a syringe in your leg.'

Agent Red looked down. It was true. Jeremiah wasn't lying. The empty syringe was indeed sticking out of his leg.

'Yow! That really hurts!' winced Agent Red.

'I know! Tell me about it.' said Jeremiah.

'Well, it sort of hurt at first but now it's okay in a nice sort of way. And I think you're right about our suits. They *are* a bit clichéd, aren't they?'

'Truth!' said Jeremiah and bumped fists with Agent Red.

Agent Purple looked at them both and shook his

head. 'Agent Red, what are you doing?' he demanded.

'Well, I'm just having a chat with my friend Jeremiah here.'

'He's a bit moody, isn't he?' said Jeremiah, nodding towards Agent Purple.

'Never stops moaning,' agreed Agent Red. 'At least you don't have to work with him.'

Jeremiah sniggered and Agent Red joined in.

'Concentrate on the truth, Agent Red!' hissed Agent Purple.

'I am,' said Agent Red. 'I can't help it. Did you know that I haven't changed my underpants in three days and at weekends I like dressing up as a clown and scaring all the neighbourhood kids?'

'I meant the truth from Jeremiah,' sighed Agent Purple.

'And you know that time when someone filled up your office drawer with fish? That was ME,' sniggered Agent Red.

'Hah! Good one!' laughed Jeremiah.

'And you know that airhorn taped under your seat when we went into that really important meeting? That was me as well!'

'Brilliant!' roared Jeremiah. 'Absolute genius!'

'And I suppose it was you who swapped the gun in my shoulder holster for a water pistol?' sighed Agent Purple.

'Yes! Yes! I'd forgotten about that one!' said Agent Red as he and Jeremiah howled with laughter.

Charlie was biting his hand hard next door, trying not to laugh.

Agent Purple reached into his shoulder holster and took out a real gun. He aimed it at Agent Red and waited. Agent Red finally noticed the gun and his laughing slowly stopped. Jeremiah was still creased up, until Agent Red nudged him.

'Spoilsport,' said Agent Red, not laughing anymore.

'Concentrate, Jeremiah,' said Agent Purple with a deadly serious look on his face. 'I want you to tell us where the third cylinder is.'

'Oooh, touchy,' said Jeremiah. 'But okay, fine I'll tell

you the truth if you really want me to.'

'YES! That's exactly what I want you to do, Jeremiah'

'Okay then. Well, I don't really love you, I think you need a shave and I'd have that wound looked at if I were you, it's oozing a bit. Shall I call Matron?'

Agent Red started sniggering again as Jeremiah went to reach for a nurse-call button by the side of his bed, but the thick leather straps were still holding him tight.

'Could you loosen these a little, please?'

'No, I don't think so,' hissed Agent Purple. 'Maybe *this* will make you focus on the answer...'

Charlie knew he should call for help but he was almost too scared to move. He reached into his jeans at the side of the bed for his mobile phone – it wasn't there. He could only watch through the window helplessly as Agent Purple took what looked like a long metal screwdriver out from his jacket pocket and pressed a button on the top. Six very thin blades sprang out. It looked a bit like one of those metal head massagers, except with another press of the button, the six thin blades started whirring round really fast.

'Wh-what's that?' stuttered Jeremiah.

'It's a *Brain Sploosher*,' said Agent Purple, proudly. 'Patent Pending.' He smiled a twisted, evil grin.

'A whattt?'

'Let me give you a demonstration.' Agent Purple pressed the switch on the screwdriver again and the long metal blades closed up. He took hold of the large yellow melon from the fruit bowl at the side of Jeremiah's bed and stabbed the screwdriver hard into it.

'A Brain Sploosher. Pretend this melon is your head. The sharp end goes in first, like this... then, I press the button and the blades spring out. Then....et Voila! Your brain gets mashed inside your own skull, and all the secrets of The Fizz are safe.'

Charlie could hear the **SPLOOSHING** noise as the blades whizzed round inside the melon. Agent Purple pressed the button on top and retracted the spinning blades. He tipped the melon upside down and smiled as little bits of yellow fruit and juice splattered onto the hospital floor.

'You see? A *Brain Sploosher*. I like it.' smiled Agent Purple.

'Well, I don't like it!' grimaced Jeremiah. 'I don't like it at all. Not one bit. And neither will Matron when she sees the mess you made on her floor...'

'I don't care what Matron thinks!' shouted Agent Purple through gritted teeth.

'Sssshhh!' winced Agent Red. 'You're speaking very loudly.'

'Sorry,' said Agent Purple quietly composing himself. He bent down and put his face up close to Jeremiah's face. It wasn't a pretty sight as Agent Purple's angry green wound looked grotesque in the moonlight, although his piercing blue eyes made up for it.

'It was you and your friend Charlie Carter's fault I got this when I fell over the bridge,' he said, running a finger down his scar. More luminous green showed through, reflecting on Jeremiah's sweaty face. 'Jeremiah, my friend. I think you get the picture, hmm? Tell me where that third cylinder of Rejoov is. Now.'

'You look beautiful when you're angry,' beamed Jeremiah.

Agent Purple span round towards his accomplice. 'This is useless. You've given him far too much of that truth serum, you idiot!'

Agent Red slapped his own face, trying to regain some composure. 'Phew, at least mine's worn off.'

'Hey look,' said Jeremiah. 'We all work for the Fizz, don't we? We're all on the same side but there's NO WAY I'm telling you that the Rejoov is inside the giant shark!' Jeremiah looked puzzled at himself. 'Hang on. Why on earth did I say that?'

'There now, that was easy, wasn't it?'

Jeremiah looked disappointed.

Agent Red turned to Agent Purple. 'The giant shark?'

'He means the pike. OUR pike. Thanks to this idiot here, it'll be all over the news by tomorrow. Are you seriously telling us that the pike has swallowed one of our cylinders?' spat Agent Purple, seething with rage.

Jeremiah squirmed in his bed. 'No! No no no no no.

NO! NOPE. Uh-uh. That shark or giant pike or whatever it is did *not* swallow up that cylinder. Nope!'

'It did, didn't it?'

'Yes' admitted Jeremiah in a little squeak.

Agent Purple threw his hands up in the air.

'Wait, wait,' spluttered Jeremiah. 'You KNOW about that... that monster?'

'Yes, of course we do.' Agent Purple drew in a sharp intake of breath. 'It's one of our experiments gone wrong, that's all. It escaped and we were hoping it would find its way out to sea and that would be the last we ever heard of it, but now.... I guess we're going to have to catch it and kill it. But unfortunately, Jeremiah, you already know too much. There's nothing else for it but I think I'll have to terminate your services with the Fizz.' Agent Purple reached for the Sploosher.

On the other side of the glass, Charlie gasped out loud. Agent Purple looked right at him and snarled. But then a low moan interrupted whatever it was that Agent Purple was going to do next. In the corridor outside, one of the sleeping Policemen was starting to move and rub his head.

'Change of plans, Agent Red. We've already been here too long. We need to go, NOW!' shouted Agent Purple, reaching for a hospital wheelchair by the door. 'We'll have to take this idiot back to the Fizz with us before he opens his big mouth.' Give him a knockout shot – and make sure it's a *big* dose!'

Both Agents were in a mad rush. Agent Purple grabbed the wheelchair then grabbed Jeremiah's detached arm out of the trolley and slung it across the big man's chest. Agent Red fumbled in his leather case and thrust another syringe into Jeremiah's arm. Jeremiah was about to protest but then his head fell to one side. Both Agents manhandled Jeremiah out of bed and plonked him into the wheelchair. As they rushed out of Jeremiah's room, the Policeman sat up with a bewildered look on his face. Agent Red stabbed him with the syringe.

'Nighty night!' said Agent Red and the Policeman went straight back to sleep. He took a set of handcuffs off the Policeman and handcuffed Jeremiah to the wheelchair with an expert ***click*** then both Agents wheeled him off down the corridor towards the hospital lifts.

Charlie slunk out of the shadows. His mouth was dry, his palms clammy - but he knew there was no choice. He *had* to follow them. He had to find out exactly what was going on. But something was funny. Funny strange, not funny ha ha. Charlie couldn't put his finger on it at first but then it dawned on him.

In their haste to get away, Agent Red had handcuffed Jeremiah's severed arm onto the wheelchair.

Charlie immediately drew up a list of Options in his head:

Option 1: This is it! This is our big chance to stop Agent Purple! I'll draw their attention whilst Jeremiah will leap up and punch their lights out. Hang on, he might be knocked out.

Option 2: I'll grab Jeremiah's severed arm and use it to knock out Agent Red and Agent Purple. Hmm, maybe. But his arm looks kinda heavy.

Option 3: I'll alert Matron, and with a small band of kung-fu Doctors trained by The Ancient Ones, we'll head off the Fizz agents and karate them both unconscious before they can get away and then I'll be the hero and be all over the News. Matron can make the tea.

Yup. Number 3 sounded like the sensible choice. Charlie took another step along the corridor and heard another ***click.*** He looked down and saw that the other Policeman had partially woken up, and in his confusion had handcuffed himself to Charlie.

The Fizz Agents wheeled Jeremiah into the lift. Agent Purple looked back at Charlie with a smirk on his face and waved 'Bye bye!' as the lift doors closed.

'You're nicked!' said the Policeman, proud to have apprehended somebody who was clearly a major criminal.

Charlie sighed and shook his head.

'No, not me. I'm one of the Good Guys. The Number One Good Guy, in fact,' explained Charlie.

'Are you?' asked the Policeman, still dazed.

'Yes, of course I am. I'm the one and only Charlie Carter,' said Charlie, proudly. 'You may well have heard of me.'

'Nope.'

Charlie looked crestfallen. He couldn't wait to go home tomorrow.

13

Here be Monsters

Charlie laid back in the hot bath his Dad had just run for him. He was home now, and safe.

His Dad had brought fresh clothes in, along with Jazz and Sam when he'd picked Charlie up from hospital, and he could hear them all messing around downstairs. Jazz and Sam had been overjoyed to see Charlie again, and although he didn't really let on, he was relieved to see his best friends, too. Charlie's thoughts drifted away, and he slipped a little bit lower in the bath, half asleep.

'Perhaps I should have had a shower instead... zzzz'

and with that, Charlie slipped further down until the bath water closed in over his head.

Further and further down he sunk, floating ever downwards into an octopus's garden, into the vivid depths where undead pirates played, and the deathly Kraken lurked.

Charlie opened his eyes and looked up as shoals of little fish circled his head. A huge ship churned the water over his head. A tanker on the way out to the Channel sounding its horn:

BARRRRRRRPPPPP!

THUUUUURRRPPPPP-BBBRRDDD!!

Charlie wasn't surprised that he could breathe and see underwater. It was his dream after all, and he could do what he liked. He looked around and saw to his surprise that he was swimming next to an old, abandoned red bus.

It was an old bus from the Eighties, but the red paint looked brand new. He swam towards the front and pressed the button to open the doors. Before he could enter, a shoal of brightly coloured fish swam out amidst a sea of bubbles, but as the bubbles cleared a terrible sight met Charlie's eyes. A human skeleton sat in the driver's seat, its hands still holding onto the steering wheel with a bony death grip. Charlie's eyes grew ever wider, as slowly the skeleton's head turned to face him.

Bubbles escaped from its bony jaw as it hissed out a chilling warning 'The Piiike isss hungggry, Charlieeee Carterrrr, hungrryy forrr youuuu.'

Charlie couldn't help but think it looked a bit like one of the air-bubble pirate toys in his Dad's aquarium.

'You cannottt escapppe the Pike, Charlie Carterrrrr. It isss cominng for youuuuuu.'

A huge shadow filled the water above the old bus. It was the Monster Pike, swimming slowly overhead. The dreadful shadow loomed closer. The pike's glowing green eyes seemed to draw Charlie towards them, then its mouth opened to reveal rows of huge, needle-sharp teeth. The bony bus-driver closed the bus doors and gave Charlie a toothy grin as it peered at him from behind the glass. The skeleton knocked on the bus doors as it laughed at Charlie's fate as the pike drew closer... closer...

KNOCK KNOCK KNOCK

'Charlie? Are you okay?' said a voice from outside the bathroom door. Charlie woke with a start as his Dad knocked on the door again. 'Charlie? You've been in there ages...'

'I'm fine, Dad,' said Charlie, breathing a huge sigh of fear mixed with relief.

'But I think I'll get out now.'

14

!!Stop Press!!

'Shall we?' asked DI Williams.

'Ready when you are, boss,' said the police officer standing next to him. She was in full uniform and had 'WPC326' on her epaulettes. 'You're looking almost smart today.'

DI Williams adjusted his tie in the mirror. 'Well, you have to make an effort if you're on TV, don't you? Mind you, I hate these things. So boring. How many Press are out there?'

'Oh, good question. Don't know actually,' shrugged

WPC326.

'Probably not many,' said the DI, dismissively. 'These live-video Q&A Sessions with the Press are always dull as ditch water.'

He admired himself in a mirror on the wall and stuck his chest out like a peacock. He tried to straighten a stray hair unsuccessfully. 'Prepare to be bored. I'll give my usual statement to a handful of bored-looking Journalists – they'll ask me about three or four questions, then we can get back to the office. Just remember to always look professional, WPC326, it is *live* TV, after all so don't forget. If anyone asks you a difficult question, probably best if you let me answer it. I've been on the Police Media Training Course, you know.'

WPC326 looked unimpressed.

'It teaches you how to present yourself properly when you're on the telly,' said the DI. 'Never ever roll your eyes on camera, and never EVER put your head in your hands. It'll look like you don't know the answer.'

'Yes, of course, boss. Thanks for the advice,' said

WPC326.

'Righto - come on then, let's do it!' said DI Williams.

The pair of them walked out of the Green Room, down a short corridor and through heavy wooden doors with a sign above them saying 'Quiet Please – Recording in Progress'. DI Williams strode out ahead of WPC326 into a brightly lit TV Studio and almost immediately wished he hadn't. He walked straight into what could only be described as a moving rugby scrum. A hundred voices all asked him questions at the same time and a thousand camera flashes went off in his face as a throng of News Teams, Camera operators and Journalists nearly knocked him off his feet. The studio was heaving. The same questions came at him over and over again, thick and fast:

'What's the latest on the missing fisherman?' 'We demand to know, DI Williams!' 'It's about time you told us all the truth!' 'What's been killing all the swimmers and fisherman on the Thames?' 'Is it true that there's a great white shark in the Thames?' 'We need to know, DI Williams!' 'It's about time you told us all the truth!'

'What's the latest on the missing fisherman?' 'Tell us about the Shark – our viewers demand to know!'

Di Williams was jostled every step of the way, but finally he managed to reach his seat on a small podium by a large LED projector. His hair was a complete mess and his tie was all over the place. The DI was clearly flustered. First, he tapped the microphone in front of him too loudly, then he spoke too closely into it. The microphone whistled and buzzed in protest. The distorted feedback made everyone quieten down.

'Good mor....'

BBBMMMMMBBBBBBBBBBB!

PPEEEEEEPPPPP!!

SCREEEEEEEE!!!

He moved back a bit and tried again. 'Well, er, thank you. Thank you all for coming. This is, er... quite a surprise. Quite a good turnout. I'll be taking questions at the end as usual....'

A flurry of the same questions from the Press hit him hard again.

'What's the latest on the missing fisherman?' 'We demand to know, DI Williams!' 'It's about time you told us all the truth!' 'What's been killing all the swimmers and fisherman on the Thames?' 'Is it true that there's a great white shark in the Thames?' 'We demand to know!' 'It's about time you told us all the truth!' 'What's the latest on the missing fisherman?' 'Tell us about the Shark – our viewers demand to know!'

'Quiet please, quiet please!' demanded DI Williams without any effect whatsoever. 'There is no such thing as a great white shark in the Thames.'

The noisy hubbub started up again with the same old unanswered questions...

'Then what's the latest on the missing fisherman?' 'We demand to know, DI Williams!' 'It's about time you told us all the truth!' 'If it's not a shark, what's been killing all the swimmers and fisherman on the Thames?' 'We've heard that there IS a great white shark in the Thames!' Is it a monster? 'We demand to know, DI Williams!' 'It's about time you told us all the truth!' 'What's the latest on the missing fisherman?'

'Tell us about the Shark – our viewers demand to know!'

On live TV, DI Williams rolled his eyes and put his head in his hands.

- - -

'Charlie! Come on, it's started!' shouted Charlie's dad up the polished wooden staircase.

Charlie, Jazz and Sam came hurtling downstairs and jostled each other as they ran into the large but cosy lounge of Charlie's farmhouse. All three crashed onto the creaking sofa and stared at the tv.

'Look!' exclaimed Jazz. 'That's DI Williams!'

'Oh yeah!' exclaimed Charlie. 'I wonder if he'll mention me...? Bound to!'

'Or me? Turn it up a bit!' shouted Sam. 'Who's got the remote?'

'Charlie has, of course.' said Charlie's dad. 'As always. How are you, Charlie? Have you found your mobile phone yet, son?'

'Nope. Lost it. Everyone sssh!' hushed Charlie.

'That phone cost a lot of money, Charlie. Have you

even looked for it, yet?'

'Dad! Shush! Ask me later. I'm trying to listen to this....' said Charlie and turned the TV volume up.

- - -

'Sergeant Williams,' began a Reporter on the TV as the rest of the assembled Journalists in the Studio fell quiet. 'My daughter was at a Riverboat Shuffle party on the Thames last night, and text me to say that one of her fellow pupils had been attacked by a Great White Shark. She came home very shaken by what she'd seen.'

'Really. A Great White....? Pfft!' scoffed DI Williams. 'Let me categorically assure everyone here that there is NOT a Great White Shark in the Thames. By the way, I'm not a Sergeant I'm a....'

'My son sent me a similar text, and he said the shark glowed in the dark!' said another Reporter.

'Ladies and Gentlemen - I've been in the Marine Policing Unit for nearly ten years now, and we've seen all sorts. Dolphins, yes. Even the odd whale or two. But fluorescent Great White Sharks – no.' He looked over at

WPC326 and shook his head. She shrugged back.

- - -

In the farmhouse, Charlie looked at Jazz and Sam.

'See, Charlie. I told you I wasn't making it up,' said Sam. Jazz nodded in agreement.

'Okay, I believe you. Both of you. I know you've seen it as well. Now hush up – let's see what else he's got to say...' said Charlie.

- - -

Back in the TV Studio, DI Williams continued to refuse to believe anything the Press were saying.

'And did anyone actually get any photos of this Great White Shark, hmm?' offered DI Williams to a silent room. 'Anyone?'

'Well, my daughter took this...' said the lady Reporter and waved her mobile phone up in the air.

'Connect her phone up to that projector, please, WPC326. Let's have a look at this monster from the deep, shall we?' scoffed DI Williams.

'Can you turn your Bluetooth on please?' WPC326

asked the Reporter, then pressed the Bluetooth button on the LED projector.

A large TV monitor sprang into life behind DI Williams. The reporter's phone connected, and a fuzzy dark photo appeared.

- - -

From Charlie's sofa, the three of them peered hard at the TV, which displayed a photo that looked like this:

'That looks like one of those joke 'Blackpool by Night' postcards I send my Gran when I'm on holiday,' laughed Sam.

'That's rubbish!' said Charlie. 'I had much better photos on my phone. I even took some video of it.'

- - -

Back in the TV Studio DI Williams rolled his eyes and tutted. 'Tch. Just as I suspected. Nothing. Righto. Can we get back to more serious stuff now, please, ladies and gentlemen?'

All the Journalists and News Teams in the Studio quietened down and looked a little embarrassed to be there. The Reporter put her mobile phone back in her pocket, but the Bluetooth connection on the LED projector remained open. Nobody noticed, but somebody else in the room must have connected a mobile phone to it.

The DI cleared his throat and smiled. 'How this lot came to be Reporters I'll never know' he muttered to himself. He stood up and addressed the Reporters.

'Let's have no more talk about Great White Sharks, okay? We know who the REAL killer is, ladies and gentlemen, but no, he doesn't have fins – he walks and talks just like you and me, well, except for the fact he's a convicted murderer and a well-known East End villain, of course. His name is John Burns, otherwise known as 'Mad Dog the Axe Murderer' and he escaped three days ago whilst being transferred to a Maximum-Security prison.' DI Williams looked around the hushed room, thankful he had regained control over the surly News Teams. A photo of Mad Dog the Axe Murderer loomed large on the monitor behind him.

- - -

'OMG, Charlie! There's a killer on the loose!' exclaimed Jazz.

'Sssh!' said Charlie and turned the TV up a bit more.

- - -

On the TV, DI Williams took a swig of water from a glass in front of him. A small bead of sweat broke out on his brow. He glanced over at WPC326 for support as he knew that what he was about to say wouldn't go down well with the gathered journalists.

'We have yet to establish his whereabouts...'

'You mean you don't know where he is?' said a Reporter wearing a permanent sneer. 'The Police have let a killer escape and now you've no idea where he is? That's just gross incompetence,' he sneered.

'... we believe that he is hiding out somewhere along the Thames. My Department, the MPU – that's the Metropolitan Police Marine Policing Unit of course....'

'You mean the *River Police*?' said the troublesome Reporter.

'...has been searching riverside properties and warehouses to find Mad Dog, and...'

'You searched any marinas, yet?' asked the Reporter.

DI Williams ignored the journalist again and raised his voice to emphasise his next statement: 'Ladies and Gentlemen, the message I have for all viewers out there is quite simple: DO NOT APPROACH THIS MAN UNDER ANY CIRCUMSTANCES!'

- - -

'Cool!' said Sam on the sofa.

'No, Sam, it is NOT cool, is it?' said Jazz. 'He's obviously crazy – killing people at random like that. And now he's escaped near here. What do you think, Charlie?'

'No,' said Charlie shaking his head. 'Mad Dog? Whoever he is, no. He's not killed all those people that have gone missing recently – well, not everyone anyway. The Police have got it all wrong. We've got a much bigger fish to catch than Mad Dog.'

'Mass murderer on the loose? Hah. All sounds a bit *fishy* to me,' said Sam, smiling.

'Do you think that DI Williams is *floundering* a bit?' laughed Jazz.

'*Cod* knows why he's blaming things on that Mad Dog bloke!' sniggered Sam. 'I think he should take the oppor-*tuna*-ty to revise his statement!'

'I think he's come up with that story just for the *halibut*!' roared Jazz.

'You two!' said Charlie, trying hard not to laugh.

'Don't *carp* on!' laughed Sam. 'I love this *plaice*!'

'I've had a *whale* of a time today!' said Jazz with tears in her eyes from laughing so much.

Charlie couldn't resist and burst out laughing with his two friends. 'Sounds like a *turtle* disaster to me!' he wheezed.

Jazz and Sam stopped laughing and looked deadly serious at Charlie.

'Turtle?' asked Jazz, straight-faced.

'That was rubbish,' said Sam. 'That's not a fish joke.'

'Oh. Okay. I thought it was okay.' frowned Charlie.

'Wahahahaha!' roared Sam, and mimed casting out a fishing rod and catching a hook in his mouth. He then writhed around the floor looking like he was a fish that had just been caught.

'We *reeled* you in there, Charlie!' roared Jazz, and all three of them rolled around the floor laughing until they all had tears in their eyes.

'Hey kids – watch this bit. Look – they're showing footage of how Mad Dog escaped.' said Charlie's dad interrupting the trio and pointing at the TV.

- - -

'Ladies and Gentlemen- this is the moment that Mad Dog made his escape. This is dashcam footage taken from a squad car....' said DI Williams, and a crystal-clear video appeared on the monitor behind, full of dates and speeds and other important Police data.

An armoured prison van lurched across the screen and barrelled at top speed into a huge metal roadsign which said 'Richmond-Upon-Thames Welcomes Careful Drivers'. The Prison Van was upended by the force of the collision, its side was torn open then it disappeared off the road at a mad angle in a cloud of flames, dirt and smoke, finishing up with a huge splash into the River Thames itself. The van submerged almost straight away, and the Police Driver could be seen clambouring out and holding on to the sirens, which was about the only bit left that wasn't underwater. Mad Dog could be seen swimming away as fast as he could. Then the footage ended.

- - -

'Now *that* was cool!' exclaimed Sam.

'Yes, okay - that really was cool!' said Jazz.

'Hey – hang on,' said Charlie, staring intently at the screen. 'How come they're showing *my* video?'

'What?' gasped Jazz. How'd they get that?

- - -

Grainy footage appeared on the monitor behind DI Williams and he pressed every button on the studio remote control to try to stop it from playing. But the footage played on.

'Where did this footage come from? Who's doing this? What is that?' he demanded.

All the Reporters in the studio looked round at one another. Everyone was shrugging at everyone else.

In the back row, away from prying eyes, a grey-haired DENT Reporter put Charlie's phone back in his pocket and enjoyed the show.

Playing on the big screen behind DI Williams head and going out live across the UK on prime-time television, was the video of Charlie's jeans underwater, then bubbles and a murky shot of Charlie's trainers swimming in fluorescent green-tinged water. Then without warning a massive green stripy shape whooshed past the camera. More bubbles, then Charlie's panicked face filled the screen. The camera focused once more, and Jeremiah came into view trying to swim away from something. A huge set of jaws opened in front of him and the throng of assembled Reporters and News Crews all gasped as they watched Jeremiah wedge the huge jaws open with a boathook.

'What's he doing?' asked one Reporter.

'He's... he's reaching into its mouth! What's he trying to get?' asked another.

'What IS that thing?' asked DI Williams.

'Well, it's not a Great White shark. It looks more like a pike to me. But it must be about thirty feet long!' said WPC326 in awe of what she was watching. 'But look at its eyes – they're glowing!'

'Might even be thirty feet long!' said another. 'Look at him! That guy is trying to get something out of its mouth. Go on my son!'

'Is this a David Attenborough programme?' asked DI Williams, not sure of what he was watching.

As one, the room started cheering for Jeremiah. 'Go on! You can do it!' In the Studio, all the News Teams were willing him on as the video Charlie had shot on his phone played to the world.

\- - -

In Charlie's lounge, Jazz hid her eyes. 'Oh no,' she said. 'I know what happens next!'

Charlie was wincing too. 'Ohhhh noooo, here it comes! Sam, don't watch this bit!'

Sam stared even harder at the TV screen.

\- - -

All the Reporters were glued to the monitor all cheering and egging Jeremiah on as they watched him fight with the monster pike. On screen, the pike was swimming in circles around Charlie, who was holding his mobile phone out in front of himself underwater. The pike's huge mouth kept trying to close and the boathook was really flexing. In the video, Jeremiah reached in and grabbed hold of his head-torch.

'Yes!' shouted one Reporter. 'He's got it! Well done that man!'

'Yayyyy!' shouted everyone.

Then the boathook snapped and the pike's huge mouth full of long wicked teeth clamped down on Jeremiah's arm. Jeremiah pushed himself away, but his arm stayed inside the pike's jaws. Blood and little bits of flesh trailed away from the pike as it swam off into the gloom of the Thames. It spat Jeremiah's arm out as it disappeared.

Everyone stopped, mid-cheer. A stunned silence filled the room.

'Ohhhh yuk,' grimaced a Reporter.

'I think I'm going to throw up,' said another.

- - -

'That was it! That was it!' shouted Sam. That's what nearly got me the other night!'

'That thing was glowing,' said Charlie's dad with a concerned look on his face.

'Bio-luminescence,' said Sam. 'We learnt about that in Biology last term.'

'Ah, so you lot *do* go to school then?' laughed Charlie's dad at his feeble attempt at humour. Nobody else laughed.

He sighed, then thought out loud 'But its eyes… glowing green eyes? I've only ever seen that once before. I think I know who's to blame for all this.' Charlie's dad walked off out of the lounge into his Study, shaking his head slowly. He shut the door behind him.

Charlie watched him go.

- - -

Back in the TV Studio, DI Williams looked pale and gripped the wooden lectern he was leaning on. He shut his eyes and wished he were anywhere else but there.

A voice at the back of the room interrupted the stunned silence.

'This is what *really* happened the other night. This is how rubbish the River Police really are!' said the grey-haired DENT Reporter, standing up. 'DI Williams – will you finally admit that you are grossly incompetent, absolutely useless and unfit to even run a bath…?'

'Oh, it's him,' whispered DI Williams to WPC326.

'Who?' she whispered back.

'Robson,' sighed DI Williams. 'That Reporter. He

applied to join the Marine Policing Unit last year and I turned him down.'

'Ohhhh, I see,' said WPC326. 'I think he's got a bit of a grudge against you.'

'You think?!' spluttered DI Williams incredulously.

Robson continued waving Charlie's mobile phone around to all the News Crews and reporters that were watching him instead of DI Williams.

'I found this, er, I mean, I was given this footage from an extremely credible source. I think it's worth its weight in gold. This is hot stuff. This is the News Story of the Year. I can send you all a link to this video so that you can show it on your own TV Networks – at a very reasonable price of course. Shall we say ten grand per download? And it'll sell a million newspapers. This is 100% incontrovertible proof that there's a monster in the Thames. Yes, that's right – there is a **Monster Pike** on the loose!'

The TV Studio erupted into pandemonium as a hundred TV Crews and Newspaper Reporters shouted their offers of money at Robson for 'his' video, and telephone lines up and down the country went into meltdown as everyone rang their news offices.

A thousand camera flashes blinded DI Williams as he slunk back in his chair.

'A Monster Pike? It's real. How was I to know?' he sighed. 'The Chief's going to fire me for sure after this.' he groaned out loud.

WPC326 leant over towards the DI and whispered in his ear.

'That went well,' she sniggered.

15

Charlie and his Dad

Charlie left Jazz and Sam watching the TV and knocked on the door of his Dad's Study.

'Hello?'

Charlie put his head round the door. 'Hi Dad,' he said in a small voice.

Charlie's dad was a slightly tanned, good-looking man with a few streaks of grey just showing through in his own neatly cut hair. He was leaning on a small bookcase and about to make a phone call. He put the phone down. 'Hey, you don't have to knock, kiddo, how you doing?

I think your friend DI Williams is in a bit of hot water there, don't you?'

'I guess so'.

'I'm serious though – how *are* you doing? You've been through a lot lately and...'

'Yeah, I'm fine, don't worry.'

'Okay, good. I'm just about worried about you and I thought that we could...'

'I'm fine. Honest,' lied Charlie. 'Hey, Dad...?'

'Yes?'

'I'm sorry about Uncle Keith.'

'Yes, that was quite a shock, wasn't it? First your mum, then her little brother.'

'About mum...'

'Yes, I know, kiddo. I'm sorry,' apologised his Dad, shaking his head. 'I'm a rubbish Dad, aren't I? I was never around for you much, and since I retired and bought this place so we could all spend more time together as a family... your mum's not here to enjoy it with us...' his voice trailed off.

'I miss her so much, Dad,' sniffed Charlie, stifling a little sob.

'I'm so sorry, Charlie.'

Charlie ran to his Dad and gave him the biggest hug he'd ever given him.

'Hey kiddo, I know I should talk to you about her a lot more. She thought the world of you, you know that, don't you? We should talk about her a lot more. You should talk about her a lot more. Perhaps *we* should talk a lot more. Don't keep it all bottled up, I guess. Neither of us talk about her very much, do we?' said his dad, wiping a tear away. 'But I know you miss her, Charlie. I miss her too. So, so much. We've both been rattling around this big old farmhouse for the last six months, all wrapped up in our own thoughts and our own little world, haven't we?'

Charlie couldn't stifle his sobs anymore and began to cry.

'But hey – you've got some good friends there,' said his Dad. 'They look out for you. You should spend more time with them. Get them to stay over tonight, then you could all go out somewhere fun tomorrow. Take your mind off things - although I don't recommend you go fishing again for a while, hah!' He tried to lighten the conversation. It didn't work.

Charlie gave a false laugh to make his Dad feel better. That didn't work either. 'Not sure I'm up to another fishing trip just yet,' snorted Charlie. 'Maybe when the time is right.'

'In your own time, kiddo.'

Charlie was silent for a while. His tears slowly ebbed away.

'The last time I saw mum, she was wearing a little silver locket around her neck.'

'Oh yes. Her photo locket. Your mum specifically wanted you to have it. I found it the other day when I was going through all the legal paperwork... sorry it's taken me so long to find it. I gave it to your Uncle Keith to give to you. Do you like it?'

'Well... that's just it. It's the most amazing thing I've

ever seen but... well, I wish *you* had given it to me, Dad. Keith the Ca...er, I mean, Uncle Keith showed it to me, but he was still wearing it round his neck when the pike came and... you know...' Charlie's voice wavered as he mimed with his hand what happened to his Uncle. 'Shooonk! And he was gone.'

'Oh, I see. So, the lockets gone as well, then.' said his Dad. 'That's a huge shame. That locket meant everything to your mum.'

'It was.... it was amazing, Dad. I can't stop thinking about it. mum always wore that locket, everywhere she went. I never knew it had a picture of me in it, though.'

'That's the whole reason she wore it everywhere.'

'Really?'

'Of course, Charlie. It had your photo in it. She always wore that locket so she could keep you close to her heart every day.'

'I didn't know that.'

'I'm so sorry it's been lost, kiddo, I really am. But hey...' Charlies Dad wiped a tear away from his eyes. 'If you want, I can get another locket for you. I'll put a photo of your mum in there... there's lots more photos of her, isn't there? All around the place.'

'I know, Dad, there's some great photos of her – but no. I don't want any of them. It has to be that photo. In *her* locket.'

'Well, it's gone now isn't it? Gone for good.'

'No – it's not.'

'Eh?'

'It hasn't gone for good,' said Charlie with a determined look on his face. 'Mum's locket is inside that fish. The monster pike...

and I'm going to get it back if it's the last thing I do.'

16

The War of the Words

'Exactly HOW are you going to get your mum's locket back, Charlie?' asked Jazz.

'I've no idea,' said Charlie, who had been gazing blankly out of his bedroom window all morning. It was another glorious day.

'Are you playing this game, or what?' asked Sam, busy cheating his way to an all-time High Score on Charlie's PlayStation.

'Nah. Not in the mood,' said Charlie without even looking around. He'd been wracking his brain about how on earth he was going to catch the monster pike, but apart from calling Tom Bruise in to help, he had no other ideas. And he knew that idea wasn't really a good one.

'Charlie. You need to get out, lighten up a bit, hmm?' coaxed Jazz, gently. She looked over at Sam, who was busy cheating at the computer game. 'I think we all need to get out instead of being cooped up here all day.'

'Yeah, fine. Whatever,' said Charlie, absent-mindedly.

'Great! What shall we do then? We can do anything! Fancy going to that new Indoor Snowboard place in town?' said Jazz excitedly.

'Nah,' said Charlie.

'How about Splashdown? That's really cool,' asked Sam.

'Nope,' said Charlie.

'Jungle World, near the park?' suggested Jazz, fingers crossed.

'Pah,' muttered Charlie.

'Well, what do you want to do then? I've run out of ideas,' shrugged Jazz.

'I want to go and get my mum's locket back.'

Jazz sighed. She so desperately wanted Charlie to lighten up and be like the old Charlie again – the old Charlie always wanted to go out and have fun and do silly, crazy things that were a laugh. But there he was, stuck under a big cloud of self-pity in his untidy bedroom. Football magazines mixed with Science magazines on the floor. Cameras, binoculars and DVD's were spread all round the room, plastic kits of World War 2 planes hung from the ceiling and movie posters adorned the walls. Three metal detectors were lying in an untidy heap by the door.

'You know,' she said, 'We never did do any proper metal detecting the other day.'

'So?' said Charlie.

'I detected that I had metal boots on!' Sam gave a cheesy grin.

'Yeah – that's the only thing you two found.'

'No it wasn't - Jazz found thingy's arm,' said Sam, causing Jazz to shudder at the memory.

'Jeremiah's arm,' said Charlie. 'I wonder how he is?'

'You know Charlie, if that thing – that monster pike thing - coughed up Jeremiah's arm,' shrugged Jazz, 'It might just have coughed up your mums locket as well?'

'What?' said Charlie and span round to look at her.

'Yeah! We could find it with the metal detectors!' shouted Sam.

'That's actually a brilliant idea!' said Charlie and jumped up in excitement. 'We'll do the usual – we'll take the electric bikes out and cycle over to Richmond, then get the Tube up to London. The detectors all fold up so can put them in our rucksacks along with some other gear. That is seriously genius! I'm glad I thought of it... Jazz, you pack the detectors up and I'll take the bikes off charge.'

Jazz rolled her eyes but knew better than to say anything.

'What do you want *me* to do?' asked Sam.

'You can stop cheating for a start!' said Charlie. 'Yeah – I saw you!'

Sam pulled a face. He'd been rumbled.

Trees as old as time hung over the towpath next to the Thames as the three of them cycled past Hampton Court along Barge Walk on their electric bikes, then up past Trowlock Island. The children whizzed past Eel Pie Island and the Twickenham Rowing Club, then barrelled along towards the outskirts of Richmond. Charlie, Jazz and Sam whooped and yelled at each other all the way. Their electric bikes made cycling fun – even more so as Sam kept turning his 'Boost' button on and shooting off ahead making motorbike noises.

Just past the bustling Richmond Bridge they stopped outside a Newsagents shop, where Charlie ducked in and bought them each some bottled water.

Two small newspaper kiosks sat on the pavement outside the Newsagents, one on either side. Both kiosks were bedecked out with Union Jack bunting and gaudy tourist-trap souvenirs. One kiosk was trying to sell the *London Gazette* with a bored looking newspaper seller standing beside it - nobody was buying that paper. The other kiosk was selling copies of the *Daily Echo* as fast as they could unwrap them to a long queue of people.

Charlie stood closer and discovered the reason why.

The London Gazette's headline read 'Mad Dog the Axe Murderer on the Loose.' The newspaper seller saw Charlie looking at his huge stack of unsold newspapers and yelled out 'Read alllll about it! Mad Dog on the loose!'

Charlie backed off and went over to read the Daily Echo newspaper. That headline was much more exciting, and they were selling loads of copies. Their headline read, in great big letters: **'MONSTER PIKE IN THE THAMES! £100,000 REWARD FOR ANY OF OUR READERS WHO CAPTURE IT: DEAD OR ALIVE'**

'Wow, Charlie, that news got out quick,' said Jazz. 'I suppose everyone knows now, don't they?'

'Yeah,' said Sam. 'It was on the radio as well this morning.'

'They shouldn't be offering a reward to catch it. It's

not just any old fish, is it? That thing will kill anyone who goes near it,' said Charlie, looking concerned.

'They're making it sound easy, like winning a goldfish at the fair,' said Sam, reading a copy of the Daily Echo.

The Daily Echo newspaper seller grabbed the copy back off Sam. 'Oi. They're 20 pence each if you want one, lad.'

'Sorry! I was only reading it,' said Sam, indignantly.

'Do you want a watch, son?' said newspaper seller.

'A watch? Cor, yes please!' said Sam.

'Okay, stand there and watch, then.' laughed the newspaper seller.

'Hah. Funny,' said Sam, clutching his stomach and miming a fake laugh.

'REEEEEAD ALL ABOUT IT!' shouted the Daily Echo newspaper seller in Sam's face. 'HUNDRED GRAND REWARD TO CATCH THE MONSTER PIKE! GET YOUR COMPETITION ENTRY FORM INSIDE!' and sold another handful of newspapers to eager passers-by.

The London Gazette newspaper seller looked daggers at his Daily Echo competitor. With a jealous 'HRRUMPH' he cleared his throat and bellowed out, 'MANIAC KILLER ON THE LOOSE! MAD DOG THE AXE MURDERER KILLS TWO FISHERMEN WHILST ON THE RUN! BUY YOUR COPY OF THE LONDON GAZETTE HERE!'

Still nobody showed the slightest bit of interest in buying The London Gazette. It was like Charlie, Jazz and Sam were watching a tennis match. The three kids stood in between the newspaper sellers as they battled it out to see who could sell the most newspapers. Their heads swung from left to right then back again as the two newspaper sellers battled it out. The Daily Echo seller smirked at his mate. The London Gazette seller looked daggers back at him.

The Daily Echo seller shouted out: 'MONSTER PIKE IN THE THAMES. HUNDRED GRAND REWARD! ENTRY FORM INSIDE' and sold twenty newspapers.

The London Gazette seller shouted: 'MANIAC KILLER KILLS TEN FISHERMEN... WITH A TOOTHBRUSH. KILLER ON THE LOOSE!' Not one newspaper sold.

The Daily Echo seller: 'THE ENGLISH JAWS! MONSTER PIKE IN THE THAMES. SPIELBERG ON STANDBY! STAR IN YOUR OWN FILM AND GET PAID A HUNDRED GRAND!' Another twenty newspapers flew off his stand.

The London Gazette seller: 'MAD DOG KILLS TWENTY FISHERMEN... IN THE NUDE! FREE PUPPY WITH EVERY COPY!' Nada. Not one single person bought any of his newspapers whatsoever.

'Are you giving away puppies?' asked Sam. 'Can I have one, please?'

'No of course I'm not,' scowled the London Gazette seller. 'I haven't really got any puppies. I'm just trying to sell more papers than him, ain't I?' he said, pointing at the man on the Daily Echo kiosk who was pocketing money as fast as he could. 'But if I told the truth, I wouldn't be in the newspaper game, now would I?'

Sam pondered on this for a moment, then looked defeated and decided he hadn't a clue what the newspaper seller was on about.

'Come on, Sam, let's go,' said Charlie. 'They're crazy making it into some sort of competition. They're going to get all sorts of idiots going out on the water who've never even been on a boat before,'

Just as Charlie went to get on his pushbike, a man wearing a full camouflage suit smelling of dry mud and maggots stumbled into him and sent Charlie flying.

'Watch where you're going, kid!'

'Rude!' muttered Charlie.

The camouflaged man bought a copy of the Daily Echo and walked back over to where Charlie was picking up his bike. Jazz and Sam gave the man a furious look. Charlie stopped them from saying anything with a single wave of his hand.

'This is going to be my lucky day!' exclaimed the

fisherman as he brushed past Charlie again, going back to his car. 'That £100K is as good as mine.'

'Really?' said Charlie, and his eyes followed the man back to where his car was parked. In the back seat was his young son, who Charlie vaguely recognised as Adam somebody-or-other from school. Adam was wearing a camouflage suit that matched his Dad's and peered out through a sea of fishing gear, landing nets and boxes of livebait. A matching camouflaged two-seater canoe was tied to the car's roof-rack.

'You think you're going to catch the pike with that?' called Charlie after the man.

'Of course I am. It's only a pike!' said the man, slamming his car door. As the car sped off, so Adam mouthed a silent 'Help me!' to Charlie. Charlie could only shrug his shoulders helplessly.

'They're going to die,' sighed Charlie to himself, shaking his head.

'Come on Charlie, leave 'em to it,' said Sam. 'We're nearly at the train station.'

'Yes, Charlie. Let's go find your mums' locket,' smiled Jazz. 'I bet we do!'

'You couple of meatheads!' laughed Charlie out loud. Then, to himself, whispered, 'What would I do without you guys?'

A red double-decker bus full of tourists beeped its horn and Charlie pulled his fallen pushbike out of the way. The bus pulled up at the bus stop next to the newspaper kiosks with its engine running next to Charlie. He gave the bus a cursory glance. The bus. The big... red... bus. Charlie looked at the bus again. It was just a bus. But there was something about it. The radiator grill looked like a big smiley fish face. Those bolts on the bonnet were its eyes and the grill was a fish's mouth. He stroked the bus with a faraway look in his glazed eyes.

The bonnet reared back and a huge mouth opened wide. Its jaws were full of sharp needle-like teeth. The big red fish-bus lunged at Charlie, who quickly pulled his arm away, then stumbled over his bike and fell to the pavement.

The bus drove off.

'Charlie? You okay?' asked Jazz as Charlie sat up, rubbing his head.

Sam was too busy laughing at his friend to help.

'Ow! Did you see that? The bus nearly bit me!'

'What are you on about, Charlie?'

'Didn't you see those teeth?'

Jazz looked at the red bus as it climbed the hill into Richmond Town Centre. Some of the tourists onboard were giving Charlie funny looks.

'The bus looks perfectly normal to me, Charlie!' said Jazz as she helped Charlie to his feet.

Sam was still laughing at Charlie as the bus disappeared over the hill.

17

Monster on the Shore

Three empty rucksacks laid next to three carelessly discarded electric bikes on the Thames shoreline. Charlie scanned the Thames with a pair of binoculars whilst Sam was struggling to hold up a telescope that was much-too-long for him.

'Can't see a thing with this.... WAHHH!!' said Sam as a huge eye looked at him from the other end. Jazz looked at him reproachfully.

'Come on you two,' she said. 'I've set all the metal detectors up and I'm going to look over there by the bridge.

It's as good a place as any. Are you coming?' she walked off and her 'beep beep beep beep beeping' disappeared round the bend of the river.

'Have you seen all this lot?' asked Charlie, focusing his binoculars on all manner of little boats and tiny dinghies that bobbed up and down on the river in front of him. 'Do they really all think they're going to catch the pike like that?'

'Got to be about a hundred boats!' said Sam, shaking his head. 'You wouldn't get me in one of those,' he said looking at the small fishing kayaks and dinghies paddling past. 'Not with the size of that pike. We need a proper boat.'

'Maybe we can borrow a boat from someone?'

'Yeah, right. Who's going to lend a bunch of kids their boat?' asked Sam.

'Hmm,' said Charlie. 'Perhaps we can build one...?'

Sam snorted out loud. 'Oops, sorry.'

'There's no way I'd get on a boat that you built!' laughed Jazz.

'Thanks for the vote of confidence,' shrugged Charlie. 'It was just an idea.'

Jazz walked off by herself and looked up at the bridge over her head. It was chock-a-block full of cars, vans and death-defying cyclists. She noticed that a lot of the vehicles had canoes strapped to the top and tutted to herself. Jazz decided to concentrate on the metal detector she was swinging to and fro – she really didn't want a repeat performance of finding something grisly again.

Unfortunately, her luck was about to run out.

As Jazz walked round one of the bridge supports, the monster was looking right at her.

It was huge. Its shiny dark grey skin was covered in barnacles and displayed scars of battles fought long ago. It looked ready to pounce on Jazz at any second as it lay half-hidden under the bridge. The beast was smiling, and it drew the terrified girl towards its crooked mouth full of pearly-white teeth. She slowly walked towards the huge jaws.

'CHARLIEEEEEE!!!'

Charlie spun round. He heard Jazz's scream but couldn't see her. He ran towards her voice as fast as he could, and Sam did his best to keep up.

'IT'S THE MONSTER! I'VE FOUND THE MONSTER!' shouted Jazz.

The two boys rounded the bend in the river running at top speed, then stopped dead. Both their mouths dropped open at the same time.

There in front of them was, indeed, a huge MONSTER. Its vast, bloated body was about thirty feet long. Large, soulless eyes stared straight at the two boys. Its huge jaws displayed rows of jagged teeth in an evil smile.

And it was smiling straight at Charlie.

He gulped hard and whispered. 'Holy Macaroni!'

18

A Monstrous Waste

It was one of those days when everything came sharply into focus. It wasn't every day that Charlie came face to face with a massive whale staring him straight in the face.

'This is Anna,' said Jazz. 'She's a bit upset.'

'Upset? She's dead,' gasped Charlie.

'In fairness, I think I'd be a bit upset too, if I were dead,' said Sam.

'No, not the whale you derps. Her! Anna...' and pointed to a lady sat on the Thames mud, her back against the whale.

It was obvious that she'd been crying for some time.

'Oh, I'm sorry, I'm sorry. I always get a bit emotional at times like these,' said Anna. She stood up and offered her latex-gloved hand to the boys. The glove looked a bit stained. 'How do you do. My name's Anna. I'm a Marine Biologist and Veterinarian. And this – this is Horace, who I've been studying for the last year. Or at least, it *was*.'

The boys gingerly shook Anna's hand and stared at the whale close-up.

The whale's huge dead eyes reflected the small figures of the boys as they crept ever nearer, aghast at what they saw in front of them. A large jagged hole had been punched in its side and a ton of plastic litter spilled out of its mouth.

'That's one big fish' croaked Charlie, dry mouthed. 'Not the first place I'd expect to see a whale - underneath a busy bridge in London. Dead or alive.'

Jazz cleared her throat. 'It's not a fish, Charlie. Whales are warm-blooded. So that means it's a mammal like you and me.'

Jazz watched Charlie with surprise as he stroked Horace affectionately. His hand traced the shape of Horace as he walked round the huge dead whale. Jazz had started to see a change in Charlie. A different side to this boy who had been so cold and aloof for the last six months. Maybe the old Charlie is coming back, she thought. Both Sam and Jazz followed Charlie and stroked the whale as well.

'Goodbye, Horace,' whispered Anna to the whale.

Jazz gave Anna a little hug. 'What a waste of a beautiful creature,' she said.

'It was hit by a boat,' explained Anna. 'Look at its side. My poor Horace has been ripped open - killed by a propeller.'

Charlie looked at the huge gash in the whale's side and shook his head. Something wasn't right. He reached up and traced the jagged edge of the wound with his fingers. He felt something embedded in the whale's flesh. The object was loose, and it gave. Charlie held his treasure up for Jazz and Sam to see. The object was smooth, shiny and about four inches long. It was ivory coloured and very sharp.

Jazz turned her nose up. 'Yuk!'

Sam said 'Cool!' but wouldn't touch it.

Anna picked through the plastic litter mound which had spilled out of the whale's mouth and let out a little sob. She held up a selection of plastic bottles and plastic bags, shaking her head at each one. It looked as though she'd already pulled out yards and yards of a thick commercial fishing net out of the whale's mouth. That was plastic, too. She held the net up to show Charlie. 'Look at this netting! It's from a trawler. It must weigh a ton. I guess if my poor Horace hadn't been hit by a boat then all this plastic in his gut would have killed him soon enough.'

'It wasn't plastic waste, or a net or a boat that killed the whale, Anna,' said Charlie.

'What do you mean? Of course it was. What else could kill a whale?' she sobbed.

'Look. See for yourself.'

Charlie held up the object he'd found. It was a long, razer-sharp tooth.

A monstrous tooth.

'You mean that thing on the news is real?' gasped Anna. 'I thought that was just fake news.'

'No, it's all true. It's a monster pike. Me and Sam here have seen it for real. Up close.'

Anna let out a little breath. 'A monster pike? Oh come on....' she winked at Jazz. 'What are these two like? A right couple of jokers, aren't they?'

'No. No, they're not,' said Jazz. 'It's true. I've seen the pike as well.'

'Seriously?' Anna's smile faded. 'That's impossible. I've studied all the marine life in this river for ten years now – there's been seals and dolphins and other whales, too. Horace only appeared last year but I've been studying him ever since. If there was such a thing as a monster pike here in the Thames, then I'd know about it.'

Charlie gave the huge tooth to Anna. 'Look. You're a marine biologist and a vet, so you know about these things. You tell me what animal this tooth is from, then.'

'But, but...' said Anna. 'That's incredible. It *is* a pike's tooth. But it shouldn't be that big.'

'My best guess is,' said Charlie in his best Sherlock Holmes voice, 'is that the monster pike hasn't been in the Thames that long. It's only just got here.' He paused for effect. 'It's all to do with Rejoov and the Fizz...'

'The what and the who?' asked Anna, clearly baffled.

'Charlie's got this theory,' said Jazz slowly, not sure if she should tell Anna anything as she didn't really know her at all. 'It's all Secret Agents and illegal smuggling and boats blowing up and stuff. But he wants to catch the pike and get his mum's locket back, anyway.'

'Ohhhhhkay then,' said Anna, with clearly still no idea what on earth they were talking about. 'And exactly how are you going to catch this so-called 'monster pike' then, eh, Charlie? Have you got yourself a little fishing net?' said Anna, almost laughing at him. 'Or perhaps you can blow it up like they did in *Jaws*....' she sniggered.

'I DON'T KNOW!' Charlie exploded. 'Why do

people always think I know everything? I haven't got an answer right now, okay? So, don't ask me. Why is it always *me* that's got to sort things out? Why am I always the one that people turn to for help? I've got my own problems too! You know, I hate my life sometimes!'

Jazz looked shocked. Maybe Charlie was only half-joking? He was shouting irrationally, and that worried her. A lot. 'Charlie...' she said. 'Anna didn't mean anything. I think...'

'I don't care, Jazz! I really don't. I don't care and I don't know, okay? I don't care about any fish, or mammal or whatever it is. I don't care that there's too much plastic slowly choking the world, I don't care what Anna thinks and I really, really, REALLY don't care about what you, Sam or my Dad thinks, okay? I miss my mum, that's all – I miss her and I want her back!'

There was a long awkward silence.

Jazz took a step towards Charlie and held his hand. Sam put his arm around Charlies shoulder's and spoke softly to his sobbing friend.

'Charlie. We're so sorry that your mum's not here anymore. We'd do anything to bring her back for you, but we can't. But *we're* still here for you, Charlie. We're not going anywhere. We're still your friends and we know that you don't mean half the nasty things you say to us -sometimes.'

Charlie slowly stopped sobbing. 'I know. I know. I really appreciate what you two do for me. I know I'm not an easy person to be around sometimes. I'm guessing that will pass in time, though. That's what I keep telling myself, anyway.' Another little sob, then Charlie added, 'Thank you guys. I really mean that.'

Anna looked embarrassed. 'I'm really sorry, Charlie,' she said. 'I truly am. I didn't know you'd lost your mum. I'm sure she was a very special person and I bet you've got some wonderful memories of her – they'll stay with you all your life, you know.'

'He's finding it hard, right now, Anna,' said Jazz, still holding onto Charlie. 'We're all a bit worried about Charlie, to be honest.'

'Ahhh, I'm fine. I'm okay,' whispered the boy teetering on the edge.

'You know,' said Anna looking at Charlie with concern, 'it's okay *not* to be okay, you know? Everyone deals with loss and grief in their own way. It takes time. It's hard and you shouldn't rush to try and get over it. Shout at the world sometimes, get angry. Let it all out. But what I would suggest though, if I may, is don't shut out the people that care for you. The memory and the pain never go away when you lose somebody special in your life – but it does get easier to deal with over time. And your friends are there for you.'

'Yeah, Charlie. You just need time, that's all,' said Sam hugging his best friend. 'And me, of course. You still need me around to make you laugh,' and he looked at Charlie cross-eyed.

'You absolute goon' laughed Charlie through his tears.

The three of them laughed. Anna joined in for a moment, then she moved slightly away and let the three best friends have their special moment together in private.

'There's definitely more to all this than meets the eye,' said Jazz. 'I think that the river is trying to tell us something. We just don't know what that something is, yet.'

There was a pause as all three of them leant against some old railings and stared into the fast-moving waters of the Thames. They all had questions swirling and whirling around their heads, but Old Father Thames said nothing and just kept rolling on by. It felt like something was about to happen. Something amazing. All three of them let the feeling wash over them and waited for someone to say something.

'I'm starving' said Sam.

Charlie spluttered out a laugh. 'You would be!'

Anna called over. 'Well, I could make you all a sandwich, I guess?'

'Really? Food? Yes please!' said Sam excitedly.

'Yes, of course. I've got a campervan parked just up the road. There's loads of food and drink in it. Come on.' Anna marched off towards the road above. The kids paused, unsure of this new person in their lives. 'Come on!' Anna called back.

'I guess it'll be alright if we all go together and get some food at Anna's old Campervan,' said Charlie, hesitantly. 'But I think she might be a bit of a weirdo 'right-on' eco-warrior so we'll probably end up with nettle soup or dandelion sandwiches.'

'Bet she's a right old hippie!' laughed Sam. 'Bet her campervan stinks and all the tyres are flat. Flower Power, man!' laughed Sam, putting the strap of his rucksack round his head like a bandana and holding his fingers up in a V-shaped 'Peace' symbol.

'You two!' said Jazz. 'I'm sure her campervan will be fine, and I am a bit peckish to be honest, so I could do with something to eat. What do you think, Charlie?'

'I think I know how I'm going to catch the pike,' he said, looking back at the dead whale.

19

None so Blind

Charlie let Jazz and Sam climb the old green steps from the Thames first, watching them slip and slide as they carefully carried their pushbikes back up to the world above.

'Green means slippery!' Charlie warned.

'Yeah okay, smart-alec,' muttered Jazz under her breath.

Just before he went up the steps, Charlie spotted the man.

He was standing in an alcove on the riverbank. He

wore a Bus Conductor's uniform and dark sunglasses. Round his neck was an old-fashioned ticket-machine on a leather strap. In his hand he held a long white cane which he waved slowly in front of him. He looked strangely out of place on the riverbank.

'Afternoon.' said the Bus Conductor, nodding in Charlie's direction. 'Fares please! Beautiful day, isn't it?'

'You're blind,' said Charlie, stating the obvious.

'Hah! That's a good one, Charlie-boy.' laughed the bus conductor. 'I might be blind but it's not me that can't see so well, is it?'

'What do you mean?'

'You've got good friends all around you, Charlie-boy. Your Dad's a good man and wants the best for you, doesn't he?'

'I... I guess so.'

'Yet you're rude to them all and treat them like you just don't care.'

'I don't.'

'You do.'

'I don't!'

'Answers staring you in the face, isn't it, Charlie-boy?'

Jazz had reached the top of the steps and put her bike down. She looked round to see Charlie still at the bottom of the steps talking to himself.

'You okay?' she called down.

'Yeah – I'll be up in a moment. Just having a chat.'

Sam had already started pedalling towards Anna's campervan.

Charlie came up the stairs at last with a puzzled look on his face. 'What do you reckon to him, then, Jazz?'

'Who?'

'That guy down there. He's a Bus Conductor – but he's blind.'

'A blind Bus Conductor? I've never seen a blind Bus Conductor before. What's he doing down there?' Jazz looked again but couldn't see anyone. 'There's nobody else down there, Charlie - you okay?'

'Me? Yeah. Of course. I'm fine. Just don't understand what he said to me, that's all.'

'What?'

'Well. He looked me straight in the eyes and said, 'There are none so blind as those who will not see.'

20

The Amazing Campervan

In the private caravan park there were caravans, campervans and motorhomes of all shapes and sizes.

Anna was there to meet them.

'Ah, here you are. Come on, I'm just over there...' she said, pointing over towards the far corner where some motorhomes and a scruffy old VW split-screen campervan were parked.

'Told you!' whispered Charlie.

'Right on, mannnn!' sniggered Sam. 'It's a little smelly old rotbox.'

'Sssh you two!' said Jazz, trying not to laugh.

Anna reached into her overalls and took out a small electronic blipper and blipped it.

A door hissed open on the biggest Motorhome the kids had ever seen. Two of its sides glided open silently which made the vehicle at least two feet wider, and a set of chrome steps automatically folded out. Anna bounded up them. The three kids followed in wide-eyed wonder.

'Wow! This is amazing!' said Jazz, looking at the beautiful paintwork and polished glass of the outside.

'This is really cool!' said Sam, as he walked up the steps of the massive motorhome and casually gave the old VW camper a sideways glance. 'We thought that scruffy old wreck was yours, not this one.'

'I didn't,' lied Charlie. 'I knew all along.'

'Don't be too, impressed, gang,' said Anna. 'That scruffy old van *is* mine.'

'Oops. I meant, er, that VW looks lovely,' said Sam, trying to get out of the hole he'd just dug himself. 'Bet it's worth a fortune to a scrap metal... er, I mean, a classic vehicle collector.

'Hmm,' said Anna and gestured them to come further inside.

Jazz giggled at Sam.

'Whose is this posh one then?' asked Charlie as all three kids crowded into the Motorhome at the top of the stairs. They stared at the inside in wonder.

The Motorhome was a complete mess.

'Has she been burgled?' whispered Sam, staring at the piles of old washing up, old clothes dotted everywhere, and books and magazines piled high.

'Can't really tell.' said Charlie. 'I think if a burglar broke in here, he'd probably tidy the place up a bit.'

Jazz grimaced at what she could see and looked for somewhere to sit down, which wasn't easy. On every surface there was a plethora of stuff. Useless detritus, some might say. There were spindly un-watered spider plants, maps, charts, pens, remnants of 'Microwave Meals for One' and packets and paper bags stuffed with who knows what.

Shoes and clothes were sticking out of every odd space available, a pile of dirty laundry took up an entire corner and an old tabby cat stared back at Charlie from between two piles of National Geographic magazines haphazardly stacked onto a stereo unit under what looked suspiciously like a brand-new and quite-possibly illegal Police-Scanning two-way radio unit.

Along one wall was a bank of big TV monitor screens, microphones and CCTV-monitors showing different views outside the campervan. It was an impressive mix of new tech and old washing-up waiting to be done.

Sam pulled a 'Bluurrgggh!' face. Jazz stifled another giggle.

Anna finished her token bit of tidying up and threw a pile of old clothes off into a corner of the Motorhome which already had another pile of clothes in it.

'The motorhome is Kane's. Kane Zeet to be precise. He runs the South African Wildlife Protection League and funds all my research. In return I look after his accounts, veterinary work and Human Resources across all his companies.

'Human Resources?' asked Charlie.

'People Management, Charlie. Kane's got a LOT of people working for him. He does some amazing work, you know - good work. He runs a multi-million-dollar operation looking after animals and their habitats around the globe. He'd be interested to talk to you, you know.'

'Me? Why?' asked Charlie.

'I text him a few minutes ago. He'd like to talk to you now if that's okay, please?'

'Erm, sure, okay' said Charlie, warily.

Anna plonked herself down in front of the bank of TV monitors and put a Bluetooth earpiece in. 'KANE MOBILE,' she said.

An electronic voice out of nowhere replied 'Request accepted. Calling Kane's mobile number now'.

'Cool,' said Sam.

As Anna waited for the call to connect, she passed each of the three kids a drink from her fridge. 'Made this myself. Hey - sit down guys, make yourself at home.'

They looked around, unsure of what was actually a seat.

'Thank you.' said Jazz and greedily glugged down a big gulp of the fizzy brown drink. She immediately wished she hadn't. Turning slightly green she made a 'cutting neck' warning sign to the boys who wisely poured their drinks into the nearest pot plant.

'Come on, come on. Where are you, Kane? Answer me!' implored Anna staring at the tv monitors. 'What do you guys want to eat?' she asked.

'Erm... we're okay actually.' smiled Charlie, but his rumbling stomach gave him away.

'HELLO?' boomed a loud disembodied voice with a heavy South African accent.

A TV monitor flickered, then Kane's face appeared huge on it. On another monitor, the three kids could see themselves. Sam waved at himself but stopped when he got a reproachful look from Jazz.

'Hi Kane. It's me, Anna.'

'Ah, yes, I can see you now. How are you? How's Horace?'

'I'm afraid he's dead,' said Anna with a small tremble in her voice. 'He'd swallowed a trawler's net and been hit by a boat and...'

'Oh, that's terrible,' interrupted Kane, who didn't look as though he'd just heard terrible news. He quickly changed the subject. 'Ah, now, who do we have here, eh?'

'These are the kids I messaged you about. This is Charlie.'

'Ah, so this is THE Charlie Carter. Nice to meet you, Charlie - I've just been hearing all about you.'

All Charlie could see on the monitor was a big fish talking to him. It was a carp wearing a man's clothes. He shook his head and the vision cleared. Kane was looking at him.

'Have you?' said Charlie. 'Who from?'

'It couldn't have been Anna, she's only just met us.' whispered Jazz.

'Who from? That doesn't matter, boy, eh?' boomed

Kane. 'The important thing is that you are safe and well, eh? You're the boy who swam with the monster pike.'

'Well, I didn't exactly swim with it...'

'The boy that saved Agent Ochre's life...' continued Kane.

'Jeremiah? No, I didn't really save his....'

'...and the boy that can think like the Pike. You know where it is, how to find it and most importantly... how to catch it. You're an important person to me, Charlie. Very.'

'Me? Important?' stuttered Charlie.

'You have a connection with the fish, eh?' said Kane. 'You can see things that others can't.'

'A connection?' exclaimed Charlie. 'I don't think so – but I have been seeing some strange things lately – I had a really weird dream about the Pike and a red London Bus for one thing. But I don't know where the pike is.'

Jazz looked worried. Sam moved closer in as though to protect Charlie from the fierce gaze of the man on the monitors.

'Rubbish!' boomed Kane. 'I've seen the footage you

took on your mobile phone. That green liquid you were swimming in when you first met the pike...'

'What about it?'

'That was REJOOV.'

'What does that matter? I don't understand, Mr Kane, sir.'

'Well, let me explain it to you then, eh, Charlie? The pike was a normal fish before those fools at the Fizz started playing around with it. They filled it full of a new, experimental rejuvenating drug called REJOOV. Must have taken them ages to think of that name, eh! Rejoov made the pike grow. Made it strong. The Fizz were trying to *weaponise* the pike - make the fish into a weapon that the military could use. But they also found that Rejoov can regenerate missing limbs and make injuries better – fast. It can make wounded soldiers fighting fit, but it has a different effect on different people. A little bit will help rejuvenate you but take too much and watch out! It's made soldiers super-strong for a while but then it slowly sends them mad. So Rejoov is banned. No-one's allowed to use it - well, not officially, eh? The Fizz must smuggle it in under cover of darkness. You got mixed up with some very bad people, Charlie. A lot of people would be in BIG trouble if it got out they were using REJOOV here in the UK, eh? Heads would roll.'

Charlie looked at Jazz and Sam. 'This is serious stuff,' he whispered.

'The problem is, Charlie – is that you've ingested some of that REJOOV, eh? Swallowed it. Only a tiny amount, not enough to have any lasting effects of course - but you're probably seeing visions, eh? You'll be drawn together, you and the pike until that one, inescapable conclusion. You might have a feeling when the fish is near – you might already know where to look for it, eh? How it feels, what its weaknesses are - and you might even know how to catch it. And that, my boy, is very valuable to me.'

Charlie, Jazz and Sam looked at each other in silence. Anna bit her lip. As usual, it was Sam that broke the silence.

'Does this mean that Charlie's got superpowers now?'

'Hah!' laughed Kane. 'No of course not! But for a week or so I'm very much hoping that he'll have an empathy with that big fish, eh? Help me catch it, that's all. But time is running out. I want to use Charlie's powers to save that fish whilst we still can.'

'Save it?' said Charlie.

'Of course. I'm a conservationist,' smiled Kane.

'I like a good chat, too,' said Sam.

'No, doofus!' said Jazz. 'Not a conversationalist, a *conservationist* – someone who saves animals. Oh, never mind. I'll do an internet search and show you what Kane does....'

Charlie peered intently at Kane's image on the monitor. 'Who ARE you, exactly? You could be anyone, for all I know. Why should I help you?'

'Yeah!' said Sam, backing up his friend.

'My intention is simple, boy - I want to catch that fish – the so-called monster pike,' said Kane. 'Just like you.'

'I don't care about the pike – I just want my mum's locket back,' said Charlie.

'Yeah!' said Sam, bravely standing behind Charlie.

'Is that so?' said Kane.

'Yeah!' said Sam.

'Anyway, how do you know so much about me?' asked Charlie

'Yeah!' said Sam.

'Well, for one thing your face is all over the News, Charlie. Your video is everywhere now. But there is another reason. I keep my ear to the ground. I talk to a LOT of people.'

'Anna couldn't have told you that much about me already – we've only just met her.' Charlie wouldn't let it go. 'What's the other reason?'

'Yeah!' said Sam

'I have friends in low places!' laughed Kane.

'Yeah!' said Sam.

'That was meant to be a joke,' said Kane, sternly.

'Oh, sorry.' Sam gave a cheesy grin.

Jazz piped up. 'Kane Zeet. Director of Zeet's South African Wildlife Protection League.'

'Yes, that's me, girl. What about it?'

'I've just searched for you online – you're also Director of Zeet's Global Hunting Ltd and Zeet's Exotic Exports. You're a Big Game Trophy Hunter!' Jazz looked shocked and hurt.

Kane looked a bit rattled.

'Ag! This girl has chutzpah, eh, Anna?'

Anna turned to Jazz. 'It's okay, Jazz. Kane's one of the good guys.'

'Really? I don't think so, look!' Jazz angrily thrust her phone towards Anna. The Google searches she'd been doing displayed pages headed with things about Kane that at first sounded great, but as she scrolled down the page, things got progressively worse:

Top Hit: Ad: Kane Zeet: Zeet's South African Wildlife Protection League: Billionaire Playboy's foundation sees four baby Rhino's re-introduced into the wild. Heavy research investment by Kane Zeet's foundation secures the future for South African

Wildlife.

Related Searches: Ad: Zeet, Kane: Zeet's Global Hunting Ltd: Trophy Hunting Tours for the true Sportsman available on four continents, all transport and ammunition supplied. No licenses required. All Visa's included. Fully inclusive prices from £30,000. Be the envy of your friends: hunt and stalk the wild animal of your dreams: lions, jaguars, giraffes, elephants etc. Two A4 photos of your kill included in the price. Taxidermy service extra: Stuffed heads from £3500, fully stuffed animal ready to display from £12,500.

Related Searches: Ad: Zeet, Kane: Zeet's Exotic Exports. Zoo's supplied, all species, all areas. Email for details. Animals exported worldwide, quotes available 24/7. Full inoculations and transport of animal all included. Lioness and two cubs available now, can ship worldwide. Paperwork not required. Any animal, anywhere. Protected species 20% extra.

'You hunt and kill animals!' Jazz snapped.

Anna squirmed in her seat. So did Kane.

'Young lady, the billionaires I take around the world contribute millions of pounds to local economies in those Countries. Their money pays for fresh water to be installed in the remotest parts of Africa, their money helps Bengal tigers to be bred in captivity and then released back into the wild. Their money pays for wolves to be reintroduced into the wilds of Canada, they've...'

'But you hunt and kill poor defenceless creatures??!!' Jazz repeated. She wasn't letting this go easily. 'You're nothing but a Trophy Hunter and a poacher!' Jazz seethed. 'You're in the Global Animal Trade. You take rich people all around the world to hunt and kill innocent animals.' she nearly spat the words out.

'Ag!' exclaimed Kane in his native South African dialect. 'It's a sport. A very lucrative sport, that's all.'

'That doesn't sound like sport, to me,' said Charlie. 'At least in a sport both sides know they're in the game. Lions, tigers and bears don't even know they're playing.'

'That's a good analogy, my boy,' said Kane. 'But don't forget – the money we get for these hunting trips helps us fund conservation projects across the world – and pays for the eco-friendly research we need to do to help save animals and their habitats. The kind of research that Anna does – expensive research.'

Anna looked at Charlie apologetically. 'It's complicated,' she said.

There was an uneasy silence in Anna's motorhome. The silence was deafening.

'Eish!' said Kane, unable to bear the tension anymore. 'Charlie – move closer to the screen will you please? You look a lot like him, eh?'

'Who?'

'Ah, it doesn't matter anymore, but you look a lot like... my son.' The mention of his own son seemed to be painful for Kane. 'I'm sorry if I have upset you, eh? But I can save this pike... WE can save this pike, together. I can help you get your mum's locket back – I have people, I have boats, I have a lot of resources at my disposal,

Charlie. I need your help. I think you need mine. Will you help me, Charlie?'

'Of course he won't!' exclaimed Jazz.

'Yeah!' said Sam loudly. 'Er, I mean NO he won't!'

Charlie was quiet for a moment. He looked around the motorhome at the three faces staring intently back at him. Anna the eco-warrior: she sounded sincere and he wanted to trust her, but he wasn't sure. Jazz, his posh friend who always told him the truth whether he wanted her to or not. And Sam – his stoopid, doofy friend who wasn't always up to speed with things but who always made him laugh. A pint-sized motormouth who was always there for Charlie. What a motley crew this was.

Charlie looked at Kane's face which loomed large on the tv monitor.

'Yes, okay, Kane. We'll help you.'

21

Rover

'Are you NUTS? Please tell me you're kidding!' implored Jazz as she walked down the steps from Anna's Motorhome.

Charlie was sitting on the grass outside.

'Charlie knows what he's doing, Jazz.' said Sam. 'Don't you, Charlie?'

'Well, to be honest – no I don't.' admitted Charlie. 'Although I did have one idea as to how to catch the pike, but who knows – half my ideas don't work. My inventions either explode, break or put me in hospital. Sometimes all three.'

'Nah, all your ideas are great, Charlie!' said Sam. 'Your rocket pack was the best.'

'That set fire to everything,' said Jazz, 'including Charlie.'

'The jet-powered moped was the best,' continued Sam.

'Oh yes, I remember that!' laughed Jazz. 'He went over the waterfall in the woods on that one – at sixty miles an hour.'

'I got some massive air on it though,' smiled Charlie at the memory.

'Got some massive bruises too,' said Jazz, 'and broke your leg.'

All three of them laughed together as Anna brought out some soft drinks and even softer biscuits.

''I'm glad you agreed to help Kane,' said Anna. 'He's a good man, really.'

Jazz scowled and tutted under her breath.

'He's going to help me get by mum's locket back,' said Charlie. 'But he mentioned something I didn't understand – he said I looked like his son. He seemed quite sad about it.'

'Ah,' said Anna.

'What did he mean that it didn't matter anymore?'

'Well,' began Anna. 'Kane's son passed away a few years ago now. He was about your age, and I guess that you remind Kane of him, that's all.'

'That's all?' asked Charlie.

'Well, no, not quite,' faltered Anna. 'It's incredibly sad really. I shouldn't really tell you about it – but it happened quite a few years ago so I guess it doesn't matter who knows about it, now. You see, Kane used to be a professional rugby player. He's always had LOTS of money, and he took his young son Morgan away with him on a month-long safari trip. But one night, it happened. *They* came for him...'

'They?'

'The Lions,' said Anna. 'Two rogue lions crept into Kane's camp in the middle of the night. They dragged Morgan out of his tent and into the middle of the scrub.

They mauled him to death. He was only twelve.'

The three kids looked at each other, open-mouthed.

'Not nice,' said Jazz.

'I'm kinda glad I said I'd help him, then,' said Charlie. 'I know what it's like to lose someone close to you.'

'Yes, you do,' said Anna. 'It was very good of you to agree to help. It takes a very long time to get over things like that – maybe Kane never will. But hey – tell me, Charlie, what did *you* mean earlier about seeing strange things lately – about the Pike and red London buses? Perhaps I can help you find out what it all means.'

'Well, I had this dream – about the pike and a London bus.'

'Cool!' said Sam. 'Did it have a Travel Card?'

'I've remembered a bit more about the dream. There were lots of buses – red ones - all stacked on top of one another in a great big pile. There was a skeleton, too – it said the pike was coming for me, but I wasn't scared.'

'You weren't?' said Anna, surprised.

'No. I wasn't scared at all – but the pike was.

Somehow, I knew it felt scared as though it knew the end was coming and it was going to die.'

'Hmm,' said Anna, in deep thought.

'I know,' said Charlie. 'Really random, eh? A big pile of buses under the water.'

'Sounds like the *Urban Reef* to me,' said Anna.

'The what?' Said Charlie.

'The Urban Reef. It's a new multi-million-pound conservation project in the Thames. It's a Charity project funded by Kane, of course. The Charity buys up old buses that are due to be scrapped, removes all the engines and oil and fuel, cranes them into the river and welds all the buses together to get one big artificial reef. It's a brilliant idea – it provides protection for many different aquatic species and we're seeing some really amazing fish calling it home already.'

'Including the monster pike.'

'Hmm, maybe,' said Anna.

'That's where we need to look, anyway,' said Charlie, with steely determination in his voice.

'Look for it? Who, us?' said Sam. 'Shouldn't we wait for Kane?'

'Nah. We can do it ourselves,' said Charlie. 'But how do we find this Urban Reef?'

'It's downriver, you can't miss it. Turn left out of the marina and you'll eventually come to it. I'll show you the exact location on my river charts. But you might find *this* useful to see it up close,' smiled Anna. 'Kids, meet Rover.'

Anna blipped a different button on her blipper again and a large panel folded out on the side of her motorhome. A chunky yellow machine looking like a fairground bumper car folded out and plonked itself on to the grass next to the bemused looking kids.

'What is *that*?' asked Charlie.

'*He's* an ROV. A Remote Operated Vehicle,' said Anna proudly.

'It's an underwater drone!' said Sam, hardly able to contain his excitement.

'You got it. Designed in Norway. Built in Germany. Paid for by Kane. They use these ROV's to inspect pipelines and oil platforms all over the North Sea. Rover here helps me look after all the whales and dolphins whenever they're in the Thames – and helps me make sure their habitat stays healthy. He's got WIFI, Bluetooth and a full-1080 HD camera onboard which you can hook up and control from an App on your mobile phone. It's state-of-the-art and easy-peasy to operate – even I can do it!' laughed Anna, stroking Rover's hard shell. 'He's only a year old and cost a fortune, but they fitted him with a full stainless-steel cage for rough conditions so he's a tad overweight. 70kg I think. It'll take at least two of you to carry Rover. I always have to borrow someone when I take him out for his 'walkie's.'

'Walkies?' asked Jazz.

'Heh! Sorry. I call it 'walkies' whenever I use Rover in the Thames. I always need a hand attaching him to my deck crane.'

'Deck crane? You mean, you've got a boat?' said Charlie, a smile slowly spreading over his face.

'Of course I have,' said Anna. 'I'm a Marine Biologist

and an aquatic veterinarian. I need a decent boat for all my research.'

'An aquatic vegetarian?' asked Sam.

'Veterinarian,' smiled Anna. 'A vet. Basically, I mend fish.'

'How big's your boat?' asked Charlie.

'The Wayfarer? She's big enough, but not huge. I can handle her by myself – just! I keep her at the Limehouse Basin Marina not far from here. She's a beauty. Wayfarer was one of the 'Little Ships' that went over to Dunkirk in World War 2. Built like a tank. She's long and low so I can get into all the canals round here, too.'

'I can't wait to see her. And to take Rover for walkies' said Charlie.

'Hey – I haven't said you can borrow him yet,' smiled Anna.

'May we?' asked Charlie.

'Please' said Jazz, nudging Charlie.

'Oh okay,' he sighed. 'Please?'

'There that didn't hurt did it?' said Jazz.

'Sure,' said Anna, throwing Charlie a big bunch of keys attached to what looked like a dayglow orange tennis ball. 'But *only* if I'm with you. Rover is worth a lot of money. We can go first thing tomorrow. If you guys can put Rover in the back of my little campervan now... you know the one Sam - my little 'smelly' campervan - then you can meet me back here tomorrow morning. We'll hook him up to my boat and take him out for a walk.'

Sam smiled his cheesy grin again. 'I don't think I called it 'smelly' as such.'

'What are we going to do when we find the monster pike tomorrow, Charlie?' asked Sam as they all struggled to lift Rover into the back of Anna's little campervan. It was getting late and they needed to get home.

'We're going to catch it of course.'

'Of course,' said Sam. 'I knew that....er, how?'

'With a net.'

'Where are we going to get a net big enough to catch that thing?' asked Jazz.

'Horace,' said Charlie.

'Horace?' said Anna, incredulously.

'We're going to put that trawler's net to good use,' said Charlie.

'Of course!' shouted Sam. 'Go Team Carter!'

'Team Carter?' groaned Charlie, slightly embarrassed.

'Yeah, that's us. I've just thought of it,' said Sam excitedly. 'I like the sound of it though. Me, you and Jazz. Team Carter!'

'Yeah, alright. Calm down.' said Jazz, equally embarrassed.

'We're not going to call ourselves Team Carter – that's daft, Sam,' said Charlie.

'I'm sure Kane would be really pleased if you can *find* the monster pike for him, Charlie. He really wants to save that fish,' said Anna. 'But I don't think you'll actually be able to *catch* the pike, will you? After all....' Her voice trailed off.

'Why not?' asked Sam.

'Well, you know. You're just a bunch of kids, aren't you...?'

All three kids turned to look at Anna. None of them were smiling.

'No, we're not just a bunch of kids,' said Charlie, sternly. 'We're a team.' He looked at Sam. 'Doing brilliant stuff and catching the bad guys - just like in one of Tom Bruise's films when he assembles a team of heroes: We are TEAM CARTER!'

Charlie, Jazz and Sam all reached out and touched their hands together. 'GO TEAM CARTER!' they all shouted as one, then burst out laughing.

It was a stupid name, thought Charlie. Stupid, childish and immature. He loved it.

Jazz watched Anna walk back off into her motorhome. 'Hmm,' she scowled to herself, then called after her. 'We'll see you back here tomorrow, Anna.' It was nice to meet you today.'

'Likewise, Jazz. I'll see all of you kids back here tomorrow.' Anna called back.

Jazz had bad feelings about Anna and Kane.

Very bad feelings.

22

The Big Game Hunter

Kane switched off the tv monitors and laughed to himself. He leant back in his large leather chair and surveyed his sumptuous office. It was lined with highly polished wood panelling and thick, expensive carpet. A wide gun cabinet filled with various makes and sizes of rifles and shotguns filled an entire wall. From every other wall, animals of all shapes and sizes stared back at Kane in silent sadness.

'You can come out of hiding now, they can't see you,' he growled.

An ugly scar moved forward into the light. Attached to the scar was Agent Purple. Attached to Agent Purple was a quiet air of menace. A green light from deep inside the scar danced and reflected around the polished wooden walls. It looked like the scar was getting worse instead of better.

'You lied. You told that kid you were going to save the pike,' sneered Agent Purple.

'Eish! Of course I'm going to save it – save it for myself so that I can put its head on my wall, eh!' laughed Kane.

'Ah, I see. Good. You had me worried for a moment there,' said Agent Purple. 'But I'll repeat our offer, Kane, for the last time. I suggest you take it. The Fizz will give you £2Million to kill this fish and retrieve our Rejoov cylinder.'

'Well, I'll repeat *my* offer, Agent Purple. It's £5Million if you want the fish disposed of as well and no questions asked. It's a big fish. It's an expensive operation, eh? Oh, and by the way – cash upfront.'

'£5Million then. That fish has got to disappear. That's

why the Fizz want you, Kane - you can hunt and trap any animal on the planet. You're the best at what you do. Do whatever you like with the fish afterwards – just get our REJOOV back and dispose of any evidence. And the boy.'

'What do you mean?' glowered Kane.

'Charlie Carter knows too much,' said Agent Purple. 'And he's cost us a LOT. He's got to disappear as well.'

'And you want me to do your dirty work for you, eh?'

'Listen, Kane. Just bring us our Rejoov cylinder back before all those weekend fishermen out there find it, okay? It must be recovered no matter *what* the cost. The Fizz can't afford to let the world know its secrets.'

'I'll see, sonny. I'll see.' Said Kane.

'No Kane. You won't 'see'. You will do exactly what we want if you know what's best for you. And DON'T call me sonny,' spat Agent Purple, moving towards Kane menacingly.

Kane didn't flinch. He stood up from his comfy leather chair and surveyed Agent Purple's green scar with some interest.

'Now *you* listen, Agent Purple. Listen carefully to what I am about to say to you. You visit me uninvited. You come to me with a problem that nobody else can solve for you. You want my expertise, my boats, my men and my weapons to hunt down an animal so bizarre its very existence threatens your whole organisation. Your attempt to weaponise a fish has backfired, and it's gotten out of control. You've lost your expensive chemical which would help you continue playing God on the battlefield - help you kill and maim more people across the globe. And now you want me to kill a child? Here you are, threatening me in my own home. You look at me like I was just another one of your lacky's to carry out your every whim. To do what you want, when you want, however you order them about.'

'What's your point, Kane?'

'My point is, Agent Purple, is that I think you've taken too much of that Rejoov. That IS what you've been doing isn't it? You're taking Rejoov and you're losing the plot. If you want my help, you ask for it in the right way. I have my own army of men. I have my own boats, my own weapons. I don't need you, the Fizz or your blood money.'

Agent Purple squinted at the sunlight outside the blinds. He looked across the rolling lawns and expensive cars being polished and buffed by Kane's staff in his opulent garages. He sniffed at the large private lake beyond the warehouses where a team of men were craning a large motoryacht and a sleek grey armoured RIB onto two low-loader lorries. A camouflaged crate with 'Type M4 CANNON 20MM AMMUNITION - KEEP DRY' written on the side and shotguns and rifles were being piled onboard.

'That's an impressive armoured RIB you have there, Kane,' nodded Agent Purple. 'I see it's fitted with the latest M4 cannon. You almost have as many toys as the Fizz...almost.'

'You can't leave any stone unturned on a hunting trip, Agent Purple. You have to be prepared for any eventuality.'

'Kane, we don't have to like each other. This is a simple business transaction. You've done very well for yourself. A big stately home in the countryside. Your own private lake stocked with fish. A sixty-foot Predator motoryacht, I do believe...'

'It's the 63-foot edition,' corrected Kane. 'The one with the twin jet drives. Very rare.'

'The deal is £5 million to kill the fish and get the REJOOV back,' said Agent Purple. 'No questions asked. The Fizz will bring our own weapons and tech along as well. If we catch it first, the deal's off. But we're not leaving any stone unturned either, so we'll be hunting it alongside you, just to keep an eye on things – we don't want you to be tempted and keep the REJOOV for yourself when you find it.'

'Of course not,' said Kane. He really didn't like Agent Purple or his tone of voice.

'Are those yours as well?' asked Agent Purple, looking at the line-up of classic cars being polished by his staff.

'The cars? Oh yes, some of them are quite rare.'

'Oh, very nice, verrrry nice,' purred Agent Purple. 'You must have very good contacts. You've got a very impressive and slick operation, here, Kane - lots of toys. Seriously, I'm very jealous. Must have cost a fortune. You must have killed an awful lot of lions in your time.'

'Yes,' said Kane. 'I used a cannon.'

Agent Purple nodded approval, then stopped as he realised Kane was teasing him.

He was very jealous of Kane's toys. The Green-Eyed Monster winked at Agent Purple from the corner of his mind's eye and whispered, *'Kane is far better than you! Kane is far better than you! Kane is far better than you!'* The monster goaded Agent Purple and fed his madness.

Agent Purple span round from the windows. Some of the luminous green liquid bubbled out from his scar and spattered onto his cheek as he spoke.

'You will help me, Kane, if you know what's good for you. We want the pike dead and the Rejoov back... *I* need it back! It's making me strong, Kane, like you wouldn't believe. I can feel it in my head, in my body - sheer power coursing through veins. It's making my mind grow, making me all-powerful. *Invincible.* I need more

REJOOV and I need it now! I will go through anyone or anything to get it back. If either you or that kid tries to double-cross me, then you'll be sorry, do you understand me?' Agent Purple ranted uncontrollably. A small green flame burned deep in his eyes.

'Nobody is trying to double-cross you, Agent Purple. I'm not. The kid's not. I think you need help, that's what you really need. I think that Rejoov stuff you've been taking is making you sick.'

'I am not sick! Nobody is going to blame me for this mess, do you hear? None of this is my making! It's all that kid's fault! Charlie Carter messed everything up, right from the start. He destroyed our retrieval operation! He destroyed our boat and killed one of our agents!'

'The kid didn't kill anyone, Agent Purple...'

'DON'T ARGUE WITH ME, KANE! I would have that Rejoov already if Charlie Carter hadn't stuck his nose in. And you... you're nothing but a two-bit illegal fur trader. I could have your operation shut down like that.' He clicked his fingers in Kane's unimpressed face.

'Watch what you say, sonny,' warned Kane.

'Don't tell me what to do, Kane! Don't call me sonny! Do you have *any* understanding what you're dealing with, Kane?'

'A mad man?' asked Kane, innocently.

'I AM NOT A MAD MAN!' shouted Agent Purple madly. 'I'LL HAVE YOUR OPERATION SHUT DOWN JUST LIKE *THAT*.' He clicked his fingers in Kane's face again. 'YES, I HAVE REJOOV IN ME. I EXPERIMENTED ON MYSELF, SO WHAT? IT HASN'T DONE ME ANY HARM! IT'S AMAZING, KANE – IT'S MADE ME UNSTOPPABLE!'

'It's made you go crazy, that's what it's done to you, sonny.'

'UNSTOPPABLE!' shouted Agent Purple again. 'And I *really* don't like being called sonny!'

'Unstoppable, eh?' said Kane, and pulled a huge loaded shotgun out from under his desk. It was the biggest and most powerful shotgun in Kane's collection. He aimed it right between Agents Purple's eyes. 'I'm fairly sure that my elephant gun here would stop you. It's got twice as much power than a normal shotgun. Would you like me to prove it?'

Agent Purple was cross-eyed as he looked at the twin barrels of the elephant gun.

'He has got to go.' Agent Purple hissed.

'Who?' asked Kane.

'CHARLIE CARTER MUST DIE!' snarled Agent Purple, taking a small step backwards.

'Yeah, yeah - whatever you say, Agent Purple,' said Kane in a slow, steady voice. 'But I suggest YOU go, right now and take your lunatic ideas with you. I've shot wild animals that have better morals than you do.'

Agent Purple slowly retreated towards the door, keeping his eyes fixed on the elephant gun in Kane's hands.

'You've got no choice, Kane. Kill the kid or we kill you.' spat Agent Purple.

'You know, I'm tired of your empty threats. You can't kill the kid, Agent Purple. That's one step too far. That's madness.'

'MADNESS?' spat Agent Purple. 'Hah! Do I really LOOK mad to you?'

'Well, now you mention it....' began Kane.

'Know this, Kane: You WILL help us. You WILL take the money and you WILL retrieve the REJOOV for the Fizz. Or your fate is sealed. You have no choice.'

Kane knew that Agent Purple was right – he didn't really have any choice. He knew that the Fizz had far reaching fingers across the globe, but that didn't stop Kane from taking an active dislike to the scar-faced man in front of him.

'Get out of my house - sonny,' said Kane, and kicked the door shut in Agent Purple's face.

23

Gone Fishin'

The camouflaged fisherman who had collided with Charlie at the newspaper kiosks was standing up in his wobbly and overloaded fishing kayak.

'Daaaaad!' whined his camouflaged son. 'I don't think you're supposed to stand up in this.'

'Adam, stop worrying. What's the worst that could happen?'

'You'll fall in and I'll have to rescue you. Again.'

With a great deal of effort, Adam's Dad steadied the tiny kayak and beamed like a Cheshire Cat. He picked up his fishing rod and with a flick of the wrist cast out into the middle of the Thames. The brightly coloured float bobbed up and down on the water.

'Bongo Baits – that's the secret. Bet none of these other guys use Bongo Baits.' He boasted to his bored looking son. 'What did that guy in the fishing shop say, Adam? *Floats and lures guaranteed for the catch of your life'* that's what he promised.'

'Dad, all you've ever caught in your whole life is a rusty old pushbike and a cold.'

'Well, I've never used Bongo Baits before, have I?'

'Can't we go home yet?' said Adam, trailing his hand in the river.

'No, we can't! Not until I've caught that pike. A hundred grand – that'd be good wouldn't it? Just to catch some old fish. That money is as good as mine!'

Adam huffed and looked down into the swirling water. A huge eye looked back up at him. Then a sleek massive shadow surged forward underneath the kayak.

'Dad....Dad...' he croaked.

'No, we are NOT going home. Nothing could make me move from this spot...'

And with that, the kayak took off at thirty miles an hour.

It was a white-water ride down the Thames. The kayak zig-zagged first one way, then the other at breakneck speed.

'YYYAAAARRGGGHHHH!!!!!' screamed Adam's Dad.

'YEEEEHAAAAAA!' laughed Adam.

About fifty metres in front of the kayak, the monster pike leapt out of the water like a vast demented dolphin with a *Bongo Baits* lure caught in its mouth. Adam's Dad gasped in amazement as he struggled to hold on to the speeding kayak.

'Did you see that? That thing must be sixty feet long! Hey – are you videoing this?'

'Yeah!' said Adam, holding on to the kayak with one hand and filming on his phone with the other. 'This is awesome, Dad – but I don't think its sixty feet long!'

Adam's Dad screamed again as the kayak just missed a paddle steamer full of tourists coming in the opposite direction. 'GET....OUT...OF...OUR...WAY!!!!'

CLICK CLICK CLICK CLICK CLICK CLICK CLICK CLICK CLICK CLICK CLICK

A hundred cameras clicked as the monster pike leapt out of the water again and again sending up huge foaming waves. With a herculean effort, the fisherman cut the line and the kayak slid across the water, up a grassy riverbank then came to an abrupt stop against a wall, covering both Adam and his Dad in fishing hooks, broken fishing rods, Bongo Bait lures and multi-coloured floats.

Adam scrambled up straight in what was left of the kayak. 'That was brilliant Dad! Can we go fishing next week, as well please?'

'Son,' said his exhausted Dad, 'I think we're gonna need a bigger float.'

24

The Evil Fizz

The Facility was a sprawling, ugly building which squatted on a bend of the Thames like an old, warty toad. It was an unassuming building – nobody ever gave it a second glance which was perfect as it hid many secrets within its thick, concrete walls.

People who knew the building nicknamed it the Fizz. But the Fizz was much more than just a building – it also gave its name to the top-secret Research & Development Company based there, working around the clock on shady projects for shady companies and shady governments all around the world.

Deep inside the Fizz were busy offices, gleaming laboratories, state-of-the-art medical facilities and a maze of underground chambers where men and women in white lab coats scurried to and fro like rats in a sewer. Huge tanks full of water contained experiments that would never see the light of day, locked vaults only accessible by the latest retina-scanning technology were hidden away from prying eyes, and computers and strange machines hummed day and night.

Level 0 at the Facility was a bland-looking carpark lined with steel and concrete, designed so that the average passer-by couldn't see the digital security cameras leading into a brightly-lit Reception Area with Italian marble floors and glass-fronted lifts to all levels. Behind the Reception Area was a screen made of bullet-proof glass and a hidden door nearly twenty metres wide which led out onto the river itself. Underneath Level 0 were three sub-basement levels hiding who-knew-what secrets from the world.

Level 1, just above the Reception Area, was devoted to huge video monitors that displayed live 3D maps and news programmes from all over the world. Level 2 was filled with computers screens watched over by shadowy figures wearing headsets who chattered incessantly to secret Operatives across the globe. Level 3 housed the Research Labs and Medical Centre. Nobody was permitted up to Level 4 unless you had a *very* good reason.

A BMW X6 skidded to a halt at the barriers at the front of the Facility and the driver briefly waved a Pass at the armed Security Guard standing next to the six steel vehicle-proof barriers which rose out of the tarmac.

'Welcome back to the Fizz, sir,' nodded the Guard, and the barriers disappeared into the floor. The car sped into the underground carpark and stopped by one of the glass-fronted lifts.

Agent Purple got out and slammed the door shut. The glass lift was already waiting for him. He got in, took a small key out of his pocket and stabbed it into the lift's control panel. He punched the button marked **4**.

'LEVEL 4 – AUTHORISED' said the lift.

Jeremiah was admiring the office that Agent Red had escorted him to. He'd been told to sit down on a large comfy ivory-leather sofa and Agent Red had sat down next to him – he'd even offered Jeremiah tea and biscuits. The office was lined with plush wood panelling and low-key lighting. Designer flowers stood in crystal vases which made the air heavy with scent. On every wooden panel hung a large oil-painting: ten stern-looking men in sober business suits stared down at Jeremiah. Under each painting was a small brass plaque which read -

AGENT X
FACILITY DIRECTOR 1982-82
RETIRED

Jeremiah noticed that the dates under each painting progressed as he looked round them all. The second from last painting was of a slightly tanned, good-looking man with neatly cut hair, leaning on a small bookcase. Jeremiah didn't know it, but the painting looked a lot like Charlie's dad in his Study. Underneath that painting the small brass plaque read:

AGENT X
FACILITY DIRECTOR 2015-2020
HONOURABLE DISCHARGE

The last oil painting was different though - it showed a woman in a sharp grey business suit. Under her painting the plaque read:

AGENT X
FACILITY DIRECTOR 2020 -

Jeremiah looked away from her stern gaze, unsure if the paintings eyes were looking back at him or not. He chose instead to stare out into the night through the floor-to-ceiling glass windows which looked onto the river. Behind the biggest oak desk he'd ever seen was an ivory-leather chair with its back to him. He wasn't sure if someone was sitting in it or not.

'Jeremiah, would you like some more biscuits?' asked Agent Red in his poshest voice.

'Why, er, thank you,' said Jeremiah trying to be equally as polite. He held the bone china teacup as delicately as he could and tried to keep his little pinky in the air. 'Wow, this office is awesome.'

'How's the arm?'

'Yeah, it's great, thank you so much,' exclaimed Jeremiah, flexing both his arms in the air and sending his tea across the wall and over Agent Red. 'Oh my, I'm sorry!'

'That's okay, Jeremiah. Or should I say, Agent Ochre.' said Agent Red trying not to be annoyed. 'I'm glad the facilities here at the Facility er, facilitated your er, re-facilitation.'

'You're being really polite! I'm so sorry about that, but I don't really do tea. All of you have been so good to me so I just want to thank you – you know, re-attaching my arm and all, not to mention the rehab. I'm amazed it's only taken a couple of days for my arm to return to normal though. Does this mean you want me for another job?'

'No, no, no, Jeremiah. We just like to look after our own, that's all,' said Agent Purple in a calm, soothing voice. 'Now, we did have to put a tiiiiiny amount of REJOOV into you, to aid with the healing process, but we didn't want to overdo it like you-know-who has....'

At that moment, Agent Purple burst into the office like a malevolent whirlwind.

'AGENT OCHRE! I WAS TOLD YOU WERE BACK ON ACTIVE DUTY. ITS ABOUT TIME! WE'VE GOT ANOTHER JOB FOR YOU. NO ARGUMENTS. MISSION STARTS 07:00 HOURS TOMORROW MORNING. AGENT RED WILL BRIEF YOU ABOUT IT ON THE WAY DOWN TO LEVEL ZERO. NOW GET UP OFF THAT SOFA AND COME WITH ME. BOTH OF YOU!'

Both Jeremiah and Agent Red looked terrified.

Agent Purple stood in front of them, dripping with sweat and wiping drips of green liquid away from his cheek. His scar looked wider than ever.

'AGENT RED, WHY HAVE YOU GOT TEA ALL OVER YOUR SUIT? COME ON, BOTH OF YOU, I NEED TO SHOW YOU HOW THE GUNBOATS WORK...!'

'Good evening, Agent Purple,' Purred a soft voice from out of nowhere.

Agent Purple stopped, mid-sentence. It was his turn to look terrified. The ivory-leather chair behind the desk turned slowly around and a woman in a sharp grey suit leant both elbows on the huge oak desk. She rested her chin on beautifully manicured hands.

'A...Agent X. Director! Ma'am. I'm sorry, I didn't know you were back in the country...'

'Evidently, Agent Purple. How have things been in my absence?'

'Oh fine, fine. I was just about to brief Agent Ochre and Agent Red here on a little job-ette I have for them in the morning...'

'Is that right, Agent Purple?' said Agent X as she

slowly stood up and walked over towards him. 'A jobette? That sounds interesting. What have you done to your face?'

'I, er, fell off a bridge, Ma'am.' He flinched as Agent X moved closer.

'Well, you'd better be more careful, hadn't you, Agent Purple? Because if you don't get that missing REJOOV back tomorrow – then you just might fall off another bridge. Capiche?'

'Oh. So, you know about the missing, er, I mean, the slightly misplaced REJOOV?' whimpered Agent Purple, looking down at his feet.

'I know *everything* Agent Purple,' she said. 'Except why you've been taking it yourself. REJOOV is too new, too strong to experiment with. We don't know the full extent of its capabilities yet. Have you found the fish yet?'

'The pike?'

'Yes, of course, the pike. THE PIKE!' she bellowed in Agent Purple's ear. 'I DON'T KNOW HOW YOU LET THAT THING ESCAPE IN THE FIRST PLACE. I presume that you have a plan in place to re-capture it?'

'Yes, yes, of course,' said Agent Purple. 'I've hired the best Big Game Hunter in the UK to track it down and kill that monster for us. He'll get our Rejoov back and dispose of the fish's carcass, no questions asked.'

'Such a shame. Such a beautiful fish,' said Agent X, looking at her reflection in the office windows. The Thames twinkled its lights in the night beyond the glass. 'Kane Zeet? You need to watch him, Agent Purple. And what about Charlie Carter...?

'I have a plan.'

'There can be no witnesses at the end of all this, Agent Purple. None.'

'I understand, Ma'am.'

'Now run along and show the boys here your new toys downstairs,' she said without turning around. 'Just make sure all of this goes away, Capiche?'

'Capiche, I mean, yes, I understand. Don't worry, Ma'am, I've got it all covered,' said Agent Purple as he ushered Agent Red and Jeremiah into the lift.

The lift doors closed behind them.

Scant seconds later, the doors opened. **'LEVEL ZERO'** announced the lift.

The three Agents got out and walked over to where a large motorboat bobbed against a hidden jetty on the water. The motorboat was so dark it was difficult to see where it ended, and the night began.

'Wow - what *is* that thing?' exclaimed Jeremiah.

'Welcome to... THE MEDUSA!' announced Agent Purple loudly, with an over exaggerated flourish. 'She's the fastest boat on the water and armed to the gills.'

'That colour!' exclaimed Jeremiah in awe, gently running his hand along the boats smooth hull. 'Incredible. I can't even make out its exact shape.'

'It's VenomBlack,' said Agent Red, proudly. 'Patent Pending. It's the darkest colour in the world – a military-grade stealth coating developed by our own boffins upstairs in the Fizz's own chemical lab. We're immensely proud of it. It's....'

'...it's a nano-tech coating that absorbs 99.957% of

visible light,' interrupted Agent Purple. 'It's my favourite colour, apart from purple, of course. I LOVE IT!' He stroked the boat with a mad look in his eyes.

Jeremiah stole a glance at Agent Red. Neither of them said what they were thinking, although Jeremiah made a subtle 'He's going crazy' gesture with his fingers. Agent Red nodded a silent agreement.

'Why's she called the Medusa?' asked Jeremiah.

'Her cannons can fire multi-headed missiles - you can choose to fire one missile or ten missiles at once,' explained Agent Red. 'She's packed with Stealth Technology: the VenomBlack paintwork and computer-designed angled sides are to evade radar and decrease thermal emissions. The hull is a very thin, lightweight composite powered by twin Whispa-Tech engines to reduce her acoustic signature - even her exhaust is muffled and filtered. Basically, Jeremiah, *nobody* can see or hear the Medusa until it's too late, and then they're paralysed with fear.'

'It's a pretty incredible boat,' nodded Jeremiah,

genuinely impressed. 'But why have you left it until now to use it?'

'We lost it.'

Jeremiah raised his eyebrows but said nothing.

'Took us ages to find it again.'

'That fish won't even hear us coming!' gloated Agent Purple. 'And by the time it does, then the Medusa here will unleash her full firepower. And if that fails, she has her baby with her, of course.'

'Her baby?' asked Jeremiah, sounding even more worried than he was before.

'That's where you come, in Jeremiah,' said Agent Purple, walking towards a large groove in the side of Medusa's hull. 'This is where Medusa keeps her baby.'

Agent Purple pressed a remote-control button and a recessed panel opened. Jeremiah peered over his shoulder and his eyes popped at what was inside.

'Whoahhhh! Now that IS cool!' gasped Jeremiah. 'What is it?'

Agent Purple gave him an evil, wicked smile.

Just then the huge metal door to the river slid back and in roared a camouflaged jet ski with a mean-looking machine-gun mounted on the front. Jeremiah watched as a familiar figure got off and walked up the jetty towards them. Two scientists in white lab-coats tied the jet ski up for the man, who looked far too important to do it himself.

'Evening, Agent Purple,' waved the man as he hurried past.

'Hey, Tom' nodded Agent Purple. 'How was it?'

'She handled like a dream,' said Tom. 'But that gun's way too small,' and pointed his fingers like a gun at Agent Purple.

Agent Purple pretended to shoot Tom back, and Tom laughed and pretended to die horribly as he disappeared up in the glass lift to Level 4.

Jeremiah stared at Agent Purple. 'Was that... was that...?'

'Who? Oh, him. Yeah. Tom Bruise, the Hollywood actor. We go way back. He does a bit of work for us now and again. We cover up his spying missions by saying it's for some film or another,' said Agent Purple, nonchalantly.

'Been doing it for years,' said Agent Red.

'Well, you guys just keep on surprising me, don't you?' said Jeremiah. 'Okay, well, I got two questions. Number One... how much are you paying me? I don't want to get my arm bit off or my boat blown up this time, so I am expecting a heavy pay cheque, okay, you get me? And Number Two... how the heck do I fit on that thing you just showed me?'

'You don't sit ON it, Jeremiah. You sit IN it,' sighed Agent Purple.

'IN it?' asked Jeremiah incredulously. 'You DO know I'm 6'6" yeah? I don't think I'll fit.'

Agent Red looked at Agent Purple.

They both stared at Jeremiah.

'Maybe we could cut your arm back off or cut both your legs off and *make* you fit....?' suggested Agent Purple. He didn't appear to be kidding.

'Ah, no, erm, okay then,' laughed Jeremiah nervously. 'I'm sure I'll fit in just fine.'

'That's what I thought,' said Agent Purple, straight-faced. 'Now let's go blow this fish and Charlie Carter to Kingdom Come.'

25

Trowlock Island

Trowlock Island was a small island that sat in the Thames full of quirky wooden cottages painted in bright colours. Each one stood on metre high stilts. Canoes and rowing boats sat outside every doorstep as Trowlock flooded completely at least three or four times a year. Electricians rewiring houses on the island had been known to pull up a floorboard only to find the River Thames swirling a few inches underneath them.

The only way to get to Trowlock Island - at any time - was by manually winching yourself over on a tiny floating chain-ferry about ten feet long. Residents had to wear waders to and from this ferry, wind themselves over to the mainland to stock up on essentials like milk and bread, then wind themselves back across the water.

Christine stepped onto the ferry with a full bag of groceries. Reginald jumped on behind her, making the small platform rock backwards and forwards in the water.

'Stop messing about, Reg!' she cried. 'I want to get to my parent's house in one piece if you don't mind.'

'Ah it's fine, don't worry, love,' said Reg and started turning the winch.

Halfway across there was a bump and the ferry stopped.

'What was that?' whispered Christine.

'Oooooh, perhaps it's that giant newt that everyone's talking about,' laughed Reg, making a face like a newt and trying to scare her.

'Giant pike, they said, not a newt!'

'Pffft. Giant newt, giant shark, monster man-eating pike. You'll believe anything you read in the papers,' scoffed Reg. 'It might even be the Creature from the Black Lagoon!'

A huge shape swam slowly underneath the ferry. The ferry turned slowly around in the water, making an ominous creaking noise as Christine and Reg clung onto the handrails.

'That's strange,' said Reg, looking genuinely nervous. 'It shouldn't be doing that. It goes straight from here to there on a chain,' he said, pointing at the two shorelines only thirty metres apart.

The ferry creaked to a halt. There was no sound apart from the river running by. Suddenly the ferry whipped back around and flung Reg into the water. Christine could only watch in horror as a huge set of jaws opened and the monster pike dragged Reg beneath the surface. A plume of water and dark red blood splashed over the ferry as Christine came to her senses. She screamed and turned the winch handle with all her might.

The ferry bumped into its docking station on Trowlock Island and Christine waded onto the flooded path that ran up between the neatly-painted houses as fast as she could. She tripped and filled her waders with water. Weighted down, she struggled the last few steps to her parent's house, half walking, half swimming. Christine didn't see the huge shape behind her, wriggling onto the flooded island like a killer whale beaching itself to grab a struggling seal. She reached the doorbell. It was an old-fashioned type, with a long metal handle you had to pull down to make it work.

Sanctuary. She'd made it!

Christine reached up to the doorbell and yanked it. The water surged behind her.

DING-A-DING-A-DING

Inside the cottage, her mum was putting the finishing touches to dinner and her dad was reading the newspapers.

'Ah, there they are,' said her mum. 'Darling, can you get the door for me, please?'

DING-A-DING-A-DING
DING-A-DING-A-DING

DING-A-DING-A-DING

'Yes, yes, yes,' said Christine's dad as he got up and walked to the front door.

DING-A-DING-A-DING

DING-A-DING-A-DING

'I'm coming, I'm coming... give me a chance!'

He opened the door. There was nobody there.

DING-A-DING-A-DING

Puzzled, he looked out, and there, only inches away from his nose, was Christine's severed hand still attached to the doorbell, dripping blood onto the welcome mat.

'Is that you, Christine?' called her mum walking over from the kitchen. 'I'm glad you're here at last, darling, I'd like you to give me a hand with dinner.'

And then she **screamed.**

26

The Little Ship

A foghorn sounded on a ship passing the Limehouse Basin Marina.

The bright full moon shone like a torch in the summer night sky. A torch beam shone through the window of the 'Wayfarer' as she bobbed up and down on her mooring. Wayfarer was a beautiful mid-sized wooden ketch built of solid oak and weighing just over twelve tons. Anna's boat had all sorts of kit on it – there were winches and wheels and echo-locators and radar domes and...

'What *is* all that stuff?' asked Sam.

'No idea,' said Charlie.

'I still think we should have asked her to borrow it first,' whispered Jazz, wearing a snood pulled up to just below her eyes.

'I did ask – she said yes,' whispered Charlie, sounding slightly muffled. He was wearing a balaclava as a cunning disguise.

'She said we could borrow it - but *only* if she was with us!' whispered Jazz.

'Did she? Oh. I only heard the 'yes' bit,' said Charlie without the slightest concern he was lying through his teeth. 'Anyway, we're only going for a quick look – I just want to see if the pike really is hiding out in the Urban Reef. We'll have all of Anna's stuff back before she even wakes up in the morning. Bring Rover over here.'

SQUEEK SQUEEK SQUEEK

Two fishing trollies lashed together squeaked up next to Charlie on the pontoons. Anna's bright yellow ROV was strapped to the top.

'This thing is REALLY heavy!' said Sam wearing a balaclava that was a bit loose for him so only one of his eyes showed.

'Tell me about it' said Jazz. 'Charlie, are you actually going to help us with Rover anytime soon?'

'Hey, I drove us here. Didn't I? I can't do all the work – I'm the brains of this outfit. Anyway, I went through all the Options and this was the best one.'

'Stealing Anna's old campervan, Rover and her boat was the best option?' asked Jazz. 'If she finds out she's going to go mad! *And* you'll get banned from driving if you get caught as you're not old enough to drive yet. Why did I let you two talk me into this?'

Charlie pulled a face at her, out of sight.

'I was right though, wasn't I?' whispered Sam. 'It was smelly.'

Charlie jumped up on the deck of the boat and grabbed the hand controls to the small deck crane. It moved round and he lowered the crane's strops over Rover. 'Seriously, Jazz, it'll be fine. We'll send Rover down to have a look at the Reef, see if the Pike's there, then whizz all her kit back to where we found it. It'll take a couple of hours, max.'

'What's the point, again?' asked Sam.

'The point,' said Charlie, 'is that I'm not letting that Kane catch the pike first. I don't trust him - he's up to something, so I want to find where the pike's hiding out, then we can come back with the net and catch it first thing tomorrow morning in the daylight.'

'You're just paranoid' said Sam. 'I thought he was alright.'

'Pppftt! Who, Kane?' said Jazz. 'He shoots anything that moves!'

'Look you two, get a move on,' said Charlie. 'Hook Rover up to the crane, I'll go and start the boat up.'

'Don't you need keys for that?' asked Sam.

'What, you mean these ones?' smiled Charlie, holding up the bunch of keys for Anna's campervan with the dayglo orange ball on it. 'Anyone who keeps a floating key fob on their keys must have a boat key on it as well!'

'Oh, very clever,' said Sam, pulling a face behind his face mask.

'Well, at least one of us is!' said Charlie. 'I'm just trying to think ahead so I can get my mum's locket back, that's all.'

'You're obsessed, Charlie,' huffed Jazz.

'NO I'M NOT – ITS MY MUMS LOCKET! SHE WANTED ME TO HAVE IT! IT'S IMPORTANT!!' shouted Charlie.

'Sssh!' hissed Jazz. 'Okay, okay.'

Not far off up at the beginning of the pontoons, a light came on in the Marina Managers house.

Sam and Jazz struggled to bring Rover onboard. As it thudded down onto the deck of Wayfarer, two big 350bhp Caterpillar diesel engines roared into life. Charlie's face beamed at his two friends from out of the boat's wheelhouse.

A face also appeared at the window of the Marina Manager's house.

'Slight flaw in the plan,' said Sam. 'Does anyone here

actually know how to use Rover?'

'Yeah, of course. Anna said she always kept about a couple of hundred metres of control cable onboard. Sam, have a look for it will you please? It's got to be in one of these lockers somewhere. It'll be just like flying a model plane. Except underwater,' said Charlie.

'Have you ever flown a model plane underwater, Charlie?' asked Jazz.

'Not yet.'

Sam opened a tall locker. A spaceman with a huge metal head leapt out at him.

'YAAAAARGH!' screamed Sam with eyes as round as saucers.

Charlie and Jazz paused for a second then burst out laughing. It was an old-fashioned diving suit, complete with a big brass diving helmet. Sam looked at them both with fear in his eyes, then looked back at the empty diving suit hanging up in the locker and breathed a sigh of relief.

'I saw my life flash before my eyes then!' he said.

'OI!!!!' came a shout from not far off. 'That's not

your boat!' The Marina Manager was hopping down the pontoons as he struggled to put his shoes on. He was still half-dressed in stripy pyjamas and a bright yellow Sowester coat.

'Charlie!' shouted Jazz.

'It's okay, I see him,' said Charlie and gunned the boats throttle levers forward. 'Let's gooooo!!'

Twin 350hp engines strained at the ropes that tied the boat fast to the cleats on the pontoons. The boat went nowhere. Fast.

'Shall I cast off?' asked Jazz.

'Cast off? We've only just got here' shouted Charlie.

'No, doofus. I meant, shall I untie the mooring ropes?'

'Oh right. Yes, cast off quick! Can't believe you forgot to do that, Jazz!' said Charlie.

Jazz and Sam jumped off the boat, untied the ropes then jumped back on. Charlie rammed the throttle levers open again and whirled the steering wheel round. The Wayfarer surged forward straight into the boat in front of it. **CRUNCHHHH!** He pulled the throttle levers back and the boat lurched backwards. It bounced off the pontoons as the Marina Manager ran towards them. **WHUMMP!!**

'Do you want me to do it?' asked Jazz.

'No, it's okay, I've got this,' said Charlie and whirled the steering wheel round the other way. 'I *can* drive, you know.'

'It's not like driving a car on your Dad's farm, Charlie – there's a knack. Here, let me...' said Jazz, shooing Charlie out of the way and sitting herself down at the helm.

Jazz turned the boat's steering, gave the throttle levers a few small nudges and the boat chugged its way off the mooring at last.

'Oi! Bring that boat back!' shouted the Marina Manager. He was now running alongside the speeding vessel on the wooden pontoons. 'That's Anna's boat, not yours!'

'She said we could borrow it!' shouted Charlie.

'I bet she said nothing of the sort you little tearaway! Now bring that boat back!'

But the Marina Managers shouts were cut short as he ran out of pontoon and fell feet-first into the water.

'GLUB!' The Marina Manager surfaced and spat out half the water in the marina. He punched the water in frustration, which only served to get him wetter and a wave went up his nose. **'BLUURRGH'** he spluttered.

'How come you know how to steer a boat, Jazz?' asked Charlie.

Jazz didn't reply, she was concentrating on steering and turning all the spotlights on. 'That's better' she sighed as the Thames lit up in front of them. 'How come you *don't* know how to steer a boat? You told me you did.'

'Well, it looks easy in all the films, doesn't it?' said Charlie. 'Just thought I'd figure it all out as I went along.'

'Jazz started her RYA Youth Training a little while ago, Charlie,' explained Sam. 'She's been learning how to drive speedboats really fast!'

'They're called RIBs,' corrected Jazz. 'Rigid Inflatable Boats. The Royal Yachting Association don't have speedboats.'

'Oh. You never told me,' said Charlie, feeling hurt at being left out of something that sounded really quite amazing.

'Well, you know...' said Jazz. 'I started the RYA scheme six months ago. About the same time as your mum.... well, you know. You had other things going on at the time, didn't you?'

Charlie was quietly impressed. He and Sam looked back as they left the still-spluttering figure of the Marina Manager climbing up an escape ladder and back onto the pontoons. He was shaking his fist at them and yelling something they didn't want to hear. Jazz navigated the Little Ship out of the Marina and into the dark waters of the Thames. Only when the Wayfarer was out in the main part of the river did she open the throttles up.

'Get the charts out, then, Sam,' said Charlie. 'Let's find out where this Urban Reef is.'

'What charts?'

'The charts. You know – the river charts. It's what us

sailors call maps. The map Anna marked up to show us where the Urban Reef is.'

'Ohhhhh, that one,' sniffed Sam.

'Oh no. Where is it?' sighed Charlie.

'In the campervan,' said Sam, moving out of Charlie's reach. Charlie went to punch him, but Sam was too fast.

'Idiot,' said Charlie.

'And since when have you been a sailor?' goaded Sam. 'The closest you've ever been to a boat was that time your Dad took you down to the model boat pond in the park. And you still managed to sink that one.'

'My Dad used to be a brilliant sailor. He taught me everything.'

'Taught you how to crash,' said Sam. 'Anyway, you once told me your Dad was a Crocodile Hunter in the Outback, not a sailor.'

'Ppfttt!' scoffed Jazz, still steering the boat. 'Charlie once told me his Dad was a Submarine Commander in the SAS.'

'And you said your Dad was an underwater welder in

the North Sea before he retired,' said Sam. 'What did he really do?'

'Well,' said Charlie, feeling unsure himself as to what his Dad really used to do. 'He did do all that, actually. He used to hunt for crocodiles in his submarine and if they ever bit the hull because then he had to get out and weld the holes back up. Underwater. A 1000 feet down. In a deep-sea diving suit like that one over there. Okay?'

Jazz and Sam looked at each other and rolled their eyes.

'What's this place we're looking for called again?' asked Jazz.

'The Urban Reef - that's what Anna called it.'

'Would that be it, then?' asked Jazz.

A large neon sign lit the Thames shoreline up. It said 'URBAN REEF – CONSERVATION IN ACTION' in huge red and blue letters ten feet high above where a small pontoon was set back from the main river.

'Yeah, that might be it.' said Charlie. He turned to look at his two friends.

'You know, I've just had a really brilliant idea.'

'Uh-oh' said Jazz and Sam together at *exactly* the same time.

27

Deep Sea Diver

'I can't see any buses,' said Sam.

'That's because they're under the water, you doughnut,' said Charlie. 'Weren't you listening?'

Jazz cut the boat's engine to a low idle, and Charlie leapt off onto the pontoon and grabbed the bow rope at the front of the boat. 'Got the hang of this now,' he said, and tied the boat up to a cleat. 'Sam – you do the stern line,' he ordered.

'Aye, aye, Cap'n, straight away, me hearty!' saluted Sam. 'Er....do the what?'

'The line at the back of the boat,' sighed Charlie. 'Landlubber.'

'I'll keelhaul me barnacles now, sir, then scrub the mainbrace at once, arrrr!' said Sam in a pirate voice and walked off to try and find what on earth Charlie was talking about.

'That rope, over there, Sam...' said Jazz, helpfully pointing out the stern line that Charlie was talking about. 'Tie it off round that cleat. It'll stop the back end from drifting out.'

'Avast behind!' said Sam, still in pirate mode. 'I'll also batten down the hatches, aye aye, Cap'n!'

Jazz laughed at Sam's stupid comments as he tied off the line, then looked around at the array of dials and switches in front of her in the boat's wheelhouse. She clicked a switch up and powerful spotlights illuminated the river underneath the boat. The long red top of a London bus could just be made out, about twenty feet under the surface.

'You two can send Rover down to have a closer look,'

said Charlie in a rather demanding voice, 'I'll be back in a minute.'

'Who made you leader of this expedition?' whispered Jazz under her breath.

With an ungainly splash, Rover hit the water and slowly sank down into the depths, pulling its long umbilical line behind it like an extra-long dog lead. Sam looked down at the four buttons on the crane's control box he was holding. It was labelled UP / DOWN / LOCK / RELEASE and he flashed a big goofy smile at Jazz.

'Oops!' he said. 'It's harder than it looks!'

'Google is your friend, Sam!' said Jazz, holding up her mobile phone. 'All the info is online if you bothered to research it properly, not just have a quick look and think you know everything. What's your name, Charlie Carter?'

'Nyahhhh,' mimed Sam, making sure Jazz couldn't see him.

'Hey!' shouted Jazz suddenly, making Sam jump a foot in the air. 'Wow! Sam! Come and have a look at this!'

Her phone was displaying the sights that Rover could

see underneath the boat. Jazz was controlling the ROV with two virtual-reality joysticks on her phone. Sam stared at the video in awe.

'It's an App to control Rover!' said Jazz. 'This is so impressive!'

Rover's bright LED lights made their way across rows of London Buses, some neatly stacked on top of each other, whilst others looked like they'd been carelessly discarded by a Giant's hand. Shoals of Carp, Roach and Bream swum amongst the billowing seagrass and rusted red metalwork, and here and there a Sea Lamprey darted away to avoid the camera's harsh glare.

'That really *is* awesome!' said Sam.

'Magical' said Jazz. 'I think I'll be a Marine Biologist one day.'

'Me too,' said Sam. 'After I've learnt how to be an Ambulance Driver of course. Hey - has Charlie seen this yet?'

'No, he's changing.'

'Into what, a sensible person?' laughed Sam.

'That'll be the day,' laughed Jazz.

Charlie strode out of the forward cabin. He was wearing the old crinkly diving suit and carrying the big heavy brass helmet. It was obvious by the look on his face that he'd heard their comments about him, but he didn't say anything.

'How do I look?' he asked.

'Just like Tom Bruise about to go on a mission!' exclaimed Sam.

'More like an elephant seal who's been ill,' said Jazz.

Sam and Jazz inspected the old suit with some wonder. The rubber was patched together here and there, and in places they could see laminated layers of tan twill. There was a half-moon pattern of what looked suspiciously like puncture marks from a shark bite. Each hole had been expertly patched up with little bits of rubber like an old bicycle innertube.

'What do you reckon happened to the diver who wore this, Charlie?' asked Jazz innocently.

'From the looks of things, I think he retired. Quite suddenly.'

'Ohhhhhkay then,' shrugged Jazz. 'Are you sure you still want to go down there?'

'Yup. My mind's made up. Rover's not spotted anything unusual, and look, I've even found a speargun so whatever happens I'll be fine. I'll just shoot the pike if it appears. And you never know, my mum's locket might just be sitting there somewhere, waiting for me to find it...

'Insane...' shrugged Jazz.

'JAZZ! IT'S MY MUM'S....'

'Shush, Charlie,' said Jazz raising a stern finger in front of Charlie's red face. 'It's okay, I know. It's important that you find it. I'm only winding you up. It's important to me and Sam you find it, too – that's why we're here and helping you, okay? You do *know* we're your best friends, right? You don't have to keep having a go at us all the time – we want you to find your mum's locket as much as you do. We're only trying to help.'

'I know. I'm really sorry, Jazz.'

'What?' exclaimed Jazz. 'Charlie Carter, THE Charlie Carter, has just said SORRY? Well I never! Sam, did you hear that? Charlie's just apologised to me!'

'What?' said Sam. He rushed over and pretended to take Charlie's temperature, then stared at him right in the face. 'This must be an Invasion of the Body Snatchers! What have you done with the REAL Charlie Carter? The REAL Charlie Carter never says sorry - to ANYONE!' Sam started hunting for the real Charlie Carter all round Charlie. He peered down the neck of the big rubber suit.

'Oh ha ha, shut up, you two,' smiled Charlie, and slammed the brass helmet over his head. As he turned the helmet round to screw it into place, Sam could only hear a few words that Charlie was saying.

'You're both a pair of num...

And also doof....

Not to mention dough....

...so there!' said Charlie. His helmet was locked tight. 'Now you can crane me into the water, if you please.'

'Aye Ayyye, Cap'n' said Sam in his pirate voice again. 'We'll lower ye down to Davy Jones Locker before ye can say Yo Ho Ho and a bottle of rum! Hey, just a thought – how did pirates know how to work all this stuff? Did *they* have Google on their mobile phones?'

'Pirates never had deep sea diver's outfits, Sam!' sighed Jazz. 'Or Google. But luckily, I do.'

'Hey Jazz – what sort of mobile phones did pirates use to have?'

'No idea...' she said, already shaking her head in preparation for an incoming bad joke.

'They had *Aye-Aye phones*!' Sam grinned. Jazz groaned.

Sam manhandled the suited-up Charlie up on deck and helped him into two massive heavily weighted metal shoes. With a *lot* of help from Google, they fixed assorted hoses, chains and other paraphernalia onto Charlie's back. Sam fixed a short rope to Charlie's suit, then attached it to the hook on the boat crane.

'What's that rope for?' asked Charlie.

'I think it's your lifeline – Google said something about it being really important,' said Sam. It's how we get you back onboard.'

'Back onboard!' Charlie exclaimed. 'Oh yes, I'd forgotten about that bit.'

'If you give a couple of sharp tugs on the lifeline, then we'll use the crane and winch you back up,' said Jazz. 'But I'll be keeping an eye on you with Rover's onboard camera, anyway.'

'Yeah,' said Sam. 'You'll be safe as houses.'

'It really worries me when you say that,' said Charlie looked really worried.

Sam attached the diving suit up to the hook of the little boat crane and swung Charlie over the water. He dangled there, helpless, and stared down at the dark water swirling under his heavy metal boots.

'Holy Macaroni! I think this must be what a maggot on a hook feels like,' whimpered Charlie, holding onto the speargun for dear life.

'You changed your mind?' called Sam.

'No, no, no... well maybe...' said Charlie with a small edge of fear on his voice. 'Just do it slowly, okay?'

'Okay' said Sam and pressed a button on the crane

controls.

Charlie shot into the water at about thirty miles an hour and disappeared with a big splash and a muffled scream. Sam nodded for a job well done. 'What else do we need to do, Jazz?'

'There was something about having to wind some wheels, but I'll have a look in a minute – I'm still taking Rover for a walk around these buses,' she said, staring at the amazing underwater world via her phone. 'Turn the intercom on, see if he's okay…'

Sam moved over to a large wooden housing on the boat's foredeck where all the cables and lines attached to Charlie's diving suit were fed from. There were two large brass wheels on each side of the wooden housing and a bank of switches next to a speaker with a microphone sticking out. Underneath the microphone was a switch labelled INTERCOM. Sam flicked it down and the switch lit up.

'Testing testing 1-2-3, can you hear me?' said Sam, tapping the mike like he'd seen them do in the movies. 'Can you hear me, Charlie?'

'Smmm! Smmm!!' shouted the distorted voice of Charlie from the loudspeaker. 'I...cannnt....beeeeth...'

'What? Say again, Charlie?' asked Sam, straining to make out what Charlie was saying.

The reception was better this time. 'Sam! I need air...!' came the urgent reply from far below. 'I can't breathe!'

Sam looked around at the wooden housing, and at the two brass wheels either side of it. On a large label under each wheel was a label which read: OXYGEN PUMP.

'Jazz...?' said Sam. 'What do we have to do with these?'

'Oh, my word!' shouted Jazz. 'That's what it said online! We've got to turn the wheels to make his air supply work!'

Jazz jumped over to the big brass wheel on the right-hand side of the wooden housing and tried to turn it by herself. It turned a few inches. Sam leapt over to the left-hand side of the wooden housing and wrestled with the brass wheel there. Slowwwwly the two brass wheels started to move together. A PSSSSHHHHTTT sound came from within the housing and the airline on the deck started to writhe like a big snake as oxygen made its way through the rubber tubing all the way down and into Charlie's diving suit.

Charlie's face appeared on Jazz's phone. He looked a bit blue but slowly colour returned to his cheeks. His voice crackled back over the speaker.

'You two goofballs!' panted Charlie. 'You've got to keep turning those wheels or else I run out of air!'

'Sorry, Charlie. The internet wasn't that clear, but we get it now,' apologised Jazz. 'It's not exactly state-of-the-art is it, this airpump? It was a bit difficult finding out what we had to do.'

'Yeah, it's a rubbishy old system, Charlie,' said Sam, with sweat running off his brow. 'Really stiff, too. I don't know how much longer we can keep turning these wheels.'

'Well, try as hard as you can for a bit longer – I'm going to have a quick look around but I'm not going to be long. I can hardly move in these bloomin' boots!'

Jazz looked at her phone and pressed TRACK on the display. The camera on Rover briefly focused on the heavy lead boots that Charlie was wearing as his footsteps churned up great muddy clouds from the bottom of the river.

'Take Rover for a walk, Charlie – he's on auto-pilot now so he'll follow you everywhere.' Jazz put her phone down so that she could still see the display, then put both her hands back on the brass wheel of the air pump. The antique wheels were difficult to turn. They needed muscle which neither Jazz nor Sam had.

Far below, Charlie looked up to see the bottom of the Wayfarer silhouetted against the moon in the night sky. He was finding it slightly hard to breathe but Rover was waiting for his new master.

'Okay, boy – let's see what's down here, shall we?' smiled Charlie at the faithful drone. Charlie turned and held out the speargun in front of him as he walked towards the stack of red buses. Rover followed close behind making little whines and whistling noises like an energetic puppy.

It was a moving, mysterious wonderland that held surprises and delights at every step and turn. Rover's powerful LED lights revealed incredible sights to Charlie. From out of the darkness, shoals of silver and blue fish darted and swirled around his head and long shards of green kelp waved drunkenly as he slowly stomped around the submerged buses. River Mussels and stripy Zebra Mussels clung together in the tide and brightly coloured algae shimmered and danced in the narrow light beam.

'Are you getting all this, Jazz?' asked Charlie, his face aglow with delight.

'Yeah! It's amazing isn't it?' came back a tinny voice inside his diving helmet. 'The Urban Reef is bringing all the plant life and fish together in one place. No wonder Anna loves it here so much.'

Charlie peered inside one of the old red London buses. Little crabs and shrimp scuttled around the floor. He went to step in but paused. He pulled the large-rubber band back on the speargun and cocked it, making sure that the weapon was ready to fire. Cautiously, he stepped onboard.

Nothing. Apart from the weeds waving in the water.

THUD!

The noise behind him made Charlie jump. He wheeled around and pressed the trigger on the speargun without thinking. Rover let out a little electronic yelp as the spear hit it right between its metal eyes. The faithful drone had followed Charlie onto the bus but was too big to fit and had bounced off. Charlie looked horrified.

'Rover!' he cried.

'The picture's gone a bit funny, Charlie,' said Jazz's voice in his ear. 'What's happened?'

'I've just shot Rover!' said Charlie as the LED lights dimmed on the drone.

'I knew he'd break it,' said Sam.

Charlie stepped off the bus and cradled Rover in his arms. 'You okay, boy? I'm so sorry about that. That's the only spear I've got though, I'm going to need it back. This might hurt a bit, boy...' and he gently took hold of the spear.

Up on the boat, Jazz could see Charlie looking directly into Rover's camera. The picture fizzed and popped as Charlie's face bobbed about on the screen. She watched a huge shoal of shimmering fish flood past Charlie, parting their silver mass just before they collided with Rover. Jazz squinted hard at the picture as she kept turning the wheels up on deck. It looked like the fish were frightened of something, almost as if they were being chased.

'Charlie...?' said Jazz, unsure of what she was seeing.

Charlie held out Rover in front of him and gently tried to pull the spear back out, but it was stuck fast. He gave it a harder tug but still the spear wouldn't move. He needed that spear for protection. Down here, in the dark at the bottom of the River Thames, Charlie was alone with his thoughts and his personal demons. He tugged with all his might on the spear. Panic started to set in. Charlie could see the shoals of silver fish as they reflected in Rover's camera lens, illuminated by the LED lights as they flashed past his head.

But there was something else.

There was a change in water pressure as though a freight train was heading his way. Charlie focused on the reflection in the camera lens and saw something huge which surged towards him from behind.

At the last second, Charlie turned around, and screamed.

A vast set of jaws opened wide as they rushed towards him.

And then it all went dark.

28

The Monster Pike

Up on the boat, all hell had broken loose.

The airlines attached to Charlie had shot across the wooden deck and had swept Sam off his feet. The safety rope, still attached to Charlie in the pike's mouth, was snagged and pulled tight over the side, making the Wayfarer list to one side. Jazz tried valiantly to wind the brass wheels on the air pump by herself, but the wheels suddenly stopped, and the boat lurched over the other way as the monster pike struggled to free itself. The force knocked Jazz over.

She reached the air pump again, but the wheels were stuck fast. Sam struggled to his feet and hit the UP button on the crane's control box, but Charlie's safety line had gone crazy. The rope twisted and pulled and violently swept across the boat's deck first going right, then left then right again, along with his air hoses and communication line. The Wayfarer was a solidly-built boat and twice as long as the monster pike but it was still being swung around by the sheer force that the fish was exerting.

'Pull Charlie up!' screamed Jazz.

'I've hit the up button!' shouted Sam. 'But it's not working!'

'Hit it again! Hit everything!' she screamed as the boat lurched around and knocked them off their feet again.

Sam pressed all the buttons on the crane's handset, but the motor started to smoke and let out an ominous howl.

'We've caught the pike!' Sam shouted. 'But I think it's going to sink us!'

'No, it's not!' shouted Jazz, crossing her fingers. 'The Wayfarer can take it.'

'Well, I'm not sure if Charlie can!' shouted Sam back at her above the din and the chaos. 'I can't get him up. The crane's broken - he's stuck down there with it!'

Jazz rushed to where her phone was being knocked around the deck by the mass of sprawling cables and ropes. Just as it was about to disappear off the deck, she grabbed it and stared in horror at the video on the screen.

Rover's camera and lights were pointed straight at Charlie. He looked like he was in a small fleshy cave with pink pulsating sides. He still had one hand gripping onto the drone's roll cage, but his head was rolling from side to side inside the brass helmet. His eyes were shut. Water surged past the camera and thousands of bubbles churned around Charlie like a swarm of angry bees in a washing machine. In the corner of her phone's screen, Jazz could make out some huge teeth.

Charlie was in the mouth of the beast. He had been swallowed whole.

'Charlie! CHARLIE!' Jazz shouted at the screen, but he didn't move.

The pike rolled and bucked underwater like a crazy fairground ride. It bit down hard, but Rover's steel cage was stuck firmly in its mouth, lodged between the beast's needle-sharp teeth. The pike shook its great head and contorted its body into all shapes trying to dislodge the drone, but Rover wouldn't budge. The pike swam back under the Wayfarer, pulling the lines taut across its decks and swinging the old boat around. It looked like any other fish caught on a fishing line - except this fish was twenty-five feet long and had glowing green eyes. The pike swam into a sea of tall kelp grass swaying gently in the river and rested its huge body, letting the flow of the river wash through it.

'It's gone underneath us!' screamed Jazz. 'Do something!'

'Like what? I don't know what to do!' shouted Sam from underneath a tangle of cables. 'Although it's all gone quiet for a minute... is Charlie okay?'

'Charlie!' Jazz screamed into her phone again at the crumpled figure of Charlie. He was lying very still inside the pike's stomach. Charlie's face was deathly pale, and Jazz feared the worst. She couldn't make out if he were breathing or not.

'Charlie!' she shouted again.

He didn't move.

'Jazz, what are we going to do if he's... if he's....' Sam's voice faltered and he couldn't finish the sentence. He'd seen the look on her face and knew he'd better stop talking. Never had he seen so much grit and determination in one person as Jazz grabbed hold of the microphone on the boat's wooden console and shouted into it.

'CHARLIE! LISTEN TO ME! LISTEN TO MY VOICE! I'M NOT GOING TO LET IT END LIKE THIS, YOU HEAR ME? YOU WILL LISTEN TO ME, MAYBE FOR THE FIRST TIME IN YOUR LIFE, BUT I REALLY MEAN THIS, CHARLIE CARTER. WAKE UP! WAKE UP NOW!'

Charlie could hear a familiar far-off voice. He raised

his head towards the sound and opened his eyes.

'He's alive!!!!' screamed Jazz with tears of joy in her eyes.

'Hey, Jazz. How you doing?' Charlie asked, bleary eyed as though he'd just woken up in the morning. 'Some dream, huh?' and closed his eyes again.

'It's not a dream Charlie,' screamed Jazz. 'WAKE UP!'

Charlie groaned and shook his head. 'Where am I?' he said, looking at the inside of his brass helmet. 'Talk to me, Jazz, give me the bad news - what's going on?'

'Well, you're about thirty feet under the river Thames wearing an old-fashioned diving suit on a boat we've stolen, the rubbishy old air pump doesn't work so you've only got about three minutes of air left, and oh - we've managed to break the crane as well.'

'Thanks, Jazz. Break it to me gently, why don't you, huh?'

'That wasn't the bad news,' said Jazz, looking at Charlie's face in the video.

'Eh?' said Charlie, his vision starting to return to normal. 'What's the bad news then?'

'You've been swallowed by the monster pike.'

'Holy Macaroni!' he said. 'Oh yes, I remember now.'

'We've sort of caught it... but it doesn't like the bait we used,' said Sam, trying to make light of the situation.

'No, I don't think it does,' said Charlie. 'You'll have to use something other than me, next time I think!'

'We can't get you out, Charlie,' said Jazz. 'Nothing works and the lines caught under the boat.' Jazz let all this bad news sink in for a moment, and she surprised herself by starting to cry. 'It's all hopeless...' she sobbed in despair.

Charlie looked at his surroundings. The stomach of the monster pike was surprisingly small. He could see its grey pulsing flesh and the outline of its backbone. He tried to move his feet but couldn't. He looked down and saw that he was still wearing the heavy metal diving boots. He bent down to unclip the boots and as they fell off, Charlie noticed a cylinder not far from him. It had REJOOV written on the side. And there was something else... something small and silver which glittered in Rover's spotlights. Something... just... out... of... reach... in the depths of the pike's stomach.

The headset inside Charlie's brass helmet crackled back into life.

'Mind you, there is some good news, though Charlie...' said Sam's tinny voice.

'What's that then?' asked Charlie.

'We've got a really good picture up here.'

Sam looked at the video coming back from Jazz's mobile phone. It was true, it was definitely high quality and they could see and hear Charlie's every move. Sam stroked the screen fondly. It was like he was saying goodbye to his friend.

'I don't know what to do, Jazz,' he said quietly. 'Charlie's going to die, and I can't do anything to save him.'

'I don't think this could get any worse.' said Jazz.

She was wrong.

Neither she nor Sam spotted two huge hairy hands which rose silently out of the forward hatch and slowly slid it open. A hunched figure of a powerfully built man squeezed itself out of the hatch and crept towards the unsuspecting kids with an axe in his hand. He towered behind them and raised the axe high up over his head.

Jazz saw the man first. She half-stifled a scream. She saw the evil glint in his eyes. She saw the huge axe, ready to smash down onto her head. Jazz raised an arm to protect herself from the axe blow – then Sam sprang in front of her, pushing Jazz behind him and out of harm's way. But there was no escape. Sam knew they were as good as dead as he stared into the killer's eyes.

The big hairy gorilla of a man gave a crooked smile as he brought the axe down in a wide arc over his head. There was no stopping the heavy blade. Sam closed his eyes and screamed. The axe connected with a loud THUNK!

Sam opened one eye.

The axe had cut the safety rope going over the side

of the boat in two, and the Wayfarer righted herself up. Only Charlie's airlines trailed over the side now.

Jazz and Sam stared at the large man in front of them, still holding the axe. He looked at them, then looked at the axe and laughed.

'Wh..who are you?' stuttered Jazz.

'Good evening,' growled the man. 'Sorry to scare you. Allow me to innerduce meself. Me names John. But if you've watched the news recently, you're gonna know me better as -

Mad Dog the Axe Murderer.'

Mad Dog stroked the axe and let out a deep, rough laugh.

Jazz and Sam gulped down a large lungful of cold night air. Both felt their hearts sink into their knees. There was no escape. It was the killer they'd seen on the News.

They were as good as dead.

29

Killer Gorilla

'You're Mad Dog the Axe Murderer?' squeaked Sam in a shaky voice. 'Then we're dead.'

'Yeah, it's me, innit?' growled the large hairy man. 'Mad Dog. Pleased ta meets yoos, yungsir and yunglady. And I can assure yoos – yoos is far from bein' dead, now ain't ya?'

Mad Dog held out his massive hairy hand towards Sam. Sam looked at it like it was a cobra about to strike, then looked at Jazz with a blank stare.

'He said he's pleased to meet us,' said Jazz, trembling.

'Ah,' said Sam. 'We're pleased to meet you too, sir. I think.'

'Likewise,' said Mad Dog as he shook Sam up and down by his hand. 'Now then, I think's yoos is in a bit of a predicament, eh, me ol' muckers? Sumfing I finks ol' Mad Dog 'ere will be able to help yoos with.'

Sam looked around the boat.

'He's talking about himself,' said Jazz. 'Says he can help us.'

'Oh right,' said Sam, shrugging. 'I've no idea what he's saying.'

'Ssh!' said Jazz. 'Don't be rude.'

Sam pulled a 'what do I do?' face.

'Pleased to meet you, Mr Mad Dog,' said Jazz, not knowing whether to shake his hand, curtsy or dive over the side of the boat to make her escape. 'Thank you for, er, your help with the rope. Can you help us get Charlie back, please?'

'I finks so,' said Mad Dog. 'I've been overhearin' all what yoos been saying froms me hidey-hole, so's I knows yoos in a bit of a pickle. Givs me yers phone.'

Jazz handed her phone straight to Mad Dog, who watched the live video feed coming from inside the monster pike. Charlie gave a feeble wave.

'He hasn't got much air left,' said Jazz. 'The underwater drone's stuck in the pike's mouth, the crane's broken and we can't turn the wheels of the air pump over there....'

'He's going to die!' wailed Sam.

'Nahhh,' growled Mad Dog. 'He ain't.'

'We can see him and hear him, Mad Dog, but he can only hear us,' explained Jazz.

'Well, just keep talkin' to im,' said Mad Dog, 'An' I'll go an see wot I can dus, eh?'

As Mad Dog walked over to the wooden console in the middle of the boat, Sam looked over at Jazz again.

'I can hardly understand what he says,' whispered Sam.

'Mad Dog said I've got to keep Charlie talking, while he's going to go and see what he can do about the whole situation,' said Jazz. 'How did you not get that?'

'I can only understand about one word out of every ten he says, said Sam, puzzled. 'Either I need a translator, or he needs to come with sub-titles.'

'Ssh!' said Jazz. 'I need to go and talk to Charlie.'

Inside the pike, Charlie looked at his air gauge. The needle was on red. His breath came in short, painful gasps as he saw his whole life flash before him.

Which, being only 12 years old so not actually having lived a long life yet, that flash didn't last very long.

In his mind's eye he saw his mum, wearing a summer dress as she danced with his Dad on the lawn. She was wearing the silver locket and laughing and dancing and twirling around. He saw his first day at senior school, the first day he met his funny but daft as a brush friend Sam and the ever-so-slightly serious Jazz who always told Charlie exactly how things were – even if he didn't want to know. He saw the day that his mum and dad had come home from the hospital, with his mum crying and his Dad trying not to. He closed his eyes slowly and saw that day in the hospice – that awful, gut-wrenchingly terrible day he'd been trying to forget about for the last six months, where his mum had said goodbye to him.

'It was a disease,' his Dad had said a few days later.

'A monster.'

And there was nothing that they could do about it. It was a monster they had no control over – but the monster had taken control over his mum. And that made Charlie angry. Charlie had taken his silent rage out on his Dad, his friends, his teachers. He'd become sullen, and difficult and unruly. He'd switched off from the world outside and only now and then would he let his friends through that tight veil of corrosive anger - and then only when he wanted to make himself feel better, not caring what his friends wanted or felt.

Charlie's words had hurt the people he cared about over the past months. First his mum had slipped away from him which he'd had no control over, of course – but then he'd let his friends slip away from him. On purpose.

Oh, his bright, beautiful, funny mum – she slipped

further and further away into the darkness of Charlie's memory, calling his name as she went. The memories played in his mind like an old black and white movie. Charlie smiled to himself, aware that his breath was becoming shallower, aware that every breath was becoming harder and harder to take. He knew that his brain was running out of oxygen, but he didn't care anymore. He'd be with his mum soon, and as scared as he was, that was all that mattered to Charlie.

'Charlie? Charlie....?' said a female voice, and Charlie opened his eyes.

'Mum?'

'No, it's me,' said Jazz, talking gently over the intercom.

'It's all very quiet down here,' said Charlie. 'I think the pike's gone to sleep. I think I'll have a quick nap, too...' and started to close his eyes.

'NO!' shouted Jazz. 'Don't close your eyes! Stay with me, Charlie, we're trying something up here....'

'I'll stay as long as I can,' smiled Charlie, deliriously.

'I've been wanting to say something to you and Sam for a while by the way. Never found the right time though.'

'Save your air, Charlie, don't speak.'

'No, its fine Jazz. Honestly. I need to tell you this.'

'Well I guess now's as good a time as any, then,' said Jazz, trying to smile. 'Unless you've got something better to do...?'

'Heh. No, I guess I haven't.'

Charlie looked up into Rover's camera and smiled at Jazz. He showed her his air gauge – the needle was below the red. Any second now, the air would be gone completely. He could just see out of the Pike's mouth, past Rover's metal casing lodged to one side, past the tangle of cables and ropes that looped around its giant teeth and beyond to where shards of moonlight and the Wayfarer's powerful underwater lights penetrated the fields of underwater seagrass.

'I think it's going to take a miracle to get me out of this one, Jazz,' rasped Charlie.

'I know,' said Jazz softly. 'This might be the last

time we get to talk to each other, Charlie Carter. I'm so sorry – I really am. I'd do anything to bring your mum back. I know it's been so hard for you. But I can't bring her back. Your Dad can't bring her back, and neither can you. You need to stop beating yourself up about it - and stop beating me and Sam up about it. We're your friends, Charlie, and I just wish sometimes you'd stop talking down to us and stop taking the mickey out of us and pushing us away all the time. We just want you to be happy, Charlie.'

'It was cancer.'

'What was?'

'It was cancer that took my mum away, Jazz. I've never been able to say the word until now. But I guess I haven't got many words left. I know I should've faced up to things a long time ago. I should've grown up and not caused my own pain to hurt you and Sam.'

Charlie started to feel light-headed.

'I haven't got much time, left, Jazz.' Charlie gasped as his air ran out. 'Listen: I've got all these wonderful people around me, caring for me, looking after me – I never said thankyou to my Dad. I never told him I loved him. I never said thankyou to anyone, I guess.'

Charlie struggled to look directly at the camera.

'Jazz – thankyou. You and Sam meant the world to me. Please remember that. I just never wanted to rely on anyone again in case you guys left me, too. Thank you so much for being there for me. Thank you for being my friends.'

'We'll be with you until the very end, Charlie,' said Jazz.

'Always,' said Sam, trying not to cry. 'Go, Team Carter.'

'Sam, you goon!' said Charlie in a feeble voice. 'Thank you for being you. Thank you for everything that you've done. I love you both, you know. I can see where I was going wrong. I can see it all now. Some of the things I said to you, I shouldn't have. I'm sorry. *That's* what I wanted to tell you two. My bestest friends in the whole wide world. I'm going to miss you....'

And with that, Charlie's voice trailed off and he closed his eyes. And Jazz knew that no matter how hard she cried, no matter what she did or said – nothing could get Charlie to open them again.

30

CHOMP!

Given any other time, Charlie would have said that the pike was a fine-looking fish. The beautiful striped markings on its huge back made it look like a green glistening underwater tiger. The way it held its smooth streamlined head made the beast look noble, almost regal. Even its gently glowing eyes held Charlie transfixed when he had first seen the giant fish. It was one of a kind. An incredible, beautiful and powerful killing machine - the likes of which the world had never seen before - and might never see again.

But Charlie felt light-headed and tired. He just wanted to sleep. And although he knew that when he *did* fall asleep it would be the end - he'd never wake up again - he still appreciated the irony: after all the fishing trips he'd been on with his Dad and with his Uncle, after all the fish he'd caught with little maggots on a hook – now here he was, trapped inside a giant fish - like a giant, wriggling maggot himself.

'That's it then,' thought Charlie as he closed his eyes. 'This is where I meet my maker. I'm going lightheaded and there's no way out. This is it. Over *and* out.'

But he didn't feel lightheaded because he was dying.

It was because his diving suit was filling up with oxygen.

Bigger and bigger the diving suit expanded until Charlie looked like he was wearing one of those inflatable Sumo-Wrestler fancy-dress costumes.

Up on the Wayfarer's deck, Mad Dog laughed out loud. Never had he had so much fun! With one mighty turn after another, he was turning the brass wheels of the air pump as fast as they could go.

More and more life-saving oxygen whooshed its way through the masses of airline which littered the Wayfarer's deck and draped over the side of the boat before they disappeared underwater, through the pike's vast jaws and into Charlie's diving suit.

Inside the pike, Charlie's suit continued to fill up with air until he looked like a human cannonball. Charlie cautiously opened one eye, puzzled that he was still alive. The monster pike began to shake, and it convulsed violently. Charlie could feel the pain it was in, and almost felt sorry for the fish. Instead of being scared, Charlie stroked the inside of the pike, and patted it.

'There, there. Ssssh. I'm sorry,' said Charlie. 'I know you're frightened. I'll try my best to look after you – but right now, you've got to let me go. I don't want to hurt you, but I need to get back to the world above.'

The pike was clearly in pain and its whole body arched as it shot around like an underwater steam train. It tried desperately hard to spit out both Rover and Charlie and water churned into its mouth. Charlie felt like he was in a washing machine on a spin cycle set to 1200rpm.

Up on Wayfarer's deck, Mad Dog was shouting instructions at the kids. 'Get ready! Don't stand near the edge! Tie that rope off there! Clear those lines!' he bellowed.

Far below, Charlie was like a bullet in a loaded gun. His diving suit was so full of air it had expanded to block the pike's stomach completely. It looked like a goldfish had swallowed a golf ball. With one mighty cough, the pike spat Charlie out through its razor-sharp teeth, puncturing the diving suit.

The air whooshed out of the diving suit. Charlie zoomed towards the surface of the water at ninety miles an hour and exploded upwards into the night sky, then careered across the surface of the river like a bouncing bomb.

WHIZZ!

WHOOOSSSSH!!

Charlie zigzagged across the surface of the water going left then right then left again as air rushed out of his deepsea diving suit making a very rude and loud farting sound:

FFFFTTTTTTTTT!

PLCCCHHHTTTTT!!!

SQUEAKKKKPPPLLCHHH!

....went his suit. Although that last one might have been Charlie himself. The monster pike was angry and chased after Charlie as he bounced across the waves. Its jaws were snapping wide open then chomping tight shut, just missing Charlie each time.

CHOMP!

CHOMP!

CHOMP!

The monster pike was closing in on Charlie, fast. Just

as its huge jaws were about to clamp down on him, so there was a loud **ZIIIIING** and then a **SHUNNNK** as a harpoon embedded itself in the back of the huge fish. Attached to the harpoon was a bright yellow buoy. The monster pike sunk beneath the waves and disappeared.

Mad Dog threw the harpoon gun down and wrapped one of the lines still attached to the speeding figure of Charlie Carter over a boat cleat. The line pinged tight and Charlie performed an amazing reverse arc over the Wayfarer before landing on Mad Dog, Jazz and Sam, sending them all flying like skittles. All four landed in a big heap on the deck and Charlie's helmet pinged off. They looked at each other in amazement.

Then they all burst out laughing.

Charlie didn't think he could stop laughing. Jazz and Sam were laughing hysterically, overjoyed that Charlie was back onboard safe and sound. Even Mad Dog was laughing out loud, which sounded much like two elephant seals having a fight.

In between laughing so much Charlie tried to

catch his breath. 'Hahahahah!!! That was brilliant! Woweeee! That was amazing! Hahahah! Whooo! Thank you! Thank you so much!' shouted Charlie, hugging Jazz and Sam as tight as he could. 'Oh, my word that was incredible. Hahahahahah!'

He turned to Mad Dog and gave him a big hug, too. Then stopped laughing.

'Er... hold on. Who are you?'

The big man stopped laughing as well and looked Charlie dead in the eyes. Charlie didn't dare to even breathe.

'Me name's John,' he rasped, 'which I don't ansers to, no more, does I, eh? Yoos can call me Mad Dog. Or, as them papers likes to call me, Mad Dog the Axe Murderer.'

Charlie's flesh went cold, and little goose bumps stood up on every surface. Charlie was so scared even his goose bumps had goose bumps. He let out an involuntary and loud gulp. 'GULP' gulped Charlie.

The big man bowed low in front of Charlie, Jazz and Sam and held the axe up in front of them.

'Ha ha ha!' laughed Mad Dog.

'Ha ha haaaa!' laughed Sam.

'Ha? Ha? Ha?' laughed Charlie. 'Jazz, why are we laughing?

'Haa haaa... oh I don't know,' said Jazz. 'But keep laughing. I think he's going to cut us up into tiny little pieces and use us for fish bait if we don't.'

HA! HA! HA! HA!!!' laughed Charlie.

He stopped laughing and gave a big cheesy grin to Mad Dog. 'Well. Ahem. How do...do...do you do, Mr Axe Murderer, erm, I mean, Mr Mad Dog. Pleased to, erm, m...m...meet you,' he stuttered.

Mad Dog thrust the axe towards Charlie.

'And that's it,' thought Charlie, for the second time that night...

'This is how I **die**.'

31

The Ballad of Mad Dog

Mad Dog gave Charlie the axe. 'ere - yoos 'ave it.'

'Er, thanks,' said Charlie, not sure that he really wanted it.

'Fand it on the bote, so it ain't mine nah, is it?' said Mad Dog. 'I aint nah feef. Im a mobbil ka mekkanik – it's me jobby, ain't I? So I've fixed yers crane and yers air pumps.'

Both Charlie and Sam looked blankly at Jazz as she handed them some dry blankets from one of the boat's cupboards. The boys were still sitting out on deck, but

Jazz went back into the wheelhouse and started Wayfarer's engine up.

Jazz called out, 'He said that he found the axe on the boat, but as it's not his, he doesn't want to keep the axe as that wouldn't be honest, would it? And he's not a feef, er, thief. He's also sorted out the problems with the crane and the air pump's working fine. Says he's a mobile motor mechanic by trade.'

'No,' said Charlie. He shivered and summoned up all his bravado. He looked Mad Dog straight in the eyes. 'You're an axe-murderer.'

'Nah, nah, nah.' Mad Dog shook his head. 'That ain't me jobby, me *trade* is it? Well, yeah, okay, mebbee it is. Axe murderer by trade!' he laughed again and Charlie and Sam looked at each other. Chills went up and down their spines and they pulled their blankets up just that little bit tighter. They were both starting to understand Mad Dog's lingo and didn't need to strain so hard to understand what he was saying now - the more he spoke, the more they understood.

'The rozzers nicked me, didn't they, for sumfing they fort I did. But I iscaped didn't I? Hahaha!!!' Mad Dog laughed like a charging rhino. 'Then I been 'oled up 'ere ever since, on this 'ere bote cos I aint dun nuffin ave I?'

'The Police arrested you for something you haven't done!' said Sam in astonishment. 'And you've been hiding out here on this boat waiting for a chance to prove your innocence?'

'That is EXACTLY what I said, young man. You've got it. Anyway, it was a bit of an accident, really.' Mad Dog explained.

'I totally understand, Mr Mad Dog, sir,' said Sam. 'It was an accident. Cool. No need to explain anymore.'

'I think there is,' said Charlie. 'Tell us about this accident...'

Mad Dog looked at Charlie with a guilty look on his face. 'Dunno if I should...'

'Jazz – can you see if you can get Rover back, please?' said Charlie, giving Mad Dog some time to think. 'Let's get Wayfarer back to the Marina, before Anna wakes up.'

'Aye, aye, Captain!' said Jazz, getting into the spirit of things. She pressed the HOME button on her phone app and the depth figures for Rover started to change. She whizzed the underwater camera round and breathed a sigh of relief. 'Rovers on his way back, and the pike's gone. No sign of it.'

'Nice one, Jazz. Well done,' said Charlie. Then he turned back to the big man sitting opposite and spoke with a much sterner voice. 'So, Mr Mad Dog, where were we? I think you owe us an explanation. I know you've just saved my life and all that, so th... th...'

'Thank you?' offered Sam.

'I know! I can say it, I can say it...' said Charlie. He breathed out, then drew a slow breath back in. With maximum effort Charlie blurted out the word 'Thank you!'

In the wheelhouse, Jazz smiled to herself. Charlie had just said thank you. Again! He obviously had to think about saying that word, but there was hope for the boy yet.

'*Thank you* for saving my life, Mad Dog. But I think you need to tell us about this accident,' demanded Charlie.

'Well, it's a long story, and it might shock you,' sighed Mad Dog.

'Nothing would shock me anymore.'

With that, Rover surfaced at the side of the boat with a loud hiss.

'Aaaarrgh!' screamed Charlie, then realised it was only the underwater drone returning home. 'Sorry – thought that was the pike then, for a minute. I bet you did too, didn't you, Sam? Sam…?' He looked over to the empty spot where Sam had been sitting.

'No, not me. I wasn't scared,' said Sam, looking out from behind Mad Dog's coat.

'Look, kids, I ain't no murderer, am I?' said Mad Dog. 'The thing is, technically I suppose I *did* stop someone from breathing - but I didn't kill him. Not on purpose, anyway. It was all a terrible accident.'

Charlie budged over and let Sam sit back down on the deck. 'Go on, he said.

'Well,' said Mad Dog. 'It was nuffing to do with me, was it? It was all *his* fault. Hatchet McKnee. You know 'im?'

All three kids shook their heads.

'He was the infamous 'Hatchet Murderer of Old London Town' that's what the papers called 'im. Hatchet McKnee would murder people with his great big hatchet, wouldn't he?'

Mad Dog made the shape of a hatchet with one of his huge, hairy hands and slammed it hard against the boat. Jazz jumped out of her skin.

'Well, what happened was this...' said Mad Dog, when a loud blast of House Music interrupted him.

The four of them looked over to where the loud music was coming from, and they chugged past a gleaming blue-hulled Princess motoryacht moored up on the far shore. The occupants were having a very loud party on board and throwing cans into the river.

'Charming,' said Mad Dog. 'Some people 'ave no respect, does they?'

All three kids shook their heads in agreement. Mad Dog continued as the sounds from the blue Princess motoryacht faded slowly away.

'Hatchet McKnee was an 'orrible bit of work, he was. A nasty villain, through and through. So, I knew he'd get 'is come-uppance one day, sooner or later, didn't I? And anyway, technically speaking, killing a killer ain't really killing someone, now, is it?'

All three kids shook their heads in agreement again. Charlie silently ummed and ahhed a bit, but kept quiet. Jazz and Sam pulled a worried face at each other.

'So anyways,' Mad Dog continued, one day Hatchet McKnee came into me garage workshop where I was working, didn't he? Now I've got all sort of fancy machinery in me workshop, all sorts of moving parts, benchsaws, hydraulic car hoists and metal crushers.'

'Ooooh' said all three kids together.

'What 'appened, I mean, what happened to Hatchet McKnee, then?' asked Charlie.

'Well. I went off to make us some tea, didn't I?'

explained Mad Dog. 'When I got back, Hatchet McKnee had fallen into the metal crusher, hadn't he? Must have leant over to have a better look and fell in.'

'Wow!' said Sam. 'Did it kill him?'

'Not the first time,' said Mad Dog. 'I had to put him in a second time! HA HA HA HA HA!!' he roared.

Charlie had a sickly expression on his face.

Jazz grimaced and her eyes opened wide.

Sam just had a puzzled look on his face. 'So what happened when the Police found his body, Mad Dog?' he asked.

'Found his body? Nah. Nobody ain't never found his body!' laughed Mad Dog. 'Mind you, I think we should all bow our heads and pays our respect to poor old Hatchett McKnee right about...... now.' Mad Dog put his hands together, closed his eyes and bowed his big hairy head.

The three kids did the same as the Wayfarer chugged underneath Tower Bridge. One of the brick arches passed by just a few metres away. One side of the arch had recently been renovated and a large patch of new brickwork could clearly be seen.

'Why are we paying our respects here, Mad Dog?'

Mad Dog nodded at the arch. 'It's Hatchet McKnee's final resting place.'

Charlie gulped. 'So the Police arrested you for killing Hatchet McKnee then?'

'Oh no, no.'

Charlie looked relieved.

'They don't know about him, yet!' laughed Mad Dog.

Charlie looked shocked.

'Nah, they locked me up 'cos they reckon I did sumfing to me neighbour, don't they? But I never – I barely even touched him.'

'Well,' said Charlie, 'I'll put in a good word for you with the Police when we get back to the Marina, Mad Dog. You *do* know you've got to hand yourself in, don't you? But you saved my life out there - I'm sure the Police will understand if you explain to them what really happened to your neighbour.'

'Of course they will,' said Sam. 'It was an accident after all.'

'Hah! I like yoos three, you know, I really do, you're funny' said Mad Dog. 'Always wished I'd had some kids of me own. Family - you know. Guess it's all too late for that now. Perhaps yoos three can be me family?'

Charlie shook Mad Dogs hand. 'Yeah, we'll be your family Mad Dog. But you know, deep down, that you've got to do the right thing.'

'Yeah, okay, Charlie. I will. But I'm always misunderstood, ain't I? I'm like that fish out there – all that fish is doing is what comes naturally to it. It ain't a bad fish, but people don't like it. They don't want it near them, not in their neighbourhoods. Yeah, it's a killer – but it's just doing that to survive, aint it?'

'You're right. I know the pike is frightened – I felt it. It's just doing what pike have done for millions of years. But we have to stop it. And we *do* have to tell the Authorities about you. I'm really sorry, but it's the right thing to do.'

'No! No! I *hates* authority!' begged Mad Dog. 'Don't do that to me, Charlie! They won't understand, will they? They never do. They call me 'Mad Dog the Axe Murderer' so they ain't gonna just smack me hand and let me off with some harsh words, are they?'

Mad Dog looked frightened and dejected.

Charlie flashed a guilty look at Jazz and Sam. 'Look, I've got to tell the Police about you, I don't have a choice... but I didn't say WHEN I was going to tell them. I can give you a day's head-start to get away if that helps?'

Mad Dog beamed a huge smile at Charlie as the boat passed a little jetty.

'Thank you, Charlie, Thank you!'

'No, Mad Dog,' Charlie said with a sad smile on his face. 'Thank *you*. You saved my life out there. We can drop you off here, if you want, before we get back to the marina?'

Jazz steered the Wayfarer over to the little jetty and expertly stopped the boat about half a metre away. Mad Dog hugged the three kids goodbye, jumped onto the jetty and started to quickly walk off. He hated long goodbyes.

'Hey, Mad Dog?' called Charlie after the rapidly disappearing figure. 'When you said that you barely even touched him - what do you mean, exactly?'

'Well what happened was, I was chopping down an apple tree for me neighbour, wasn't I? And me axe slightly touched him - it was a tiny little scratch that was all. And the newspapers fink it's far better to call me *Mad Dog the Axe Murderer*' rather than *'Mad Dog the Person Who Only Ever Slightly Touched Somebody With An Axe'* don't they, eh?'

Mad Dog was nearly at the top of jetty's bridge by now. A dark grey shadow against the swirling early morning grey mist.

'So how many times did you touch him with the axe, then, Mad Dog?' called Charlie to the disappearing figure.

'Thirty-eight!' came the answer out of nowhere.

32

A Moment of Doubt

Charlie pulled a 'Hmmmm' suspicious sort of face and looked back at both Jazz and...another empty space.

'Where's Sam?' asked Charlie.

Sam was nowhere to be seen again. Jazz pointed towards the stern of the boat and bit her lip. 'He's gone back there, Charlie. I think you should go and talk to him.'

'Me?'

'Yes, you. Go on.'

'Okay,' said Charlie, puzzled. 'Can you get us home

okay, Jazz? I want to get this boat and Rover back in his kennel before anyone spots that we've gone.'

'Of course I can. The Marina's not far away now,' said Jazz as she nudged the Wayfarer round in the direction of the Marina and nodded towards the back of the boat. 'Now go see Sam.'

Sam was sobbing quietly when Charlie found him. He was tucked right in at the back of the boat, trying to make himself as small as possible.

'Sam! What's the matter? What's up?'

Sam's red eyes and blotchy face looked up at Charlie.

'I thought you were dead back there. And it was my fault! I was stupid and I thought I could sort all those pumps out but I couldn't as I wasn't strong enough and I didn't know what I was doing and I nearly killed you out there and you're my best friend. You. Charlie Carter. My best friend in the whole world.' Sam sobbed and great big wet tears stained his cheeks.

'Woah! Whoahhh!' comforted Charlie and put his arm around the sobbing boy. 'What are you talking about? The crane broke down because we overloaded it, then the wheels on the air pump broke because they're so old and antiquated. I was surprised they still worked at all. But it's not your fault – I talked you into all this. And you know why?'

'No, why?' sniffed Sam.

'Because I *wanted* you around. It's brilliant when you're around, in fact. It wouldn't be the same without you, would it? You're great. You make me laugh. You're my best friend. I love it when we go off on our stupid adventures - I can't go on adventures by myself, now, can I?'

'Yes, but...' sobbed Sam. '...you're good at EVERYTHING, Charlie. I can't even turn a simple wheel without messing up.'

'You've got it all wrong, Sam. I can't do half the things you think I can do. I always doubt myself. The only difference between me and everyone else is that I'm not afraid to have a go. But half the time I mess up - and mess up big time.'

Sam laughed.

'You *know* I mess up, Sam!' laughed Charlie. 'You've seen me do it! How many times was I in hospital last year because I'd had an accident....?'

'Me and Jazz were trying to figure that out. We reckoned it was about once a month!'

'Hah, yeah!' Charlie smiled. 'That's the only thing I can do better than you, Sam. Fail harder and faster.'

Both boys laughed.

'Look at me, Sam. I'm the boy from nowhere - still going nowhere.'

Sam smiled as Charlie ruffled his hair. 'And I definitely can't make everyone laugh like you can, now can I, eh? That's a real gift. I'm really jealous of you on that one.'

'You? Charlie Carter? Jealous of me? How on earth can you be jealous of me?'

'Because,' said Charlie, taking Sam's shoulders and looking him straight in the face, 'You're the nicest, most honest, trustworthy and loyal friend anyone could ever ask for, Sam. You've got the heart of a lion, and the bravery to match. I have faith in you, you know that? I wish I was more like you. I wish *everyone* was more like you in this crazy world of ours,' explained Charlie. 'Without you, I'd be nothing.'

Sam beamed with pride and felt at least an inch taller. Charlie gave him another big hug and playfully wrestled him in a headlock towards the boat's wheelhouse where Jazz had been watching them from. All three of them hugged each other tight.

'Both of you - thank you for being my friends. Thank you from the bottom of my heart.' said Charlie. And he meant it.

'Now come on you two,' said Jazz with a tear in her eye. 'The sun will be up in a bit and we've got to get all this stuff back before anyone notices.'

'Ah, you worry too much, Jazz,' said Charlie. 'Nobody will have noticed.'

33

Fish 'n' Ships

The Wayfarer chugged slowly past a sign which read **The Limehouse Basin Marina** in big letters.

'We're back!' Jazz called to the boys who were busy trying to sort out the mass of cables and ropes and buoys and fenders and all sorts of other stuff which were strewn around the boat. They had no idea what did what.

'What's this?' asked Sam, holding up something so that Charlie could see it.

'No idea,' said Charlie, holding up something else. 'Where does this go?'

'No idea,' said Sam.

'Come on you two, hurry up. We'll be back at Wayfarer's berth soon,' called out Jazz as she steered the boat parallel to the pontoons. She could see the empty berth where they took the Wayfarer from and steered the boat towards it. But the sun was rising, and it was getting light. Quickly.

'Hey, Charlie – do I look like Anna?' asked Sam, holding a knot of old rope over his head and fluttering his eyes at Charlie.

Charlie looked up from trying to tidy the boat up and laughed at Sam's really bad impression of Anna.... just as they slowly chugged past Anna, the Marina Manager, DI Williams and Charlie's dad all standing in a line on the pontoons.

All four were watching them in stone-cold silence.

Anna had red eyes where she'd been crying. The Marina Manager had caught a cold and was wiping his runny nose. DI Williams stood there with his arms folded and Charlie's dad was shaking his head.

'I think they may have noticed, Charlie,' whispered Sam.

'You think?' said Charlie.

Not far from Wayfarer's berth there were two black and white Police patrol boats moored up. Parked on the marina's green slipway was a black and white police car with METROPOLITAN MARINE POLICE UNIT written down the side and DI WILLIAMS written underneath the driver's door mirror.

Anna, the Marine Manager, DI Williams and Charlie's dad walked slowly down the pontoons keeping pace with the boat. All of them had a look like thunder on their faces. Jazz pointed the Wayfarer's nose into the berth where they'd taken her from only a few hours before. It felt like they'd been out to sea for days rather than only a mile down the Thames. The Marina Manager helped tie the Wayfarer up, in between sneezes.

'Charlie! What on earth do you think you were doing?' shouted his Dad. 'If you knew the trouble you've caused – DI Williams here was going to issue a

Warrant for your Arrest!'

'Yes, Charlie! I was going to issue....' began DI Williams.

'So, I think you owe Anna here a huge apology, my lad!' continued Charlie's dad, cutting DI Williams off.

Anna was still looking at her boat. 'I'm speechless,' she said. 'What on earth happened?'

'I'm really sorry, Anna. We, er, I mean, *I* borrowed your boat. I made Jazz and Sam come along with me. Still, no harm done, eh?' said Charlie, raising a hand and presenting the Wayfarer back to Anna. 'The old girls done us good, she's been a brilliant boat!' Charlie turned around to see the boat for himself. It was the first time he'd seen it properly in the daylight.

The Wayfarer looked like it had been in a warzone. It had cable marks all down its side and the anchor chain had gouged out some woodwork. The boat crane was still smoking slightly. One of the brass wheels to the air pump was hanging off. The diving suit that Charlie had worn had been carelessly discarded over the wheelhouse and the brass diving helmet had a big dent in it. Rover had been pulled back onboard upside down, and all its paintwork was scratched by huge teeth marks.

'See, it's not too bad,' grinned Charlie, sheepishly.

And with that, the Wayfarer's echo-sounder and top mast fell off and crashed to the deck.

'Ooh,' said Charlie, pursing his lips. 'I think I might just need to review my Options, here.'

Option 1: I'll tell them we were hit by a tidal wave. They have those 'tidal bores' on the Severn River, don't they, so I bet they have tidal waves on the Thames. Or,

Option 2: A band of marauding Pirates came along and made us take the boat. Hmmm... not sure if there's pirates on the Thames these days.

Option 3: Tell the truth. Yes, that's it. I'll grow up, take responsibility for my own actions and tell them the truth. What could possibly go wrong?

'Okay,' Charlie thought, and took a deep breath.

'Here goes.'

'I wanted to find the monster pike before Kane as I'm not sure he is who he say he is and you know I had a funny sort of feeling that I knew where the monster pike was so I went out looking for it with Rover but I wasn't going to go into the water AT ALL but I found an old diving suit and I thought I knew how it worked so there I was walking round the buses underwater you know the Urban Reef in these great big heavy brass boots and it was quite safe because Jazz and Sam could still see and hear me and it's amazing what I could see down there but then I got swallowed up by the monster pike and I nearly died but Jazz and Sam kept talking to me so I didn't BUT THEN Mad Dog the escaped axe-murderer appeared and saved me by blowing up my diving suit full of air like a MASSIVE balloon so the pike had to spit me out and I shot up and over the boat and went about a hundred feet in the air.'

Charlie blurted it all out in one breath.

'Hmm. Sounds plausible,' said Charlie's dad.

'You're nicked!' said DI Williams.

'You're not arresting my boy,' said Charlie's dad quietly in DI Williams ear. 'I'm pulling Rank on you and that's the end of it. By the way, I wouldn't park your car there.'

'Oh, come on! What a load of flim-flam!' guffawed DI Williams. 'I've never heard so much rubbish in all my life. Surely you don't believe a word of what Charlie just said?'

'Or I'll make sure you get busted down to patrolling Milton Keynes – on a bicycle.' continued Charlie's dad to DI Williams, making sure no-one else could hear.

'Huh. Okay, I won't arrest him,' sighed DI Williams, but he wasn't happy. 'You're not even working for the Government anymore, let alone the Police,' he muttered.

'Yes, but you know I still have friends...' warned Charlies Dad with a thin smile on his face. DI Williams pulled a face back but knew when to shut up.

'And,' said Charlie proudly. 'I said thankyou to Jazz and Sam. I think I've grown up. I learnt some valuable lessons last night.'

'Now THAT'S a load of rubbish,' said Charlie's dad.

'Hey no, I believe him,' said DI Williams. 'Your lad's a good kid, you know.'

'Kane's not going to be happy when he sees his boat,' Anna whined. 'Luckily, he's miles away.

ARRRROOOO GAAAAA!!

The piercing siren subsided and somebody with a booming South African accent shouted, 'Ahoy there! Looks like someone had a wild time last night!'

'Kane!' groaned Anna. 'Oh no, now we're all for it.'

Kane's luxury motoryacht the *Poseidon* loomed towards them out of the early morning mist. His other boat, the *Neptune* armoured RIB, roared up behind it. Kane barked instructions at his crew to tie both boats up, then jumped off onto the pontoons and sprang over to the group like an eager schoolboy going on a school-trip.

'Hello everyone, I'm Kane. Kane Zeet. Honoured to meet you all.'

'Kane, sir, I'm so sorry about your boat,' said Charlie, thinking it better to get a pre-emptive apology in first.

'Hey, yes, that's quite a mess you've made of my boat, eh?' nodded Kane, looking almost impressed at the carnage. Then he turned to Charlie and gave out a loud laugh. 'Heh! Bet you had great fun! Wish I'd been there to see it all. But that's life, kid, so don't worry - it'll all get fixed. Anna, would you check the Wayfarer out please? Let me know how much it'll be to fix her back up.'

Anna did as she was told, and Jazz and Sam helped her onboard.

'I'm guessing you must be Charlie Carter – I'm really pleased to meet you at last.' Kane's face beamed as he shook Charlie's hand really hard up and down. 'You ready for today, eh?'

'What's happening today, sir?'

'Hey, just call me Kane, no need to call me sir, eh?'

beamed Kane and ruffled Charlie's hair as his crew tied the Poseidon and the armoured RIB Neptune up to the pontoons.

'I hope you have a license for all this,' said DI Williams, looking at the gun on Neptune.

'Hey, Sergeant, I have a license for everything,' beamed Kane.

'I'm not a Sergeant....'

WHAAARRRRR RRRPPPPPPP!

The VenomBlack *Medusa* glided to a halt alongside the opposite pontoon. It was like the shadow of a cloud moving silently across the water. Without its siren you wouldn't know it was there. Agent Purple looked down from the *Medusa's* cockpit and sounded the siren again, seemingly just to annoy DI Williams on purpose.

WHAARRRRRP PPPPP-P-P-P-P!

With a whoosh of powerful side-thrusters the MEDUSA held itself alongside the pontoon on autopilot. Agent Purple and Agent Red stepped down onto the pontoon and brushed down their suits.

'Hello Charlie,' Agent Purple called over. His green scar glowed in the morning light.

'Hi,' Charlie called back, looking worried. 'What are you doing here?'

'Hasn't Kane told you, yet?' shouted Agent Purple. 'We're all here today to make sure we catch that fish – the monster pike. And finish it.'

Agent Red gave a little snigger at the side of Agent Purple. 'And finish you, too, Charlie Carter,' he smirked.

'Ssh!' hissed Agent Purple.

Jazz and Sam got off the Wayfarer and stood by Charlie. He rounded on Kane.

'Finish it? Does he mean you're all here to try and kill it? Kane – are you working with Agent Purple? You said you were going to save it...'

'I'll explain it to you later, but just stay away from him,

eh?' warned Kane, ushering Charlie behind him. 'He's a nasty piece of work that one. Come on, you three - let me show you round my new toy instead.'

Onboard Kane's POSEIDON everything was thick carpet and polished wood. Jazz and Sam marvelled at the opulence and little marble statues dotted around the glossy motoryacht. Here and there were beautifully framed photographs of Kane and his family in far-off places, and expensive artwork hung from the immaculate walls.

'It's all really posh!' said Sam.

'Huh,' shrugged Jazz. 'He's only rich because he kills and smuggles animals around the world illegally.'

'I'm going to look round all the boats here, Jazz. You coming too?' said Sam excitedly.

'Yup. Don't want to stay here,' she said, looking down her nose at Kane's obvious wealth. 'Looks like Charlie's staying though.'

'Sir,' began Charlie, then saw Kane about to correct him. 'Kane, I mean. Look, I said I'd help you - but you said you'd save the pike, not kill it.'

'Eh, you're a brave man, Charlie,' said Kane as he sat down on one of his cream leather sofas. 'That thing out there nearly killed you, yet here you are still wanting to save it. Why?'

'Because it's the right thing to do. It's not evil – it's just doing what a pike does. Hunt and eat.'

'Pah! The right thing to do eh?' laughed Kane. 'It's an animal, that's all it is. An animal that shouldn't exist, by rights. It's an experiment - the Fizz pumped it full of REJOOV just to see what happened. It got out of control, that's what happened! The beast escaped and they can't catch it. Hah! That fish took the top-secret chemical they were developing for the Government. Yes, Charlie – the British Government. They hoped REJOOV could be used on the battlefield, help our brave boys and girls regrow arms and legs that had been blown off in war, Charlie – but REJOOV has nasty side-effects, side-effects that they're finding out about the hard way. They need that cylinder full of Rejoov back so they can develop it, make it better. Safer. Surely, you'd want to help with that, eh?'

'Yes, I guess so,' said Charlie, unsure if he really did want to help or not.

'Look, I'll level with you, eh? It takes years to make REJOOV, and there's only one cylinder of it left in the whole world – and its inside that fish. The Fizz are paying me a fortune to get it back. They want me to catch the pike and get rid of it for them, so that's what I'm going to do. I don't have much choice in the matter. Agent Purple made that quite clear.'

'Why don't they just catch the pike themselves if it's so important to them?'

'Hah! The Fizz? They couldn't catch a cold, that lot. They're good at a lot of things – fishing is *not* one of them, eh? Personally, I think Agent Purple wants it back for himself. You need to stay away from him, Charlie, is that clear? But either way, they need me to catch the pike for them – but to do that, I need to know where it is, first, eh? And that's where you come in. You seem to have an affinity with the fish. You know how to find it - I know how to catch it.'

'I know how to catch it as well,' said Charlie as he picked up a photograph of a young lad off the side of Kane's desk. 'Is this your son?'

'Yes. That is my wonderful son Morgan. Or perhaps I should say, it *was*. He was a fine lad.' Kane wiped his eye where a solitary tear had started to run down his cheek. 'But he's not with us anymore, I'm afraid.'

'He looked a lot like me.'

'You remind me a lot of him, Charlie, in more ways than one. He was brave and fun and full of life, too. We had lots of adventures together, until....' Kane's voice trailed off.

'I heard he passed away while you were on a Safari together.'

'Oh, I see. You have been talking to Anna, eh?'

'And because he passed away – that's why you hunt animals?' asked Charlie.

'Passed away! PASSED AWAY!?' Kane roared. 'IT WAS THE LIONS. They came into the campsite to get him, Charlie. Took my son away from me, the lions - and killed him. My beautiful son.'

Kane took the photograph of his son and stared at it for what seemed like ages. Then he put it down and turned to Charlie.

'I couldn't save him, Charlie. I can't save that big fish either, eh? But I can save you. Listen to me when I tell you – have nothing to do with this hunt. Stay away from Agent Purple, okay, Charlie? He means to hurt you – or worse. His mind has been clouded by too much REJOOV. He's been using it on himself - but he's gone crazy. Don't trust him, don't turn your back on him. Promise me that.'

'I thought you wanted my help to find the pike...'

'Ah, the MONSTER PIKE, eh? Yes, I did, but... perhaps some things are not worth risking your life for, eh, Charlie? I've changed my mind. I'll catch the pike myself. It might take me longer, but my reason to live has long gone...' he looked over at his son's photograph again. 'I'm old, Charlie. My doctor tells me they found something on my last check-up that, by all accounts may mean I only have a year or two of life left. Your life is just beginning...'

'But...'

Charlie was interrupted by shouting from outside. He and Kane looked out of the Poseidon's windows across to where DI Williams' car was slowly sliding down the boat ramp. A few other people were running across the pontoons towards it. But it was too late. With a smooth SPLOSH, DI William's car slid down the green ramp and into the water.

'Hah!' laughed Kane out loud. 'That DI Williams, eh? He doesn't have much luck, does he? Why does everyone park on a green ramp in a marina? Schoolboy error, eh?'

'Green means slippery...' smiled Charlie. 'Everyone knows that.'

With all the commotion going on outside, nobody noticed a blip appear on one of the Police boat's sonar screens.

!BLIP!

The blip got closer.

!BLIP!

Agent Purple watched DI Williams as he tried to get his car out of the marina. The more he tried, the deeper it sank until only its roof was above the waterline. Agent Purple allowed himself a little smile as he ran his finger down his green scar and turned to get back on his boat, the Medusa.

'Hello, Agent Purple,' said Charlie's dad, standing next to the Medusa and running his own finger down a mysterious groove in its hull.

'Don't touch that!' hissed Agent Purple.

Charlie's dad looked hard at Agent Purple. He kept his finger in the groove. Onboard the Medusa, Agent Red went to look out, saw who it was, and quickly ducked back down below.

'Please.' said Agent Purple with false courtesy. 'Sir.'

'That's better,' said Charlie's dad not taking his eyes off Agent Purple. 'What have you done to your face?'

'It was...an accident.'

'The great Agent Purple had an accident?' laughed Charlie's dad. 'And how did you manage that, exactly?'

'I don't have to tell you anything, *Mister* Carter,' sneered Agent Purple. 'You're *not* my Boss anymore... Sir.'

Charlie's dad made a quick movement towards Agent Purple as though he was going to punch him. It was a dummy, but Agent Purple still flinched.

'You're putting a lot of effort in to catching a fish,' said Charlie's dad. 'That REJOOV must be worth an awful lot to you.'

'What do you know about REJOOV?'

'I know it's been banned in fifteen countries. I know it's illegal to develop anywhere in Europe – so where are you getting it from?'

Agent Purple smirked. 'I told, you *Mister* Carter. You're not the boss of the Fizz anymore. I don't have to tell you anything.' A little line of green pus oozed out of his scar and Agent Purple absent-mindedly wiped it away with his hand. 'If I told you – I'd have to kill you.' he laughed at his own joke.

'You'll tell me why you want to kill my son,' said Charlie's dad looking directly at Agent Purple.

Agent Purple's little smirk disappeared off his face. 'Charlie Carter is your son? Of course! I should have known.'

'You go anywhere near my son, Agent Purple, and I will hunt you down and kill you like the scum you are.'

'Then tell him not to get in our way again,' said Agent Purple. 'He has already cost the life of one of my Agents and lost me, I mean, the Fizz, a valuable consignment of REJOOV.'

'The Fizz don't need that REJOOV as much as *you*, do they?' said Charlie's dad taking a step towards Agent Purple. More green pus oozed out of Agent Purple's scar. 'You need it. Look at you – you're full of REJOOV. What on earth have you done to yourself? You've lost the plot. You only need the REJOOV back so that you can get your next fix. How desperate you must be, to threaten the life of a small, harmless boy.'

'I had to know what it did to a human,' hissed Agent Purple and squared up to Charlie's dad, his face full of hate and venom. 'And it feels.... Incredible. Don't get involved with things that are no longer your business, *Mister* Carter.'

Small waves hit the Medusa, and Charlie's dad took his eyes off the green scar for a moment. Agent Purple took the opportunity to quickly get back onboard, leaving Charlie's dad alone on the pontoons.

!BLIP! !BLIP!

A shout came up from one of the Police Boats. A Police Officer looked out. 'Sir! DI Williams, Sir!' cried WPC326 as she looked at the sonar screens. 'I've got a blip!'

'Oh, I'm sorry to hear that,' DI Williams called back absent-mindedly, 'But we've got no time for medical problems now, young lady.'

'No, I mean I've got a blip on the sonar! There's something big coming this way!'

'The monster pike!' shouted DI Williams.

!BLIP! !BLIP!

Kane leant over the side of his motoryacht. 'Quick – everyone, get back onboard the boats!'

All the boat crews jumped onto their own boats. Fast hands untied ropes and cast off. Lights, tv monitors and flickering screens were turned on as everyone rushed to get their boat off the pontoons first. It was a right commotion, and on every boat flickering sonar screens and fish-finders showed that a huge shape had appeared underwater just outside the marina.

!BLIP!

!BLIP!

!BLIP!

Agent Purple's boat *the Medusa* was first out of the marina, all whisper-jets and thrusters going full throttle. It was uncannily quiet, but still churned up the water round the pontoons.

The two Marine Police boats sped out next, sirens

blaring and DI Williams holding onto one of the boat's sides and trying not to fall in. 'Follow that boat!' he shouted to WPC326. 'We've got to try and not let this lot get out of hand!'

'OH MY GOD, KANE, IT'S HERE!!' shouted Anna excitedly as she jumped onto Kane's *Poseidon*. Charlie jumped off as Kane thrust the throttles wide open. The huge luxury motoryacht sped off its mooring towards the open waters of the Thames, quickly followed by Kane's other boat, the much smaller armoured RIB *Neptune*. Onboard the Poseidon, Kane picked up his elephant gun.

'You've brought your shotgun!' exclaimed Anna.

'Old Faithful!' shouted Kane, stroking the elephant gun. 'I'm sure that the Fizz may have more exotic toys than me, but this old girl has stopped charging Rhino's in Africa and mad elephants in India – it'll easily stop the pike!'

Kane's two boats sped out of the Marina and passed Charlie, Sam and Jazz who were left behind on the pontoons as they bobbed up and down in the wash.

Charlie's dad joined the three kids and watched all the boats leave the marina.

'Time to die!' shouted Kane above the roar of the Poseidon's engines.

'Guess he doesn't need me to find the pike now,' said Charlie, disappointed. 'The pike's found him.'

'We need you,' said Sam. 'So, what's the plan?'

On the back of the Poseidon, Anna was waving to Charlie. No, wait. She wasn't waving. Charlie looked hard at her - she was *pointing*. Anna was pointing towards the other side of the marina and trying to mime something about a big square.

'What's she pointing at?' asked Jazz.

All three looked towards where Anna was pointing. Her old campervan was still parked half in, half out a parking bay where Charlie had left it last night. He wasn't a bad driver, bearing in mind that he'd only ever driven his Dad's old tractors and cars on the farm recently, it's just that he couldn't quite fully see over the steering wheel yet.

'Did you leave the back door of her campervan open, Charlie?' asked Jazz.

'No, I didn't. I made very sure to lock it.'

'Then why is it wide open?'

- - -

Charlie peeked into the back of the old campervan. Jazz, Sam and Charlie's dad gathered behind and looked over his shoulder.

'Dad,' said Charlie. 'I had this really good idea the other day...'

'Uh-oh,' said his Dad.

'You any good with rigging up nets?'

Somebody had bundled a huge fishing net inside the back of Anna's campervan. It was the one from the whale.

'Thanks, Horace,' said Charlie.

'Thanks, Anna,' said Jazz. 'Perhaps I was wrong about her.'

'What are we going to do with the net?' asked Sam.

'Look,' said Charlie, and they all followed his gaze.

The *Wayfarer* was still moored against the pontoons.

34

The Hunt is on!

Jazz watched Charlie and his Dad load the heavy net onto the Wayfarer, and they started connecting it up to the sides of the boat. Charlie threaded a rope all along the edge as Charlie's dad hooked one end of the net up to the boat crane. Sam had caught his feet up in the net and was trying to untangle himself.

'I hope the crane will still work, Dad' panted Charlie.

'Are you sure *any* of this 'catch the pike with a big net' idea of yours is going to work, son?' asked his Dad, looking at the state of the boat. 'You know how big the pike is, more than anyone.'

'Of course! Don't my ideas always work?' smiled Charlie.

Charlie's dad, Sam and Jazz all looked at each other but said nothing.

'I recking she knew we were going to steal her campervan – and her boat,' said Jazz as she watched Sam still struggling to get out of the net.

'You think so?' said Charlie.

'Yeah – she showed us how to work Rover and told us where her boat was moored.'

'Hmm. Maybe.'

'Why didn't she help us in person, then?' asked Sam, finally freeing one foot from under the net.

'She couldn't be seen to be helping us, could she?' said Jazz. 'She knows Kane is being paid a lot of money to catch the pike.'

'...and kill it,' said Charlie.

'Exactly,' said Jazz. 'She could only help us without Kane knowing that she did.'

'You kids have got it all figured out, haven't you?' said Charlie's dad. 'But please – just be careful around Agent Purple. He's gone round the twist.'

'Can someone figure out how to get me out of this net, please?' asked Sam, with his other foot still trapped. Jazz finally relented and strode over to Sam and freed him in two easy moves.

'Doofus,' she tutted.

- - -

'Blimey!' shouted DI Williams. 'I've never seen anything like it!'

He looked around at all the boats as they sped down the same wide stretch of the Thames, leaping from wake to foamy wake. Boats of all shapes and sizes had joined in the hunt as well, all eager to catch the monster pike first. The Thames was littered with dinghies and RIBs and even a few big old barges, each had fishing rods and lines and hooks everywhere. But nobody had come prepared quite like Kane and Agent Purple.

'This has got to be the biggest speedboat chase in the

WORLD!' DI Williams shouted with glee. 'We must be doing thirty knots. Isn't this exciting! Although possibly all quite illegal.' he said to WPC326 onboard the Police boat.

They were watching the blip on the sonar screens. 'At least we're catching up with the pike, although these sonar screens aren't that accurate, are they? It's hard to tell exactly where it is.

Ahead of them, the great fish leapt clear out of the water and kept on going.

'Wow!' exclaimed WPC326. 'It's fast - it must be doing about 25 knots!'

The monster pike sped towards a boat with three fishermen onboard. They desperately tried to manoeuvre their boat out of its way, but like a speeding submarine just breaking the surface, the pike slammed into their boat and almost cut it in two. Their boat sank instantly as the pike sped round in a great circle.

!!!BOOM!!! !!!BOOM!!!

'What on earth...??!!' shouted DI Williams as two small barrels shot out the back of the Medusa.

!!!BOOM!!! !!!BOOM!!!

A great plume of water leapt sixty feet into the sky. Depth charges! Agent Purple was grinning from ear to ear.

'Fire the multi-shots!' roared Agent Purple.

!!!BOOM!!! !!!BOOM!!! !!!BOOM!!! !!!BOOM!!! !!!BOOM!!! !!!BOOM!!! !!!BOOM!!! !!!BOOM!!! !!!BOOM!!! !!!BOOM!!! !!!BOOM!!! !!!BOOM!!!

A multitude of missiles and depth charges fired from the Medusa. The pike changed direction and weaved through the bombardment, leaping out of the water and heading straight for Kane's boat.

'Stand by for impact!' shouted Kane.

CRUMP!

The pike hit Kane's 30-tonne motoryacht and made it rock sideways, but it was only a glancing blow and the Poseidon turned sharply and gave chase. All around, boats were changing direction to follow the monster pike. Some boats hit others, fishing lines were being tangled up and people were falling overboard. It was chaos out on the water.

Agents Purple's boat the Medusa turned quickly and quietly, followed by Kane's armoured RIB the Neptune and then the Poseidon.

DI Williams scowled at Kane and Agent Purple as they shot past the much slower Police boats. The Skipper of the Neptune gunned the throttle wide open and the crewman manning the gun trained his sights on the monster pike, but the huge fish disappeared below the waterline.

'Don't let it get away!' shouted Kane. 'I want the pike's head on my wall by tonight!'

Kane's armoured RIB roared round and the skipper gunned the throttle wide open. It drew up almost level with the monster pike.

'Shoot that fish!' demanded Kane.

But the pike sensed the danger it was in and dived. A wave caught the RIB just as the gunner fired off a volley of shots.

The first volley of shots missed the pike by a mile and cut a little fishing boat in half. The anglers in it leapt out in different directions. The second volley of shots also missed the pike and strafed a passing disco boat. Fairy lights, disco speakers, glass and wood shattered everywhere as partygoers screamed and took cover.

The two Police Boats roared up to the disco boat, and DI Williams grabbed a loud-hailer.

'IS EVERYONE ALL RIGHT?' he shouted to the people onboard, then he leant back into the Police boat and shouted, 'I THINK EVERYONE'S OKAY!' before realising he was still holding the loud-hailer.

Kane rolled his eyes. 'There! The pike's there! I can see the yellow buoy that's still attached to its back!' he yelled.

The armoured RIB roared around again and bounced off the wake of Agent Purples boat. As the RIB bounced in the air, so the gunner fell onto the rocket launcher at the side of the boat and mistakenly fired off two rockets.

HMS Belfast, a floating tourist attraction which had

sat at the side of the Thames since 1971 took the full brunt of the accidental attack. The rockets pierced its grey hull and grey smoke began to belch from a hatch on its deck. Hundreds of tourists screamed and ran off as fast as they could. All was quiet for a few seconds apart from a fizzing sound coming from deep within HMS Belfast.

And then...

KA-

BOO-

OOM

HMS Belfast erupted in a huge explosion. Thousands of fish were blown up into the air, then fell back out of the sky onto Kane's beautiful motoryacht. Kane sat on his expensive leather sofa covered with smelly fish and put his head in his hands. He wasn't having a good day.

Agent Purple's boat was a lot closer and the powerful explosion tore into the Medusa. He put his hands up to try and shield himself, but it was too late, and the blast blew him across the deck.

The explosion also startled the pike. Underwater shockwaves bounced off its huge body and rocked it from side to side. The pike knew it needed to leave this place. It needed to hide and sought refuge in the nearest place out of the main part of the river.

Onboard the damaged Medusa, Agent Purple staggered to his feet and clutched his head. He studied the banks of bleeping monitors and sonar screens as sparks and smoke began to fill the cockpit. Agent Red appeared out of the carnage and stared in horror at Agent Purple.

'Boss, your face...' he gasped.

'Don't worry about it, get after the pike – it's turning back towards the marina!' shouted Agent Purple, his face hidden by smoke. 'We'll trap it there. Get after it NOWWWWWWW!'

Charlie onboard the Wayfarer was just leaving the marina when the pike hurtled in and circled the pontoons, desperately looking for a way out.

From the Wayfarer's large wheelhouse, Charlie could see the full size of the enormous fish as it squeezed past them. In the shallow water the pike's tiger-like green and black stripes glistened in the sunlight.

'That's one beautiful fish,' whispered Charlie to himself.

'That's as big as a Great White,' said Charlie's dad. 'Not sure if this net's big enough.'

'I think it is – just,' said Charlie, and crossed his fingers.

Jazz heaved the Wayfarer's steering wheel hard round and positioned it between two pontoons so that the pike couldn't swim past them or underneath. Sam came running in to the wheelhouse with grease all over his hands.

'The crane works fine, Charlie,' he said. 'and the nets all hooked up to it.'

'Is it hooked up properly?'

'Did it myself,' said Sam looking at Charlie's dad. 'With a little help, maybe.'

'Okay, Dad, Sam – get ready to drop the net when I say so. Jazz... what are you doing?'

'I'm steering the boat, what does it look like?'

'Oh yes, okay... well, everyone get ready then!'

'What are *you* doing exactly?' asked Jazz.

'Me? Well I'm going to...'

'YOU'RE GOING TO DIE, CHARLIE CARTER! EVERYONE FREEZE AND PUT YOUR HANDS UP!'

All four of them in the Wayfarer's wheelhouse froze. Agent Purple stood in the doorway. They had their backs to him. Big mistake. Behind him, the Medusa was right alongside the Wayfarer. Charlie cursed to himself that he hadn't even seen the big VenomBlack boat arrive. Jazz and Charlie's dad put their hands up without turning around.

'Excuse me,' asked Sam. 'Do you want me to freeze *then* put my hands up? Or put my hands up *then* freeze?' He and Charlie looked at each other and sniggered. They both slowly turned around at the same time - but what they saw made their mouths drop wide open and their blood run cold.

Agent Purple was pointing a semi-automatic pistol straight at them. But that wasn't what shook Charlie and Sam to their very core. Most of the flesh on Agent Purple's head had been torn away by the explosion. Only his eyes remained intact and a few, tattered shreds of skin dangled here and there. It was as though somebody had shredded his face with a potato peeler to reveal his skull underneath.

And his skull was a bright, burning luminous green.

'One false move, Charlie Carter, and everybody is going to have

A

REALLY

BAD

DAY.'

Agent Purple wasn't kidding. His finger on the trigger tightened.

So did Charlie's bottom.

35

Death of a Legend

'Holy Macaroni...' gasped Charlie.

'What's the matter, kid?' hissed Agent Purple. 'Haven't you ever seen a man with his face blown off before and a luminous green skull?'

'Well no, but...'

'But nothing. Get this old wreck of a boat out of my way and let me get to that fish. I need my REJOOV back and I need it back NOW.'

'Well it wasn't just you I was frightened of,' said Charlie, and pointed behind Agent Purple. 'It was *that*...'

'You think I'm going to fall for that one?' laughed Agent Purple. 'That's the oldest trick in the book, Charlie. Pathetic. I'll give you to the count of THREE to move this boat out of the way.'

'1...

2...'

A big blue Princess motor yacht rammed into Agent Purple's Medusa at full speed.

‼WHAAAMMM‼

Charlie's dad grappled Agent Purple to the floor and the pistol went off. Twice.

Agent Purple stood up. Two small holes oozed bright green liquid out of his chest. He looked down at them in wonder as they healed up almost immediately. And laughed.

Mad Dog yelled 'Wahoooo!' at the top of his voice as he slammed the blue Princess into reverse, then punched the throttle forward and rammed the Medusa as hard as he could again. The Medusa folded up as it was squashed between the Princess and the sturdy wooden hull of the Wayfarer. All the partygoers on the blue Princess whooped and cheered as they held on tight.

'Nicely done, Mad Dog!' said one.

'Good shot!' said another.

'Don't scratch my Daddy's boat, will you...?' called a voice from the back of the crowd.

Mad Dog pulled an 'oops too late' face as he shouted at everyone onboard the Princess, 'Okay, everyone off. This here's me last stop. Gotta go help me ol' mate Charlie!'

The partygoers swayed as they got off the blue Princess and whooped and wobbled their way up the pontoons. Mad Dog smiled and waved at Charlie onboard the Wayfarer.

Onboard the Medusa things were in a bad way. The boat had listed to one side and started to take on water. Its thin, stealth-tech hull had split open. The theory that it didn't need to have a thick hull because it couldn't be seen by the enemy wasn't holding up so well. Its designers had never taken into account the Mad Dog factor. The 20mm cannon on its foredeck had been bent into a useless shape, its missile launchers now rendered useless. Agent Red was still onboard, and he struggled over to a row of buttons inside the cockpit. He pressed one then collapsed to the floor.

The mysterious groove on the side of the *Medusa's* hull hissed and opened. A twenty-foot long black-and-white killer whale slid out into the water.

It was a man-made killer whale, made of steel and armoured glass and a whole lot of hate. A powerful waterjet engine sat just above the killer whale's tail. Where its head should have been was a glass cockpit. Inside sat Jeremiah.

'So, the Fizz finally got the Orca project working,' said Charlie's dad as a huge whine filled the air. 'Looks amazing. Hope for their sake it's built better than their Medusa.'

Jeremiah fired up the Orca's engine and as it zipped

past, he pointed out his good-as-new arm to Charlie. Charlie nodded and gave him a thumbs-up sign. He was glad to see Jeremiah was still alive and looked to be in good shape. Jazz and Sam looked on, open-mouthed as the killer-whale shaped mini-sub whirred past them.

'Whose side is Jeremiah on, do you think?'

'It's a shame, but I guess he's still working for the Fizz, by the look of it. Where's Agent Purple?' asked Charlie, looking around nervously.

'Legged it up the pontoons,' said Charlie's dad.

'He was shot, though! And he had a gun...'

'Not anymore,' said Charlie's dad, holding up Agent Purple's semi-automatic pistol.

Jazz whirled into action. She reversed the Wayfarer away from the sinking Medusa as DI Williams and the two Police boats turned up, followed by Kane on the Poseidon.

'What have I missed?' shouted DI Williams over to Charlie.

'Oh, nothing much,' smiled Charlie.

The steel Orca leapt out of the water. Jeremiah nodded a cheery 'hello' at DI William's stunned face as the monster pike leapt out of the water close behind the mini-sub.

'Mini-sub' said Charlie, as he pointed at the Orca. 'Being chased by the monster pike.'

'Okayyyyyy,' said DI Williams, too stunned to say anything else.

Jeremiah stabbed at an array of flashing buttons and lights in front of him as he steered the Orca around the marina. The pike was close behind, and every now and again it tried to take a massive bite out of the steel killer whale. Jeremiah pushed the Orca's throttle forward and the mini-subs powerful jet engine snapped his head back with the force of the acceleration.

'I've gotta get me one of these!' Jeremiah whooped.

The Orca dived and Jeremiah laughed like a child with a new toy. His laughter stopped dead when he looked over to his side.

The monster pike was swimming next to the Orca.

It was at least eight feet longer than the mini-sub and could swim just as fast. Jeremiah gently steered the Orca away from the pike, in a tight circle underwater and then pointed the mini-sub straight back at it. He pressed a switch hard on the console and yelled as a sleek silver fish sped towards the pike.

'Fire One!'

The torpedo missed the monster pike completely.

Up above, Mad Dog saw the silver torpedo streaking round in the water towards Charlie's boat and shouted a warning. Without a second thought, he gunned the throttles of the big blue Princess wide open and put himself between the silver torpedo and Charlie Carter.

!!KERRR-

BLAAAM!!

The torpedo had a devastating effect on the Princess. Jagged bits of blue plastic hull from Mad Dog's boat rained down on the Wayfarer's wheelhouse. Charlie's dad leapt over the three kids at the last second and held them tight. Eventually, the blue rain stopped.

'Is everyone okay? Charlie... are you alright?' asked Charlie's dad, shaking some smouldering bits of wreckage off his shirt.

'Yes, I'm fine Dad, I'm fine. Thanks,' said Charlie. His Dad looked back at him with genuine concern on his face. 'Don't worry about me, check the others – please.'

'Okay, Charlie, will do. Jazz, how's you?'

'I'm okay thanks' said Jazz.

'Sam?'

'Aye aye, all present and correct, Sir,' said Sam, saluting like a pirate.

'Where's Mad Dog?' asked Charlie.

Charlie looked around through the acrid smoke. Little bits of blue flaming wreckage were floating around the marina. Over on the slipway the figure of Mad Dog lay very still. Charlie leapt off the Wayfarer and ran as fast as he could down the pontoons.

'Mad Dog! Mad Dog!' screamed Charlie. 'Somebody call an ambulance!'

He scuffed to a halt and cradled Mad Dog's head. It was bruised and bloodied. Some of his clothes had been torn to shreds in the blast and Charlie could see a terrible chest wound. Tears ran down Charlie's face as he pushed some burning wreckage away.

'Mad Dog!'

The big man groaned and gasped a big lungful of painful air. He could only just manage to open his eyes. A small crowd had gathered around them.

'Is that you, Charlie?' he whispered hoarsely. 'Charlie, me boy?'

'Don't speak, Mad Dog. We've called an ambulance.'

'Ahh, no time for that now, Charlie. Are yoos okay? Did I saves yoo?' whispered Mad Dog, closing his eyes.

'Don't close your eyes, Mad Dog. Stay with me...!'

Mad Dog blinked. 'Ahhh, Charlie. You know

sumfing? When you gotta go, you gotta go.'

'No! I don't want to lose you, Mad Dog! You're not going anywhere. You just saved my life. That's twice now.'

'Nahhhh son, you got it all wrong, ain't yoos? Yoo saved mine,' smiled Mad Dog, wincing in pain.

'What? How do you mean?'

'Don't you get it, Charlie? *You* saved *me*, not the other way around. All I ever wanted in me whole life was to be an 'ero. To 'ave me own family. Be a good man and do sumfing good for a change.' Mad Dog groaned and coughed up some blood.

'You ARE a good man, Mad Dog.' whispered Charlie.

'Well, you know what? I finks yoos is right, so maybe I is. Maybe I'll be remembered that way, too, eh? That would be good. Ol' Mad Dog – an 'ero! Now, Charlie - go save that fish.' The big man looked up at Charlie and smiled.

Charlie looked across to where he could see blue lights and sirens coming from far away. When he looked back down, Mad Dog had shut his eyes for the last time.

'You're the biggest hero I've ever met,' smiled Charlie through a veil of stinging tears. 'Thank you, Mad Dog... thank you.'

The sirens were screaming and the fires were howling as Charlie Carter sobbed into a dead man's chest. A rumble of distant summer thunder heralded the passing of a hero.

36

Punch it, Sulu!

The monster pike took fright at the explosion. Instinct cut in and it fled up a small waterway that led out of the Limehouse Basin Marina and, just maybe, to freedom.

The waterway was the entrance to the Regents Canal - a long canal that traversed most of London. It passed many well-known landmarks along its narrow, shallow length. At its deepest the canal was only six feet deep - in some places it was only three or four feet deep. Not that the pike knew this – all it knew was that it had to escape the flaming carnage of the marina.

It fled. It looked like a submarine as it swam along the canal with only its back and huge dorsal fin above the water line. It created a huge wake behind it as it swam, yearning to find deeper water and freedom.

'Follow that fish!' Kane commanded. He looked at his Mariner's Charts onboard the Poseidon and grunted 'It's as good as dead. That canal's a dead end – it only goes to Little Venice. We'll corner the pike and kill it there!'

At that command, all the boats charged into the canal entrance after the monster pike.

The first boat to go in was Jeremiah in the *Orca,* the killer mini-sub. The big man wrestled with the fake fish's controls as it bounced around in the wake caused by the fleeing pike.

The second boat into the canal was Kane's armoured RIB the *Neptune*, which was quickly followed by Kane himself on the *Poseidon* and then DI Williams and WPC326 onboard one of the Police boats. DI Williams scowled after Kane and glanced back at the other Police boat which was being swamped by a horde of sightseers and rubber-neckers clicking away on a thousand different cameras. They were also trying to move the remains of the Medusa, the Fizz's half-submerged boat. Agent Purple was nowhere to be seen. The flotilla of boats charged off down the canal after the monster pike, which was in the lead by at least a hundred metres.

'Charlie...?' said a softly spoke voice.

Charlie's dad rested his hands on his son's still sobbing shoulders. Charlie's red eyes looked up.

'Do you want me to take you home, son?'

'No, I don't!' came the angry reply. 'Sorry. I mean, no thanks, Dad.'

Two Paramedics appeared, and along with the Police they took over Mad Dog's lifeless body. Jazz and Sam came over and gave Charlie a big hug.

'They're all going after the pike, Charlie. Kane said he was going to corner it and kill it at Little Venice,' said Jazz. 'That's where Regent's Canal ends.'

Charlie allowed himself to be gently walked away from Mad Dog's body. He stole a glance back at the big guy. 'If that's where they're all going, then that's where we're going, too. Erm, please? If that's okay with everyone? But they've got a bit of a head start on us.'

'Slow and steady...' began Charlies Dad.

'Wins the race.' said Charlie, with a steely look of determination. 'Come on. Let's go!'

Jazz took the helm of the *Wayfarer* again and started the engines up. Charlie and his Dad undid the ropes holding the little cruiser onto the pontoons and threw them to Sam onboard. Sam tied the ropes up as best he could, and Charlie and his Dad jumped onboard as Jazz steered the *Wayfarer* over towards the entrance to Regent's Canal.

Charlie stepped into the wheelhouse and stood next to Jazz. She was doing a great job at steering and nudged the throttles gently as she'd been taught to do, carefully turning the wheel and nursing the Wayfarer until its bow lined up with the entrance to the canal. The old boat had been through a lot recently.

'You know the radar domes fallen off, don't you?' she asked.

'Yup,' said Charlie, and put on a Captain's hat he'd found hanging up behind the door.

'And the sonar's gone and I think one engine's playing up,' she added.

'Yes, I know. How much power can I have?'

'She canna take much more, Captain!' said Sam. If we push her too hard, she's gonna blow!'

'Everybody hold on,' said Charlie, with a look of grim determination on his face. 'We're going to give her all she's got.'

Jazz looked nervously at Charlie but gripped the throttle controls ready for his command. Charlie looked at her and bit his lip, unsure if this was the right thing to do or not. His moment of doubt didn't last long. The boat lined up perfectly with the canal entrance.

'It's now or never, Captain,' said Jazz.

'Let's get them,' shouted Sam. 'Go Team Carter!'

Charlie gripped the back of the chair Jazz was sitting on and pointed dead ahead.

'PUNCH IT, SULU!' he shouted, remembering all

the Star Trek episodes he'd watched with his dad.

Jazz thrust the throttle controls hard open. The Wayfarer's twin props sent up a huge plume of water and the little ship surged forward into Regent's Canal.

'Wahooooo!' shouted Sam, having to be stopped from falling backwards overboard by Charlie's dad. He steadied himself and shouted 'This is brilliant! Warp Factor Ten, Cap'n!' as the scenery blurred past.

Jazz turned to Charlie inside the wheelhouse. 'Two things. One: What's he going on about?

'He loves Star Trek and all the old sci-fi films,' laughed Charlie out loud, looking over at his crazy friend.

'And Two...'

'What?' said Charlie, still laughing.

'Take that silly hat off.'

Charlie rolled his eyes and threw the Captain's hat out of the window. It bobbed up and down on the big waves as the Wayfarer sped along the canal towards its destiny with fate.

37

I, Monster

Agent Purple stared at what was left of his face in a glass shopfront and let out a pitiful groan at the terrible sight.

His bullet wounds had healed but he'd run from the Marina in pain. The Rejoov inside his body was running low – it was critical he retrieved that last cylinder back so he could take some more. Every time he took Rejoov, it made him feel powerful, strong – unstoppable. But the effect only lasted for a while. He needed more, and soon.

He cursed the fact he'd been disarmed so easily on the

boat – Charlie's dad may have retired from the Fizz, but he still knew how to handle himself. Agent Purple knew he should have been more careful, but not everyone could have survived that explosion. Even if most of the skin on his head had been burnt off and he'd been shot, at least he was still alive. And he was going to get that REJOOV cylinder back, even if it meant wiping out anyone and everyone who stood in his way.

The people inside the shop screamed as Agent Purple's luminous green skull stared in. He recoiled back from the window, shocked by their reaction at first - then leered at them like Frankenstein's monster scaring the local villagers on purpose.

'YAAAAHHHH!' he roared at the shoppers as they ran off.

Agent Purple laughed to himself – it felt good to frighten people. But then he caught sight of his green reflection again and yelled angrily at what he'd become. He shouted his frustration at the monstrous image in the shop window.

'CHARLIE CARTER, YOU DID THIS TO ME! YOU WILL PAY FOR THIS! I AM COMING FOR YOU, CHARLIE. TODAY WILL BE YOUR LAST!'

BLATTT BLATTT BLATTT BLATTT

A bright red Ducati Monster 1200S motorbike roared around the corner of the street. With a single blow, Agent Purple knocked the rider off and jumped onboard. He aimed the motorbike in the direction of Regent's Canal and roared off at breakneck speed.

BLATTT

BLATTT

VROOOO-OOMM**MM!**

38

The Promise

The great fish swam for its life. It could swim at twenty miles an hour normally, but when hunting or if frightened it could manage short bursts of over thirty miles an hour.

Today it wasn't hunting. It was frightened.

It **whooshed** up the Regent's Canal past playing fields and football stadiums, under the Mile End Road, under the A107 where nestled the Viktor Wynd Museum of Curiosities then **slooooshed** past the Narrowboat Pub.

Diners at the windows gazed in awe as the great beast swam past, impressed at its speed. They marvelled at the pike's beautiful colours and gently glowing eyes which shimmered just beneath the surface of the canal. Unable to go back because of its relentless pursuers, the Monster Pike never slowed until it felt a natural resistance in the water. Ahead of it lay the narrow Eastern entrance to the 200-year-old Islington Canal Tunnel. At 878metres long and only ten feet wide, instinctively the huge fish knew that the tunnel could lead to its salvation – or become a deadly mile-long death trap.

Behind the Monster Pike its pursuers in their motorboats roared around the bend of the canal and into view.

The great fish knew it had no choice. It launched itself into the tunnel like a dark-green missile. A huge bow-wave surged ahead of it like a mega-tsunami or a humongous washing machine set at maximum spin speed. In front of the pike and behind it, this tube of fast-flowing water filled the narrow space of the Islington Canal Tunnel completely from roof to floor. A huge tube of water which was now travelling through the tunnel at thirty miles an hour.

Behind the pike, the flotilla of motorboats was fast approaching the narrow entrance to the tunnel.

Jeremiah in his black and white Orca whizzed straight into the tunnel mouth. He couldn't submerge as the water was too shallow. The metal fins of the Orca touched the brick sides of the narrow tunnel every now and again. Ahead of him he could see a huge wall of water flowing behind the fleeing fish.

Kane's armoured RIB sped into the tunnel. The crew had to duck as they went in. Just behind them, DI Williams in the black and white River Police Boat roared up to the entrance.

'DI Williams!' shouted WPC326, driving the police boat. 'I don't think we're going to fit!'

'Of course we will!' DI Williams shouted back. 'There's plenty of room, so don't stop - that's an ORDER!'

The noise of the River Police boat hitting both sides

of the tunnel echoed along its whole length. People walking nearby clenched their teeth and wore pained expressions. WPC326 just shrugged and held the throttle wide open. There were black and white scuff marks down both sides of the tunnel.

DI Williams sobbed to himself. 'There goes my pension,' he sighed.

Kane's boat just behind the River Police boat came to a sudden stop. Kane knew that there was no way his big motoryacht was going to fit into that tunnel, so threw the thrusters into reverse.

'Stop, stop, stop!' he shouted at his boat. 'Ag! We're going to lose the pike!'

'What are we going to do?' asked Anna, as Kane's huge motoryacht gently bobbed in the middle of the canal.

It was now nothing more than an expensive white elephant. Kane hit the steering wheel in frustration. He had to have that fish! He kicked his elephant gun on the floor beside him. That was just a useless toy now, as well.

The gun wasn't going to kill anything today. Charlie's boat appeared round the bend of the canal behind Kane. The Big Game Hunter's eyes lit up.

'Permission to come aboard, please, Charlie?' asked Kane, pointing his elephant gun at Charlie as the Wayfarer came to a gentle stop behind the Poseidon. 'Your boat can get through this tunnel. Mine can't.'

Jazz flashed a warning glance at Charlie. Charlie's dad pulled a face and Sam clenched his knuckles around the side handrail.

'Permission denied. We're going to save the pike,' yelled Charlie, 'Not kill it.'

'You've got my gunboat and Jeremiah right on its tail, Charlie,' gestured Kane with his elephant gun. 'If you really want to save that pike then you'd better let me onboard.' He stepped forward.

'No!'

Kane stopped, mid-step. 'Ag! What? You can see I have a gun, eh, Charlie?'

'I don't care,' said Charlie, coming out on deck and

standing between Kane and his friends. 'You're not coming onboard MY boat until you promise me that you will NOT kill the pike!'

Behind Charlie's back, Sam smiled a big grin at Jazz. They bumped fists and said a silent 'Yes!'

'I think you'll find, Charlie...' said Kane, still standing on his motoryacht but edging slowly towards Charlie, '...that you are actually standing on one of MY boats, eh?'

Charlie looked around at the Wayfarer and kicked himself. He realised that Kane was right. The Wayfarer did belong to Kane.

'He's got a good point, Charlie,' whispered Jazz. 'And a big gun.'

'What choice do I have?' Charlie yelled.

'None at all, kid,' laughed Kane as he helped Anna step off the Poseidon and onto the Wayfarer. Kane still waved his elephant gun out in front of him, careful not to get too close to Charlie's dad.

'Okay – you can come onboard, but you have to

promise me one thing...' said Charlie to Kane, who was already onboard the Wayfarer.

'What's that, eh?' said Kane.

'You have to PROMISE me one thing, you will help me save the pike.'

'Ag, I don't know if I can do that, Charlie.'

Charlie stood still on the front of the Wayfarer's deck refusing to budge and let Kane walk past. He said nothing but silently glared at Kane. The two of them stared at each other for what seemed an eternity.

'Eish, you're a brave boy, Charlie Carter. A brave boy.' Kane broke the staring match and looked away first. 'Okay, look, we are wasting time. I will *promise* you that I will do what I can – and what is right - when the time comes. But I cannot promise you anything else, eh?'

Charlie moved to the side and let Kane and Anna walk past. They sat down just outside the boat's wheelhouse. All the while Kane kept a wary eye on Charlie's dad.

'Now come on, eh? Let's get this boat moving. Go, go!' Kane shouted towards Jazz.

Jazz didn't move her hand on the throttle. She looked at Charlie, still standing on the bow. He bit his lip and hid his hands. They were visibly shaking. It took a few moments to compose himself, but then he slowly nodded at Jazz.

'Okay. Team Carter. Let's go.'

Jazz slowly nudged the throttle controls forward.

'Go for it, Jazz,' said Charlie.

She pushed them forward all the way and the Wayfarer thundered into Islington tunnel.

At the other end of the long tunnel all was peace and quiet.

A couple were enjoying a sunny picnic in a little wooden rowing boat, bobbing about on the water. The man wore a loud stripy blazer, bowtie and immaculately ironed trousers with turnups over expensive two-tone boating shoes. The lady was dressed head to toe in pink. Their own little world was simply idyllic. Nothing could spoil it.

'Ah, I love these gentle little river paddles, Andrea,

my little honey bun!' he waxed lyrical. 'London is so delightful in the Summer.'

'Oh, I know, my little pudding-bunny,' purred Andrea in excitement. 'I do love these wonderful picnic trips up the canal with you.'

'Ah, my little sugar-plum fury. Shall I open the Champers, my little love-dumpling?'

'Oh, I could simply eat you up, you gorgeous scrummy little man,' squealed Andrea. 'You are truly scrumptious!' and bent forward to give him a little peck on the cheek.

A ten-foot high wall of water exploded out of the tunnel mouth and put a stop to all their fluffy-wuffy sickly-wickly bunny-wunny-ness.

Their rowing boat capsized and threw the screaming couple into the canal as a million gallons of water containing an angry twenty-five feet long fish full of teeth charged past them at thirty miles an hour.

!!BOOOOMMMM-

SPLOOOSSHHFF!!

'Yaaahhh! Help me, my little love-bunny! I can't swim!' wailed Royston.

The bedraggled Andrea spat out half the river and looked across at her struggling boyfriend. In a somewhat different and coarse voice, she shouted encouragement at him.

'Oh, stand up, you numpty! The water's only four foot deep here.'

39

Purple Reign

The Monster Pike wasn't stopping for anything. It knew it had to lose its pursuers or die; it was as simple as that. But it was tired and slowing down. It was alone, frightened and confused.

The beast swam for miles along the canal. All the while the flotilla of murderous motorboats trailed behind it, sometimes close, sometimes far away as the pike found hidden pockets of strength within its tired body. As it surged around the tight bend near to St. Pancras train station it accidentally hit the wall of the canal by the

London Zoo at thirty miles an hour.

Slightly stunned, the great pike lay still for a moment and floated in the water. Surely there was another way out? Surely this wasn't the end of the canal? The great fish could feel movement in the water ahead and turned its great length towards what it hoped was open water.

Another tunnel on the canal loomed ahead.

The great fish swam for its life. It was almost a third out of the water now, its great belly painfully rubbed the bottom of the shallow canal. With a mighty swish of its tail the pike was in the tunnel and another, smaller, tidal bore ran ahead and behind it.

This tunnel though, was much shorter. It was the Maida Hill Canal Tunnel in West London which had dull yellow lights dotted along its ceiling side-by-side with overhead high-voltage cables. At only 249 metres long it took a normal barge a couple of minutes to go through it at a steady *chug chug chug* of six miles an hour. The Monster Pike swam it in only a few seconds then burst out of the end of the tunnel in another great tube of water.

Again, the Orca, the Neptune and DI William's Police boat stormed into the canal tunnel behind it.

A minute later, Charlie's boat motored into view and Jazz slowed the boat down to make sure they were lined up with the entrance to the tunnel. On the right of the tunnel's entrance steps disappeared up to the road above, and next to the steps was a sloping blue metal structure angled like a ramp which towered over the canal. This was where the high-voltage power cables came up from under the towpath and connected to the National Power Grid overhead.

The front of the Wayfarer was now slowly creeping into the tunnels entrance.

BLAT!

BLAT!

BLATT!

VROOMMM!!

A shiny red Ducati Monster 1200s skidded around the road above the tunnel entrance, then blasted down a narrow alley before thudding down the stairs to the canal.

The motorbike jumped onto the canal towpath and roared up level with the Wayfarer. Agent Purple's green skull glared at Charlie, then looked up at the angled blue ramp of the sub-station. Agent Purple gunned the motorbike away from the boat, then skidded round 180 degrees and wrenched the Ducati's throttle wide open. The motorbike roared towards the blue ramp at sixty miles an hour, then soared into the air across the canal and landed on the boat's deck with a massive

KER-THUD

Charlie's dad and Kane were sent scattering.

The Wayfarer disappeared fully into the tunnel.

Inside, the heat was stifling. Agent Purple's luminous green skull reflected off the brickwork as he snatched up Kane's elephant gun and waved it around at everyone.

'Keep going!' bellowed Agent Purple to the terrified Jazz at the wheel.

Sam ushered Anna into the wheelhouse behind him whilst Kane staggered to his feet. Charlie's dad was lying on the boat's wooden deck with a broken arm.

'Make any sudden movements *Mister* Carter, and your son will have a burial at sea!' hissed Agent Purple.

'Touch one hair on his head and nowhere on earth will be safe for you.' warned Charlie's dad, and groaned as he clutched his arm. 'The Fizz will help *me*, not you.'

'You've gone mad, Agent Purple!' shouted Charlie. 'You've taken too much REJOOV – look what it's done to you!'

'I don't care. I just want that monster pike!' roared Agent Purple.

'*You're* the monster – not the pike,' said Charlie, staring at the green skull.

'You've done this to me, Charlie Carter, YOU! You've caused me so much pain and now I've come to give YOU some of that pain back!' snarled Agent Purple, his green skull contorted with hate.

'Pain?' said Charlie in a quiet voice. 'Pain? What do you know about pain? How much pain do you think I've had to suffer these last few months? I've lost my mum!

I've been through more pain than you can *ever* give me. You can threaten me all you like, shoot me if you want – but don't EVER threaten my family or my friends. I've had enough, Agent Purple. You have no idea what *real* pain is!'

'Well in that case, I know this is going to hurt you a lot more than it is me, then!' roared Agent Purple, now fully in the grip of his terrible madness. He pointed the elephant gun straight at Charlie and went to pull the trigger.

Kane butted in and waved his hand in front of the barrels. 'Ag, Agent Purple. Be careful with that, eh?' he said, trying to buy Charlie some more time. 'It's not just an ordinary shotgun – it's an elephant gun. It'll take the ceiling down if you fire it in here.'

Agent Purple whirled around and pointed the gun straight at Kane. He spat out the words, 'Don't tell me what to do, old man! I've had enough of you...' and raised the gun up to his shoulder.

And that's when Charlie saw his chance. He leapt for

the boat's steering wheel and wrenched it round, hard. The Wayfarer hit the tunnel wall and stopped dead, sending everyone flying. Agent Purple stumbled forward, and Kane grabbed at the elephant gun. For a moment, the 'old man' had the better of Agent Purple and managed to point the gun away from everyone and straight up at the tunnel ceiling.

'You're stronger than you look, old man!' sneered Agent Purple. His grinning green skull pressed close to Kane's face as the pair wrestled with the gun.

'Springboks. Front row prop,' growled Kane. 'Beat that – sonny!'

Agent Purple's smile vanished a moment before Kane head-butted his green skull. But his finger was still on the trigger and the gun went off.

The blast blew a wide hole in the tunnel's ceiling and a high-voltage power cable swung down. Huge showers of orange sparks shot out as brickwork and masonry fell around their heads. Agent Purple threw Kane away from him like a discarded jacket. The Big Game Hunter skidded across the wooden deck on his back. Agent Purple laughed as he stood up straight and pointed both barrels of the elephant gun at Kane again.

'Still one shot left, I believe, Kane!'

And that was when one of the high-voltage cables wrapped itself around Agent Purple. He dropped the elephant gun and screamed as 11,000 volts surged through him, frying his body from the inside. Everyone on the boat shielded their faces as the high-voltage explosion lit up the tunnel. Orange flames licked out of Agent Purple's green skull, his suit caught on fire and grey wispy smoke engulfed his body. His charred remains fell over the back of the boat along with the power lines, which sizzled and popped in the water.

In the streets above and across the tunnel's ceiling, all the lights went out. Block by block, people's tv's switched off. Fridges, kettles and washing machines came to an abrupt stop.

For a moment, it looked like *The Day The Earth Stood Still*.

Inside the Wayfarer's wheelhouse, Jazz and Sam stared at Agent Purple's lifeless body floating face down in the canal at the back of the Wayfarer. Then they turned to stare at each other.

'Dead?'

'Looks like it.'

'Can't say I'm too sad, to be honest.'

'Me neither.'

Slowly they turned their stare towards the metal throttle levers.

'Go on then, get us out of here,' said Sam.

'You touch them first!' exclaimed Jazz.

'No way am I touching them!' said Sam. 'They're metal.'

Charlie came in and pushed the throttles open. 'They're safe to touch, you goofballs - all the powers blown. Come on. There may still be time.'

40

Big Trouble in Little Venice

The monster pike was really slowing down now.

The great fish had nearly run out of steam. Apart from its immense size the pike looked as helpless and defeated as an ordinary fish that had spent the last of its energy on the end of an angler's rod.

The canal in Little Venice was bordered on both sides by gorgeous town houses and quirky little street cafes, where artists sat side by side with the rich and famous. A hidden gem that sparkled in the heart of London.

All this meant nothing to the monster pike.

All it cared about was survival. It was an innocent animal just trying to survive in a world it hadn't asked to be in. The great fish sensed it was unique. And alone. An unwanted by-product of man's constant search for new technologies, the fish was nothing but an accident that had gotten out of control. It knew it had reached the end of its journey. There was nowhere left to turn.

BLAAAAMM!

'Yeehaa!' shouted Jeremiah as his torpedo exploded against the wall behind the pike, bringing down a ton of masonry. Startled, the pike darted away as fast as its tired body would let it.

'Fire!'

Another torpedo from Jeremiah's Orca missed the pike by inches and blew up the road bridge at Westbourne Terrace, which collapsed into the water below. Jeremiah steered the Orca round in a tight semi-circle and saw Kane's armoured RIB the Neptune heading towards the pike.

'Fire!' smiled Jeremiah. 'That's the last one - don't say I never did anything for you, Charlie Carter.'

The little silver fish left the Orca and whirled towards the Neptune. It hit the armoured RIB's hull just as the Skipper was about to fire at the pike. The explosion split the Neptune in half and raised it ten metres out of the water, but an accidental burst of fire from its cannons hit a waterside café scattering diners in all directions. Stray bullets hit the Police boat which sent DI Williams and his crew diving for cover.

'STOP FIRING!' shouted DI Williams from a loudhailer. 'THAT'S AN ORDER!'

Jeremiah switched off the Orca, and it came to a rest on the canal floor, the cockpit just sticking up out of the water. He clamboured out and waded towards the side of the canal, dragging the two semi-conscious men from the armoured RIB behind him.

'We've got nothing left to fire, anyway!' said Jeremiah.

'Well, there you are then. Good,' said DI Williams. 'Look at all the damage you've caused, Jeremiah. I have to say, you know – you're a terrible shot.'

Jeremiah laughed. 'I hit every single thing I aimed for.'

'But you missed the pike every time.'

'Never said I was aiming for the pike, did I?'

'You mean...?'

'That's right - I missed it on...'

'No! No, no, no. Don't say it...' warned DI Williams.

'Oh, come on - it's funny.'

'I know what you're going to say - and it is NOT funny.'

'I'm gonna say it anyway...'

'Say it and I'll arrest you!' warned DI Williams.

'Arrest me? What for?'

'I'll think of something. How about *Crimes against Comedy* for a start.'

Jeremiah couldn't resist it any longer as he knew he was going to be arrested no matter what. 'I missed the monster pike on *porpoise*,' and burst out laughing.

WPC326 on the Police boat giggled at Jeremiah's terrible joke. Even the two semi-conscious men from the

Neptune spluttered out a little laugh. That joke was truly awful!

'Right – that's it, you're all NICKED!' smiled DI Williams. 'Every single one of you, so there.' He felt quite pleased with himself that he was *finally* getting to arrest someone.

WPC326 had just hauled Jeremiah and the two men from the Neptune onboard the Police boat when Charlie and the Wayfarer rounded the corner. The huge net was dangling over the side of the Wayfarer, just below the waterline.

'Charlie!' shouted DI Williams, pointing towards the pike 'Watch out – it's still loose!'

The Monster Pike knew it was cornered. The collapsed bridge had cut off its only other escape route, apart from the direction it came in. It turned to face the only way out. The Wayfarer stood in its way. The pike could see a narrow gap between the boat and the canal wall. It knew this was its last chance at freedom.

'Steady...!' whispered Charlie.

The pike summoned up every last ounce of energy it had and surged forward with all its might.

'Steady!' said Charlie, a bit louder this time.

The pike powered its way into the narrow gap between the Wayfarer and the canal wall. Three tons of furious fish tried to wriggle its way past the Wayfarer in a gap that wasn't quite wide enough.

'NOW!' shouted Charlie.

Sam hit the button on the boat crane. The winch whined and smoked in protest. But it worked. The long net down the side of the Wayfarer snapped upwards. The boat rocked from side to side, sending everyone flying as the pike struggled to break free. Waves crashed over the side and drenched everyone onboard.

Charlie's dad saved Anna as she fell and they both ended up on the floor of the boat. Kane grabbed onto his elephant gun but fell over the side rail and into the canal. Charlie, Jazz and Sam fell together in a crumpled heap.

The net groaned and stretched - but it didn't break. It held onto its prize catch tightly. The Wayfarer steadied itself. The waves in the canal slowly subsided.

Charlie cautiously peered over the side of the boat. Jazz and Sam joined him.

'Whoahhhhh!' said Sam. 'That's awesome.'

'Oh, my word,' said Jazz. 'That *is* incredible.'

'I've done it! I've caught it!' smiled Charlie. 'Er, I mean... *we've* caught it!'

All three looked down at the net.

The Monster Pike looked back up at them.

41

The Beast Must Die

The monster pike was half in, half out of the net.

The huge fish was an awesome sight to behold. Its beautiful black and green stripes along its broad back glistened in the sunlight. Its massive striped head with its rows of fearsome teeth looked magnificent. The pike's fins were iridescent in the sunlight and displayed deep shimmering shades of reds and greens and purples. Its underbelly was scarred from where it had rubbed against the bottom of the canal. Its fight was gone. It had been caught, and its energy was spent. It ceased struggling, too tired to put up any more resistance. It lowered its head, subdued in captivity.

Charlie leaned over the Wayfarer's handrails and reached down to the pike. Its soft glowing eyes looked back up at Charlie. It seemed to be imploring him for mercy. Charlie stroke the huge fish's skin. It felt warm and smooth. As he touched the pike, so a jolt went through Charlie's body. In a few fleeting seconds he could feel what the pike could feel and could see into its mind's eye. Charlie saw the moment when the young pike was first caught and put into the huge water tank at the Fizz HQ. He saw the Fizz scientists in white laboratory coats scuttle around the tank and experiment on the pike with large, painful injections of Rejoov, he felt its pain, he felt its fear. He watched the Fizz make it grow and grow into the monster it was today. He could feel its longing to escape, to seek freedom and sanctuary, he could feel its longing to once again see overhanging trees and calm rustling reed beds with the summer sun warming its broad back. Charlie knew the pike just wanted to escape its tormentors and to not be hunted. To be free.

A large figure leapt up out of the water.

'YYYYAAAAAAH!!!'

It was Kane – still clutching his shotgun. The Big Game Hunter quickly waded round to where the pike lay caught in the net. He pointed the shotgun at the Pike and rested both barrels against its head. Kane's finger went to press the trigger.

'NO!' screamed Charlie. 'NO!'

Kane paused. His trigger finger loosened slightly, and he took a long, hard look at the pike for the first time.

Time stood still for Kane. For a moment, it seemed that the world stopped turning. The shouts from above him died away. He was lost in the beauty of the great fish.

The pike was huge. Its scales shimmered a rainbow of different colours in the sunlight and its great eyes were a soft, mesmerising green, drawing Kane deep into their glowing depths. Its long, iridescent orange and green dorsal fin rose slowly up and down on its broad, ridged back and its red and purple gills breathed slowly in and out.

The pike knew that these would be its last ever breaths. It had been beaten. Its quest for freedom was over. It was totally at the mercy of the Big Game Hunter. It was only a fish, Kane kept telling himself - but what a fish! The Monster Pike had a haunting beauty that transcended time and place. It was the most beautiful animal Kane had ever seen.

It might also have been the most unique animal he'd ever seen. Its sheer size and colourings were impressive. A one-off. An unnatural animal in an unnatural world. Nothing else quite like it had ever been on earth, and probably nothing else like it would ever be again. But it was just an animal. Animals had taken his precious son away.

And that's why the pike had to die.

Kane pressed the shotgun harder against the pike's head and his finger tightened on the trigger again.

'NO, KANE, NO!' screamed Charlie. 'Please! You promised me! You PROMISED!'

Sweat broke out on Kane's brow. He looked back up at Charlie, and for a moment Kane saw his own son, Morgan, looking down and begging him not to kill this huge, beautiful animal. This incredible but defenceless animal.

'KANE!' shouted Charlie. 'LISTEN TO ME! I'D DO ANYTHING TO BRING YOUR SON BACK, I REALLY WOULD. BUT I CAN'T. NOTHING CAN. I CAN'T BRING MORGAN BACK, KANE, YOU CAN'T BRING HIM BACK - YOU HAVE TO LET HIM GO!'

'Ah, Morgan my boy...' whispered Kane. He shook his head and the vision passed.

Charlie reached down and put his hand on the pike's broad head. He stopped shouting and spoke to Kane in a slow, calm voice, edged with tears.

'You have to let your son go, Kane. Enjoy the memory of him. You don't have to kill any more animals in revenge for Morgan's death. It's not the pike's fault - he's no more a monster than me or you. Morgan has gone, Kane, nothing can bring him back. Just be thankful for those precious memories you have – treasure them. Be thankful that he was ever there in the first place. You don't need to do this…. please!'

'It hurts, Charlie,' whispered Kane. 'It hurts.'

'I know it does, I know. But you have to let go of your anger and your hurt. Morgan will always be there – nestled in your heart and just a mere thought away.'

Kane looked up at Charlie then looked slowly back at the pike.

His finger trembled on the trigger.

42

No Swimming

Kane's old mud-splattered Land Rover pulled up on a small hill overlooking Kane's massive private lake.

Deep beds of water reeds rustled in the breeze and swallows dipped and played across the rippled surface of the water in the warm evening light. Every now and again one of the birds touched the water with its beak and formed a small ring which grew wider and wider.

Across the other side of the lake sat Kane's beautiful mansion house with a wide gravel drive sweeping up to its tall columns and heavy oak front door. Kane's staff were out polishing his collection of vintage cars behind the security gates. A lorry marked 'County Auctioneers' was being loaded up with stuffed animal heads and all the vintage guns from Kane's private collection.

Charlie got out of the Land Rover driver's seat and stretched his legs. He took off two blocks of wood which were tied to the bottom of his feet. It was the only way he could reach the car's pedals.

'At least you're getting better at driving,' said Jazz, getting out of the passenger side. 'Promise me you won't drive on the road though yet, until you pass your test?'

'Charlie doesn't need to pass a test,' said Sam, struggling out the back of the Land Rover with an armful of long wooden posts. 'His driving's awesome.'

'Promise me,' said Jazz.

'I promise. Don't worry,' said Charlie and took out a hammer and a box of screws.

The three of them left the Land Rover and walked down to the side of the lake where a group of men were hammering in wooden posts at regularly spaced intervals, then fixing red warning signs up.

'Did you bring me some more posts, eh?' boomed a gruff South African voice.

'Sam's got them,' said Charlie. 'I've brought some more screws. Can we help you put the signs up, please?'

'Of course,' said Kane. 'That would be a big help, eh? How's your Dad?'

'Oh, he's fine,' said Charlie. 'Sends his regards. Told me not to drive your Land Rover.'

Kane laughed as he brought over a sledgehammer to where Sam was holding one of the posts upright.

'When I nod my head, hit it!' said Sam.

'Don't tempt me,' laughed Kane and gave Sam a playful cuff on his head. He laughed again as Sam went cross-eyed and pretended to be knocked out. Kane hadn't felt as good as this for a long time. He hammered the post into the ground.

Jazz brought over one of the red signs and held it straight as Charlie screwed the sign onto the post. The four of them stood back to admire their handywork.

The sign said:

DANGER
NO SWIMMING
and definitely....
NO FISHING!

'You know they're taking away all of your stuffed animal heads?' asked Charlie. 'And all your gun collection.'

'Of course. I don't want to see them again,' sighed Kane wistfully. 'I'm giving it all up, Charlie my boy. You taught me a good lesson, eh? I don't need to hunt animals to make up for my son not being around anymore. Forgive but don't forget, eh? You know, I might take up fishing instead...'

Out on the lake the surface rippled for a moment and

a huge dorsal fin broke the surface. A large green striped back shimmered in the evening sun. Then all was still again.

Charlie laughed. The sunlight glinted on something around his neck.

'And of course, we managed to get your mum's locket back. All good, eh?'

'Thank you for not hurting the pike, Kane,' said Charlie, touching his mum's precious locket. 'Especially as you had five million reasons why you should kill it.'

'Ah, you gave me one *big* reason that was better than those five million ones, as to why I should save it,' said the ex-Big Game Hunter looking straight at a puzzled Charlie. 'You saved my life - it was the least I could do for you,' laughed Kane. 'I did my bit. Got the REJOOV cylinder back for the Fizz, so they were, shall we say, *very* happy with me. I said I'd dispose of the pike for them – I never said where or how. And now that Agent Purple has gone, the Fizz might just do some good with that REJOOV, eh?'

'So, the Fizz still paid you, then?' asked Jazz.

Kane didn't say yes or no, but his big smile spoke volumes. 'Heh! Maybe. But you know, we might have hurt the pike a little bit - that was some delicate operation, eh? Getting that cylinder and your locket back out of its stomach. No mean feat, I can tell you. Anna's a good vet. You know, I think she wanted to save the pike as much as you did.'

'Thank you, Kane, it means a lot to me,' smiled Charlie. 'Thank you very much.'

Jazz and Sam looked at each other. 'Wow!' they said.

'He said 'thankyou' again,' beamed Jazz. 'Wonders will never cease!

'I know,' said Sam. 'He's getting the hang of it now. The old Charlie Carter is back!'

'When Anna operated on the pike, she found something else, too,' said Kane.

'Did she find Charlie's Uncle? Or his head?' asked Sam.

'Eish - you kids! No, she didn't find anything like

that. She found something far more important.'

'What was that?' asked Charlie.

'Well, for one thing, the monster pike is a she, not a he,' said Kane, enjoying the suspense. 'And *she* is pregnant.'

'That was a brave fish,' said Sam and Jazz thumped him.

Kane hugged the three kids as if they were his own, and smiled. 'You crazy kids! You know,' said Kane. 'You guys can come here as often as you want and see how she's doing. We'll take good care of her. I think I'm going to have an interesting retirement. All's well that ends well, eh?'

'Well....' said Charlie. 'Not quite. I've got one last thing to do.'

He took a small round wreath out the back of the Land Rover. It was a very handsome looking wreath. A small handwritten label on it read *'Dear Mad Dog. RIP. You were a true Hero. Love from your new family, Charlie, Jazz and Sam x'*

Charlie gently threw the wreath onto the lake and watched it move slowly away from the shore. Jazz and Sam joined Charlie and they gave him a big hug.

'You know, said Charlie holding his mum's locket. 'I'll always miss my mum, more than words can ever say - but she'll always be with me, just like I said to Kane - nestled in my heart and just a thought away. What I'd really hate is if I couldn't see you guys. Thank you for being there for me.'

'It's good to have you back, Charlie,' said Jazz.

'Team Carter!' yelled Sam.

'TEAM CARTER!' shouted all three of them as one.

'Holy Macaroni!' shouted Charlie, running towards the Land Rover. 'C'mon!! Let's get out of this place and go have some FUN!'

43

Jacks

The monster pike liked its new home.

The man-made lake was stocked full of carp, tench and barble. Ducks and Canada Geese nested on its shores. There was enough food to last a lifetime. The great fish broke the surface and felt the sun warm its back. It wasn't being hunted anymore – nor ever would be again. A movement in its stomach signalled that it was time. The pike shuddered and a cloud of baby pike - *Jacks* - whooshed out into the cold deep waters of the lake.

The teeny-tiny little Jacks tumbled out. Fuelled by the tiny amount of Rejoov in their huge mother, each one straightened and swam freely for their very first time within seconds of being born. And in a few more seconds, each one of the Jacks doubled in ferocity.

A large carp swam lazily through this cloud of baby pike and gulped down as many as it could, then swam off having had its fill. After a few metres it stopped dead in the water. The carp convulsed and a strange look came over its fishy face. A tiny Jack swam out through a hole it had just eaten in the side of the carp.

Then another.

Then another.

The carp was eaten from the inside out in a flash.

Little bits of flesh filled the water which was lit with shafts of sunlight from above. In seconds, all that was left of the carp were its bare bones, picked clean as thirty Jacks swam back to the safety of their mother.

The big beautiful pike swam slowly off into the gloom.

Epilogue

Hooked

The Thames was much quieter now at night. And safer.

For the moment.

Deep in its murky depths a silver cylinder sat in the river mud, rocking slowly from side to side in the tide. From an almost unnoticeable hole in its side leaked a tiny but regular cloud of green liquid.

A Lamprey eel slithered towards the cylinder. The Lamprey was a metre long, ancient, nightmarish eel with a funnel-like sucking mouth full of hooked, razor-sharp teeth. It was an invasive species and hundreds had found a home in the Thames. It fed by clinging onto other fish with its teeth, eating them alive. The process would sometimes take days.

The eel swam up to the small split in the cylinder's casing and clamped its mouth over the hole.

And fed.

ABOUT THE AUTHOR

David Rogers

CHOMP! Charlie Carter and the Monster Pike is the action-packed debut children's novel from author David Rogers. David lives in deepest darkest Dorset with his horse-mad wife Jean, their two cockapoos Freddie and Jimmy, two cats and two horses. Although only the horses aren't allowed indoors. Ever.

As you read this, David is writing his follow-up novel *REARGUNNER! Charlie Carter and the Ghost Bomber* and Jean is probably trying to sneak her horses upstairs out of the rain. Again.

Please keep checking the facebook page Charlie Carter Adventures for news and updates on Charlie and his friends Sam and Jazz.